The Grill on Murray Avenue

A Story of Innocence

JOHANNA MCKENZIE

To Enrique

for your faith, encouragement, and friendship

CONTENTS

CHAPTER 1

"Our strength often increases in proportion to the obstacles imposed upon it."

—*Paul de Rapin*

Deciding to try one more time, I somehow drag myself onto a bus. About twenty minutes later, I wind up at Gullifty's restaurant on Murray Avenue in Squirrel Hill. "I wish I could help you," the nice-looking elderly hostess with the smart glasses tells me, "but we already have a waiting list for this summer of about forty." I just look at her blankly.

******

MUCH TO MY SURPRISE, I've been having a terrible time finding a waitressing job. I think the problem is that I waited too long to start looking, not that I haven't been giving it my best effort. In fact, I've already been to an extensive, prying, and uncomfortable interview at The Balcony, a rather exclusive second-floor restaurant that overlooks Walnut Street in Shadyside, and which doubles as a jazz club in the after-dinner hours, but I haven't heard back from them. Eat'n Park on Murray Avenue offered me a position, but I'd have to work the graveyard shift, at least for the first few months. I considered it—but just for a moment. And earlier today I made the mistake of inquiring about a job at Cappy's, a tiny bar-and-grill also on Walnut Street, during the lunch rush. "Let me give you a bit of advice, honey," the manager told me as she rang up one bill after another, "you keep showing up at this time of day looking for a job and you're not going to get too damn far…"

Realizing that nothing will completely comfort me but a nice, strong pot of Earl Grey, I decide to head to The Coffee Tree Roasters on Forbes. On most other occasions I would have gone to the 61C on Murray, but I need serenity right now, not a lot of stimulation.

Walking past the various shops and establishments, including a couple of bookstores, a drugstore, a Chinese restaurant, a wine and spirits shop, a hair salon, and the Squirrel Hill Post Office, I try to enjoy the nice weather and to think positively, telling myself for what seems like the hundredth time that if I just keep at it, something fortuitous will come to me.

I walk a bit farther, having just glanced across the street at the Manor Theatre to check out what movies are playing, when to my left, a place I've never noticed before catches my attention. It is just a diminutive red-brick building, closed in on one side by a flower shop, and on the other by a tiny Russian restaurant, and so easy to pass right by without a second thought. But on its front window, which is very large in comparison to the overall size of the façade, "The Grill on Murray Avenue" presents itself in bold, proud, fancy letters, a deep shade of alluring red. "Oh yeah," I mumble, pausing for a moment. "I remember someone in one of my classes mentioning that a new bar-and-grill was opening up around here. This must be it."

Curious, I walk up to the window, surround my face with my hands to block out the sun, and peer inside. I really can't see all that much, except for the outline of a bar and a bunch of dimmed overhead lights, but out of nowhere a very warm sensation washes over me… Should I try this place too?

I decide against it. I just don't think I can tolerate another rejection today, and besides, it is getting late and my pot of tea is waiting for me.

I keep walking. Just as I get to the corner of Murray and Forbes, though, the pedestrian light turns red, so I wait, using the time to observe all of the passersby, as I'm inclined to do. I can't, however, keep myself from glancing back at the new bar-and-grill.

Should I?

Should I?

I can't resist.

My feet take me back to the little brick place I'd had no intention of giving a chance. ∎

CHAPTER 2

I pull open the large gray door and step inside, pause for a moment in the short corridor—my heart running—and then slowly walk forward. The first person I see is an attractive, dark-haired, stocky man dressed in khaki shorts, a light blue Oxford shirt, sexy, lightweight glasses, a thin goatee and mustache, and a lot of Italian masculinity.

Things are looking good so far.

"What can I do for ya?" he asks, having looked up from the newspaper that is spread out in front of him at the end of the bar, and which he is gripping firmly with both hands. He is standing, not sitting, with his legs spread rather far apart, like a linebacker preparing to make a tackle.

"Hi… I…uh…I was wondering if…if you had any openings for waitresses right now," I manage to get out.

His face crinkles up a bit. "I don't think we have an opening *right* now, but…" He looks around for a moment. "Hey, Cath, come here for a second, would ya?"

A short, attractive woman with very long, red, wavy hair that is pulled away from her face in a high ponytail finishes wiping a table and walks up to the bar. She tucks the damp rag between her dark blue apron and her swollen belly. Her fingernails are long and painted bright red as well. She smiles at me and then raises her eyebrows as she looks at him.

"When is Renee planning to leave—in a month or two?" he asks her.

"Oh no, Nick, I don't think so," she says, shaking her head. "In a couple of weeks actually." She turns toward me. "Are you looking for a job?"

"Yes, I am," I answer. (I can't help but feel a tingling of hope.)

"Do you have any experience?" Nick quickly adds.

"Oh yes, I do," I say. "About a year's worth."

He nods slowly.

"Oh good," the woman says, grabbing a pad of paper and a pen from behind the bar and handing them to me. "Why don't you take these and write down all of your contact info and your past experience, where you worked and for how long, and all of that stuff. Okay? You can take a seat at one of the tables up front if you want."

"Okay. Thanks," I say, taking the paper and pen from her, and also trying to take in as much of the place as possible.

I sit down at a table, facing away from the bar, and proceed to print the following as neatly as I can, a bit surprised that they don't have a formal application, but also quite impressed with it at the same time:

<u>Contact Information</u>
Jenna McCartney, 412-365-4956
Chatham College
Box 334
Woodland Rd.
Pittsburgh, PA 15232

<u>Waitressing Experience</u>
The Coach Room Restaurant, Bedford, PA:
June 1991–September 1991

Ed's Steak House, Bedford, PA:
June 1992–September 1992

The Sunshine Inn, Raystown, PA:
June 1993–September 1993

I read it over a couple of times, making sure that I haven't made any mistakes, and then I walk cautiously up to the bar.

"All set?" Nick asks.

"Yes, I am." I hand the pen and pad of paper to him.

He glances at it. "Okay, well, we'll give you a call if we're interested. Thanks for stopping—"

"Can I take a look at that?" my redhead advocate calls, suddenly appearing from the back of the restaurant with a bowlful of golden french fries sitting upon a tray she is supporting with her left hand. "Just let me deliver this and I'll be right there."

She quickly drops off the fries to a couple sitting in one of the booths and returns to the bar, leaning her tray against the side of it and wiping her hands on her apron.

"Okay," she says, taking my "résumé" from Nick's hands, "let's see here." She looks at it for a while. "Okay. Jenna, is it?"

"Yes. Jenna," I reply.

"Oh, good… Okay, well, this looks great. It looks like you have sufficient experience, so what I'll do is I'll give this to Bobby, the owner, and if he's interested he'll give you a call. We may need some help, starting in a few weeks. The other daytime person, who works just part-time, is probably going to be leaving soon to do her horse-showing business full-time…and then, as you can see," she says as she lightly pats her stomach, "I'm going to be out of commission for quite a while myself… Oh, and by the way, I'm Cathy, and this is my husband, Nick. He's the waitstaff manager."

I shake their hands, feeling very happy, but also feeling rather guilty for having found Nick so attractive.

"Thank you so much," I say.

"No problem. Someone should be in touch," Cathy answers. "And don't worry… I'll definitely put in a good word for you." ∎

CHAPTER 3

I sit in a spacious and comfortable Regent Square living room, relaxing after having tucked in bed the sweet little boy and girl I'm babysitting, a job I got through my college's babysitting hotline. I am so happy for the work and the money, but I know that these occasional assignments aren't going to be enough to pay for my rent and food for the summer.

Oh well. Why worry about it now? I can spend my time more wisely. Of course there's always the option to take out my collection of Hawthorne tales and reread "Sights from a Steeple," one of my favorites. Before that, though, I'll check to see what my buddy Teeli is up to. She had said something about maybe going out together for a cup of coffee later tonight.

I call the room that we are sharing for the summer on campus in Woodland Hall, but no one answers, so I decide to find out if there are any messages. I punch in the access code and listen.

Beeeeep. "Hey, Freddie, this is Teeli." ("Freddie" is one of the nicknames that Teeli has chosen for me; in fact, I hardly ever hear her call me by my real name.) "I'm already at the C." (She has nicknamed the 61C Cafe as well, although this nickname seems to fit its object much better than mine does me.) "I decided to go early and do some work for my American History class. When you get finished babysitting, why don't you meet me here? Okay, Freddie?… Okay. I hope to see you then. Bye, Freddie… Bye."

I absolutely love meeting Teeli for coffee, and especially at the C, so of course I'll meet her there if the couple I'm babysitting for doesn't get back too—

Beeeeep. "Oh! Someone else must have called," I blurt out. I wait for a few seconds, and then:

"Hello. This message is for Jenna McCartney. Jenna, this is Bobby Allman, from The Grill on Murray Avenue…" I jump up off the window seat and almost knock the phone to the floor. "I was wondering if you were still looking for a waitressing job and would like to come in for an interview. If so, please give me a call at five-two-one, twelve-twenty-two. Thanks. Hope to talk to you soon."

"Awesome!" I exclaim, completely forgetting that the two little ones are in bed, and listening to the message again so that I can jot down the phone number and make sure that I haven't been imagining things. To my utter delight, I really haven't, so I call Mr. Allman back immediately and we set up a time to meet, not this coming Monday but the Monday after that, at noon.

I can't wait to tell Teeli the good news. ■

CHAPTER 4

Figuring that finding a parking spot near The Grill at noon will be difficult, I decide to walk. Besides, I've walked from Chatham's campus to Squirrel Hill many times before (mainly to pick up odds and ends from Revco), and the walk is short—only about fifteen to twenty minutes, depending on the pace you take. Also, I think that the walk may help to clear my mind and settle my nerves a bit.

On the way there, I feel somewhat uneasy, but good overall, thinking about how intensely I prepared for the interview. Over the past week, I spent hours reviewing all my notes from previous interviews, and I even checked out a few more interview-technique books from the library. I just hope I haven't failed to anticipate any difficult questions. So, as I put one foot in front of the other, I once again go over the answers that I've prepared to countless questions—What's the first thing you say when you walk up to a new table? Do you tend to write down all the details of your orders or keep a lot of the info in your head? How would you handle a complaint from a customer?—but as soon as I arrive at The Grill's entrance, I feel tense again. I summon the courage to pull open the heavy door, though, as I did a few weeks ago, and walk inside.

I glance around for a moment, looking for either Nick or Cathy, but coming toward me instead is an attractive man, about five-seven or so, with dark hair, a trim build, and long arms. He is comfortably dressed in jeans and a polo shirt, and appears to be in his mid-thirties. What I particularly notice about him, however, is the way he walks. It's as if he doesn't have to put any effort into it at all—as if his muscles are made out of a stretchy and pliable, but shapely, kind of rubber. Suddenly I feel much more at ease. "Hi," he says, gently shaking my hand, "you must be Jenna… It's nice to meet you… I'm Bobby…" He motions to the front. "How about we sit over here at this two-seater."

"Okay."

We sit down and begin talking, and from the start, I can't believe how easy this interview is. In fact, it isn't even like a real interview. Instead of asking me about my work experience and what I think makes a good server—the type of things you would expect to be asked during an interview for a waitressing job—he asks me when I would be available to work and if I would just want to work for the summer or perhaps would want to stay on for longer. And then, just like that (we haven't even been sitting here for ten minutes), he tells me that the job pays two-eighty an hour plus tips ("a much higher hourly rate than most places around here," he adds), and that I can start working the day shift, Monday through Friday, from eleven a.m. to five-thirty p.m., if I'm interested, starting the following Monday. I can't help but get the feeling that he decided to offer me the job even before he met me, just as long as when he did meet me I didn't come across as either a supreme dolt or a serial killer, or something else to that extreme.

So, having an especially good feeling about the place, as I did initially, I accept the offer on the spot, my usual heavy dose of indecision for once, and surprisingly, absent. Then

I get up from my seat, smile at him warmly, shake his hand, push my chair into the table, and walk out the door, so happy I'll be coming back. ■

CURT

Each morning when I arrive, there he is, huddling behind the bar—all six-foot-two of him—filling the shiny sinks: one with warm, sudsy water, and the other with steamy, hot rinse water, covering him in a heady mist. On the deep-maroon, tan-topped bar in front of him lounge four or five lemons upon a white plastic cutting board—some whole, some divided, others in triangular, juicy pieces—a glistening, sharp knife beside them, the fresh citrus and fruity soap scents mixing together and permeating the air. And through the old, dusty TV that sits high upon the beer cooler, the energizing theme song of *The Price Is Right* greets me, reminding me of sweet summer mornings as a child when my father, my younger brother, and I would sit in the living room in my home in the middle of PA, where I grew up, happily watching the show and playing the games together.

I never knew that walking into work could make you feel so good (I've read and heard so much to the contrary), but here I am, Monday through Friday, welcomed with a "Hi honey" from Curt (a Tom Selleck look-alike if I do say so myself), wonderful smells, and fond reminders of home.

That's really great, you say, but what about the rest of the day, until my shift ends at five-thirty? Well, it seems crazy, but I have no complaints about that either. When Curt is busy bartending and the bell rings in the kitchen, I bring out his food and hand it to him, allowing him to personally deliver it to his customers, which I can tell he prefers. And during the lunch rush, from about noon to two, when I am usually quite frazzled, he clears off the dirty tables and booths and resets them while I take orders and dart around.

Even better, he talks kindly to me and, without ever acting bothered, answers any questions I have (such a big help when starting a new job!), always explaining any rules and procedures he thinks I should know. It's especially enjoyable watching, in the midst of all this explaining, how he so familiarly interacts with all of his friends who stop by often, in some cases every day, to have a refreshing drink or a tasty bite to eat, or just to chat and say hello. After working with him for a while, though, it's no wonder that so many people come in specifically to see him—the other benefits secondary. A cup of just-brewed coffee gently placed in front of one friend, a hand firmly placed into the hand of another, a wink of an eye so full of recognition, a cocktail given a little more "spirit" than usual. He may be too busy to talk to his friends sometimes, but that doesn't mean they're not communicating.

When he does have time to talk, though, he's so natural and laid back, that you just want to tell him more. Plus, he is so generous, in so many ways (with his attention, for example), but especially with his money. He's not a bit hesitant about sharing it with anyone who needs it—or really *doesn't* need it, for that matter. If he sees you out anywhere in a social situation, whether at The Decade (the well-loved historic rock and roll bar at the corner of Atwood and Sennott streets, near Pitt), Buffalo Blues (the new blues bar and restaurant on South Highland Avenue in Shadyside, which Curt really digs), or Nick's Fat City (the hip hangout on East Carson Street in the South Side, which features a live band practically every night and has autographed guitars hanging all over the walls), he's always the first person to offer to buy you a drink. "Give all of my good friends here a drink," he'll tell the bartender, motioning to us with a swoop of his hand.

Then there's his family. His brother, sister-in-law, and two-year-old niece (so cute!) often come from Ohio, where they live, to visit. I've waited on them a few times, and each time I do, Curt secretly takes me aside and whispers in my ear, "If they say they're ready for the check, just tell them that it's been taken care of." Curt's brother, in response, calls from the first booth in the nonsmoking section, closest to the bar, where they always like to sit (he must have an uncanny ability to overhear), "Oh, c'mon, Curt; you don't have to take care of the check *again—really*." But there's no use in arguing; Curt *never* lets them pay. What's more, he always offers to babysit his niece so that his brother and sister-in-law can go out on the town and spend some time alone together and enjoy Pittsburgh. It's obvious that he dearly loves the little girl, because he constantly sweetly smiles and baby-talks to her as he hunches down on his knee and takes her tiny hand.

What impresses me most about him, however, and what I'm most grateful to him for—which is something he's certainly not required to do—is that (right from my first day) he welcomes me into his circle of friends, introducing me to them like I'm his long-lost buddy: "I'd like you to meet my friend Jenna here, the newest addition to our group." He even takes the time to tell me funny stories about crazy situations they've gotten into together, supplying that history of feelings and never-again moments—through the inflections in his voice, the excitement in his eyes, the laughs that won't stop—that ties all of them so securely to one another.

Yes, there's Craig Newbert (aka Globy), the main bartender at The Decade, whom Curt seems to particularly identify with; Dom, the owner of The Decade, who saunters to the bar in his expensive suit and shiny rings, with his attractive gray hair slicked back, sitting sideways on his seat and sipping a whiskey on the rocks; Mark, a cute, black-haired, short, and stocky all-American type of guy who works down the street at the Heads Together bookstore and stops to see Curt after his daily afternoon errand to the post office and before he reluctantly goes back to work; Craig Brockle, an *In Pittsburgh* employee who helps out at The Decade checking IDs and collecting the cover; Joe Fish and his ornery father, Firpo—the owners of the seafood store and restaurant down the hill on Murray—who are Italian, well-fed, relaxed, friendly, and always clad in stained white butcher clothes and aprons, and also always smelling like Joe's nickname; Zeech, the exuberant, big-bellied owner of the kosher store, also down the street, who insists on leaving through The Grill's back door, especially after sunset; Freddie (there's another one), the Black, tiny, extremely skinny, almost-not-there cook from The Squirrel Cage—the always-crowded, hip hangout around the corner on Forbes Avenue—who never looks sad; Pops, also a cook at The Cage—Black, tall, elegant, and friendly—who walks in so easily, smiles, and calls me "old blue eyes," which tickles me; Walter, the successful Squirrel Hill lawyer who enjoys The Grill's drinks and social aspect more than anyone I've seen; and JoAnn (short, full, curly brown hair and glasses) and Kitty (very short, straight, stark black hair—cropped at her chin—and glasses), the two eccentric ladies who work up the block at the insurance agency. Sure, the two of them are very particular about things—"Just a glass of water, half full, no ice, for me," says JoAnn; "And a cup of coffee…it *has* to be steaming and filled right to the edge…for me," says Kitty—but they've been so nice to me that it makes me want to cry.

I guess I wasn't wrong, then, when I first got the feeling that The Grill is an intimate, exclusive club, with no instructions, bylaws, or rules that are written on paper or verbally expressed, but with ideals that are instinctively felt within the hearts and souls of each member: to be happy, friendly, and supportive of each other. And I feel so fortunate that Curt has accepted me into this unusual bunch and has encouraged others, by his actions and demeanor, to do the same.

I couldn't be enjoying my new job and the summer any more than I already am, and I have Curt in part (a *great* part, that is) to thank. ∎

BETH

She's got it all together.

Tall (close to six foot), shapely (rather voluptuous, actually), fair-skinned, pretty, intelligent, and well-spoken, with brown eyes and abundant hair that she pulls loosely back in a low ponytail, she has her own sense of style while on the job. Instead of wearing khaki shorts or pants as most of us waitresses always do, she wears a short, wraparound khaki skirt, which shows off her long legs. But what is most noticeable about her is that she has a great deal of common sense, is very confident, determined, and focused, and knows exactly what she wants first before anything else: a good, stable career. She is attending the University of Pittsburgh, where she is pursuing a business and computer science degree, and she is working at The Grill to put herself through school, which I can particularly relate to. I remember that I instantly felt a connection to her and felt comfortable talking to her.

We met not too long ago. Whereas I waitress during the day, Monday through Friday, and occasionally on Saturday, she usually waitresses on Wednesday and Sunday evenings and hostesses for a few hours on Saturday evenings. But our paths cross in that in-between time, when she is just arriving for work and I am doing all of the necessary restocking jobs before I can leave. From the start, she has been extremely kind and very helpful in any way that she possibly can be.

But how could I not like her?

The first time we met, you know what she said to me?

"Hi, I'm Beth. It's very nice to meet you… I hear that you are a dancer." ■

MAKING A STATEMENT

In walks a thin, middle-aged, gray-haired man with glasses and the current issue of the *Pittsburgh Post-Gazette*. He smiles at us pleasantly, sits down in the back booth, props a menu up in his hands, and starts studying it.

In no time at all, here comes Cathy—suddenly. She hurriedly approaches the man, grabs his folded paper, reaches past him and across the table (in a shockingly easy manner, in fact, even though she is almost nine months pregnant), and, with as much force as I've seen from just about anyone, obliterates a fly on the wall, and with much success.

You would think that the squished fly would adhere to the wall, but it doesn't. Rather, it falls to the table, right beside the man's hands.

I've never seen such a look of repulsion and disgust on someone's face, but there it is.

"Are you *crazy*?!" he yells, utterly taken aback. "How could you do something like that?"

He stares at her for a moment more, but then he yanks his *Post-Gazette* from her hand, finds his way out of the booth, stands up, and storms out the door.

Today is Cathy's last day at The Grill—at least for now. She shrugs her shoulders. ■

THE PERFECT SOLUTION

About a month into my new job, I approach her with a question.

It is an early Wednesday evening around five, and, as I've gotten into the habit of doing before leaving each day, I decide to check the schedule that Bobby posts each week in the kitchen on the wall directly above the soup and sauce bins. The schedule isn't anything fancy, just a piece of white paper with a handmade grid that Bobby creates with the aid of a ruler. On the left-hand side, in list form, are all of the employees' names, and across the top, each in its own column, is a day of the week.

I stop in front of the soup area and look up, studying the schedule. As has been the case for the past four weeks, the box that falls under the Monday column and corresponds with my name says "10:30 to 5:30," as do the boxes for Tuesday through Friday. However, this time, as I glance at the boxes under Saturday and Sunday, which are usually empty, something is different. The box under the Saturday column says "Bus, 6 to ?" I look away and then look back at the schedule once again, sure that my eyes are playing tricks on me, particularly because I hadn't noticed anything there when I had checked earlier in the week. But as I review the schedule one more time, I realize that my eyes haven't deceived me.

"Bus, six to question mark" I slowly read, as about four

surges of adrenaline shoot through me, one to each limb. Immediately, images of me wearing a full-length, spattered apron; my hair in tangles and sticking to my greasy face; dashing, exhausted, from table to table; carrying a heavy, large, gray bin, full of dirty dishes till the wee hours of the morning; no one else left in the restaurant but worn-out, disheveled me flood my mind. *Bobby!* my inner voice screams, *I don't want to* BUS *tables—I took this job to be a waitress!*

I stand there, not able to move, completely inundated with the unexpected change in my duties. My mind starts racing, and I wonder why I feel so uncomfortable, especially since I don't think that bussing is beneath me or that I shouldn't help out wherever I am needed. What, then, is the problem?

Not able to immediately figure it out, I continue standing there, and for quite a while, in fact, until I am momentarily knocked out of my dilemma by the sound of someone walking up the basement steps toward the kitchen. I suddenly realize that I must look rather foolish. I figure that it must be Bobby, because I was told that he was going to help out in the kitchen that night, as he does when it's necessary. Not wanting to run into him just then, knowing that I want to say something to him about the schedule but not knowing exactly what to say, I quickly walk out into the restaurant, looking down at the floor (to gain more speed, I guess), just missing him before he makes it to the top of the steps. Bobby is extremely nice and gentle, and I have no reason to be afraid of talking to him, but he is the boss, after all, and I've worked here for only a month. I then realize that I am walking rather fast, so I tell myself to slow down.

Once I do so, I glance up, and there, standing close to the ancillary bar, is Beth. (The ancillary bar is simply a small counter that lines the wall near the entranceway, and it is very close to the main bar.) She is getting ready for her shift, tying the strings of her dark blue apron around her waist, which she has to wrap around and tie in the front of her since the strings are so long.

Then it hits me. Why don't you ask Beth about it before you go to Bobby? She's worked here for a couple of years and will probably know why he put you down to bus tables. Plus, she's really easy to talk to.

"Hey, Beth," I say, trying to act casual as I sit down on one of the ancillary bar's stools. "How's it going?"

"Oh, not too bad... I guess you're getting ready to go home?"

"Oh yeah, my shift's just about over. It was slow today, so I got most of my side work done early," I reply.

"That's good... Oh, but I mean the part about you getting your side work done early," she says, lightly laughing.

"Yeah, hopefully it'll be busier tomorrow," I say, acting as if I don't have a care in the world, when in all actuality I am totally preoccupied with asking her about the schedule. Finally, though, I succeed in getting the words out. "Beth, uh, do you, uh, mind if I ask you about something?"

"Do I mind? Of course not. What's up?" she says, finishing with her apron and looking right at me.

"Well," I begin, lowering my voice, "I just noticed that Bobby put me down to bus tables on Saturday night, and he must have just added it to the schedule last night or earlier today because I don't remember seeing it earlier in the week. And he didn't even say anything to me about it... I mean, I realize that our schedules aren't set in stone and he's the boss and can change them, and of course I bus my own tables during the day—it's part of the job—but I didn't know that I was going to have to bus tables on a

Saturday night…"

"Oh—" Beth replies, having listened intently to everything I said. "I don't think Bobby meant that he wants you to just bus tables. He probably wants you to hostess."

"Hostess?... Then why did he put *bus* on the schedule?" I ask.

"Well, hostessing here doesn't just mean that you'll greet people and lead them to their seats. It also includes helping the waiters and waitresses in any way you can, like delivering food for them, taking drink orders, and also bussing tables and resetting them whenever it's necessary—you know, all the same stuff you do when you waitress. It's really not that much different, except that you won't be taking the main food orders, and you're asked to dress up a little. And, instead of getting two-eighty an hour, you get five. It's really not so bad," she says, her face bright and encouraging.

"Oh," I say, starting to feel quite a bit better about the situation.

"And," Beth continues, "you only need to work until whoever's waiting tables that night feels that they can handle things without your help. When they let you know that, you just need to check with the bartender if it's okay for you to be finished, and then you're all done!"

"How long does the shift usually last?"

"Sometimes two hours, sometimes four or five, depending on how busy it is."

"So it's a pretty short shift then."

"Oh yeah…it's actually really nice. You get to come in and make a few bucks, but you don't have to spend your entire evening here, especially on a weekend… Oh—and about Bobby not letting you know that he was going to put you down for hostessing…he does stuff like that a lot. He probably had every intention of telling you about it and explaining to you what was expected of you, but it most likely slipped his mind. In fact," she says, smiling and shaking her head, "he may not even have realized that you've never hostessed before. You know how lackadaisical he can be sometimes."

"Yeah, I have noticed that," I say, nodding. "But, Beth, to be honest with you, I really…I just really don't want to work on Saturday night. I just don't think—I don't think I'm ready for it." I look down for a moment and then back up at her.

She smiles at me thoughtfully. "Oh, Jenna, I'm sure that you'll be just fine. Everyone says how well you've been doing so far, you know."

"Yeah. I know. But I—"

"Jenna—" Beth's eyes light up suddenly. "I don't mean to interrupt, but I just thought of something. I have to work the day shift on Saturday, from eleven to five-thirty, like I usually do. If you wouldn't mind switching with me and working during the day, I could hostess for you on Saturday night…"

"*Really?*" I say, feeling like I've just been rescued from a bunch of turbulent waves. "That would be so great for me, Beth, but…but…but I really don't want you to have to adjust your schedule for—"

"Oh, no, Jenna, believe me—you'd be doing *me* such a big favor as well. I don't think I've slept in on a Saturday for months, and I'm just so exhausted. To be able to sleep in on Saturday morning, leisurely drink a cup of coffee and read the paper when I get up, and then study for a few hours in the afternoon before I come in here—that just sounds wonderful…" she says, her eyes quite dreamy.

"Well, okay, Beth. Okay. It sounds like it will work out really well for both of us, so let's go ahead and do it."

"Great!" she says, the gratitude emanating from her.

"We should check with Bobby, though, to make sure it's okay. He usually doesn't have a problem with this kind of stuff, but it's best to mention it to him… But, don't you worry about it. I'll take care of that tonight before I leave."

"Thanks so much, Beth," I say, removing my apron, "and thanks for explaining things to me. Have a really nice night."

"You too, Jenna. I'll see you Saturday," she replies, giving me an appreciative wink. ∎

MY FRIEND

He appears in the entranceway and pauses—his right hand resting in the pocket of his khaki pants, his black leather jacket hanging comfortably, and the current issue of *The Economist* held close to him—looking just as natural as ever, as if that's exactly where he should be at exactly this moment.

With a nod of his head and a smile he gestures to the front and seats himself at the two-seater closest to the window, opening his magazine to the movie reviews. I greet him with a Beck's Dark and a short funnel-shaped glass, placing them gently in front of him on a small, square napkin.

"Hey there, Mariano. Nice to see you today."

"So nice to see you too, Jenna…as always," he says, pouring some of the dark, rich, creamy-looking beer into his glass. "Say, do you have a second, Jenna? Before you get too busy?"

"You bet," I answer. I slide halfway onto the seat across from him, placing my little round tray on the small, maroon table and resting my arms on top of it. "I'm all ears."

"Great. Well, would you be up for dinner and another movie tonight?" he asks in his slightly accented English. "Take a break after working so hard on a Saturday? I just read a great review of *Il Postino* and can't wait to see it."

"*Il Postino… Il Postino…* Oh, I can't say I know anything

about it. I mean, I don't recall seeing any previews about it. But it certainly sounds interesting. What's it about?"

"Well…it's about Pablo Neruda, about the friendship that develops between him and his Italian postman, and about…about…the intense love of the postman for a village wai—"

"Really!? Your favorite poet! How great!… But oh gosh, Mariano, I'm sorry. I cut you off. You were saying?"

"No, no. That's just fine, Jenna. That's just fine. You finish what you were saying."

"Yeah? No, please…please… You finish."

He shakes his head.

"Oh, well then. Okay… Well, he's the one you told me about from Chile…the one who described love as being—how did it go?—something like, 'Love is a war of lightning, and two bodies ruined by a single sweetness…' That one?"

He tries to hide it, but he looks a bit shocked. "Yes. Yes. That's the one. Good, good memory, my friend," he replies, shaking his head.

"Well, it's a powerful, passionate, thought-provoking quote, you know? Not one that's easy to forget…"

"Oh, yes, I know. There's certainly no doubt about that. All of his work is like that. And yes, I've been so eager to see the film for weeks now, having read so much of his poetry and so much about him since I can remember… So, what do you think, my friend? Interested?"

"I'll be ready by seven," I say, touching his hand softly. He picks up his glass, motions it toward me, and takes a drink as I stand up and walk back to the bar. ∎

HOW IRONIC

I'm laying a fresh, crisp, white filter into the black plastic container that disconnects with a *twist* from the coffeemaker, when he approaches me and taps me lightly on the shoulder. Between the thumb and index finger of his right hand, a stack of quarters are tightly held.

"Hey…Jenna?… You'll be okay for a couple of minutes, won't you?" he asks. "I just have to step across the street for a moment, to plug the meter."

"Oh sure, Curt—I'll be just fine," I reply, looking up at him. Suddenly feeling concerned, however, I add, "I'm not trying to be nosy or anything, but doesn't that get quite expensive? You *do* have to feed that thing every two hours or so, don't you?… I mean…isn't there someplace free or less expensive you could park?"

"Yeah—" he immediately answers, the corners of his mouth beginning to turn upward, a mischievous glimmer in his eyes, "a few blocks away, on Northumberland Street, in front of my apartment." ∎

CRAIG NEWBERT (aka GLOBY)

He has that kind of mysterious sexiness that you can't quite describe, the stuff of Nicolas Cage. And he looks particularly attractive when he smiles, which accentuates his always-there mustache. Plus, he is friendly and easygoing, coming into The Grill at least twice a week, around three or four o'clock or so (when the place is rather empty), to hang out with Curt for a while and to drink a few cups of coffee before he has to leave to go to work.

As soon as he sits down on the bar stool, Curt gently places a clean, empty, white stoneware mug in front of him, then a napkin, a spoon, a little oblong plastic container full of sugar and sweetener, and a white stoneware dish filled with tiny, individual containers of half and half. "Just a minute for the coffee, buddy." As usual, each and every time Craig comes in, Curt dumps out whatever coffee is sitting on the burner, and he brews a fresh, steaming pot. And each and every time Craig gets up to leave—"Well, you know what time it is, Curt"—whether he has been sitting there for half an hour or two, has drunk one cup of coffee or four, he reaches into his pocket, takes out his wallet, and places a five-dollar tip on the bar. It's unmistakable how much they care for each other, in their masculine, unassuming way.

Craig is a bartender just like Curt, and he mainly works

the evening shifts at The Decade. From what they're telling me, though, he hasn't always been a bartender. Out of all The Grill's employees, and out of all its regulars, he seems to have had the most unordinary career. "You're kidding!" I respond to Curt and Craig, quickly turning around to look at them when I hear them talking about it (my back was toward them because I was punching an order into the computer next to the bar). "You mean that you used to be on those competitions on TV that my dad and I watched together when I was a kid?"

"Yeah, Jenna, you got it," Craig replies. But I just stand there, looking blankly at him. (I've learned, from past experience, to question my gullible nature.)

"Really, Jenna, we're not kidding," Curt says, laughing. "We're not lying. Craig here, my buddy here—he used to be one."

"No way," I say. "No way." I'm sure these two are having some fun with me, as they've done many times before.

"Yes, *way*," Curt says, laughing even harder. "He used to be a professional bowler."

A professional bowler? No—well, maybe. But then, no. I just don't believe them. As Jewel inquires "Who will save your soul?" through the overhead speakers, I walk away incredulous, shaking my head, sure they are pulling my leg.

Who will save your soul indeed. ■

BREAKING THE RULES

lacing one foot after another, she makes it in, her eyes on the floor. Her short, full hair is stiffly curled and dyed a lackluster shade of brown, and a drab, gray dress with a skinny, cracked belt hangs on her stout body, sometimes covered over with an off-white, dingy shawl. A musty, old smell accompanies her also. Her lips, however, are painted a red that's quite shocking.

"Hi, honey, how are you?" she says as her eyes, the same color as her dress, look up at me expectantly, a soft, kind, natural smile on her face. "You are going to be my waitress today, aren't you, honey?"

We've become rather friendly. Ever since the first time she came in to eat, which is now a weekly occurrence, I've felt compassion for her. She usually arrives around two, when business is slow, and we chat for a few minutes. I slide into the seat across from her, and we talk—mainly—about me, she never wanting to give up too much information, always so insatiably curious about my dancing and my writing, and all that I hope to achieve.

When I'm not free to chat any longer, either because a new customer has come in or I am starting to feel guilty for sitting down on the job (especially today, the first day I've ever worked with Nick…he's filling in for Curt), she orders a glass of Pepsi with a straw, and a grilled chicken sandwich, topped with lettuce, tomato, raw onion, and mayo. She doesn't like any of the side dishes we offer—french fries, coleslaw, potato salad, or applesauce—so she asks if she can have a side salad with Italian dressing instead. "Okay, honey? Okay?"

"Oh, okay, Olivia…okay. No problem. Let me get that for you," I reply—week after week, in fact—always feeling a little twinge of uneasiness, but always agreeing to it anyway.

I head to the kitchen and take out one of the already prepared salads from the cooler, unwrap it from its plastic covering, fluff its contents up a bit so it looks fresh and appetizing, pour a bit of the golden specked-with-spices Italian dressing into a small plastic container and place it on the edge of the glass plate, and then deliver the salad to my friend.

"Thanks, honey, thanks," she says, looking down at it warmly. "That's just fine, honey."

She proceeds to slowly eat her salad and then the rest of her lunch when it's ready, the entire time gazing around the restaurant and watching me work, seemingly so content to be in the presence of another, to have some activity to entertain her.

About an hour later, having briefly checked on her every now and then, I stop at her table. As usual, nothing remains on her plate or in her glass, which have been pushed to the side. "You enjoyed it, I take it?" I ask her.

"That I did, honey. That I did," she says, grabbing her torn, overused pocketbook from beside her and placing it in front of her on the table. She then reaches inside and, with no searching at all, suddenly retrieves a sleek, beautiful, shiny, silver tube, its top adorned with the engraving of a playful sprite.

"Can't forget this," she says, turning the tube, allowing the glistening red to rise, applying the color to her lips without a mirror, with the skill and accuracy of a surgeon.

"Certainly not," I say, watching her intently.

She rolls her lips inward for a smoothing final touch, placing the tube in the exact spot she found it. Then she hands me ten dollars. I reach into my left-hand apron pocket, fingering through the bills that are in there. I find her bill and walk up to the bar.

"May I get some change, please?" I ask Nick as I hand the rectangular white bill to him, with the money placed on top of it.

"Sure," he says, taking the bill and money from me and turning toward the cash register. But instead of running the bill through the register and getting the change, as he usually does, he looks down at the bill, as if he is studying it.

What's so interesting?

He turns back around toward me and looks up. Staring at me and not moving a muscle, he says, "Jenna, you *do* know that you're not permitted to substitute a salad for the side dishes, don't you, unless you charge two dollars extra?"

I pause for a moment, taken off guard. "Oh yeah... Yeah, Nick... Sorry about that," I finally reply. "I do know that."

He stares at me for a while again, apparently not exactly sure how to react. "Well...well... We'll let it go this time," he eventually says, turning to his register and opening it with its familiar *ding!* "But please don't do it again. If we start doing it for one person, Jenna, we'll have to do it for everyone... Okay, Jenna? Understand me, Jenna?"

"Okay, Nick," I say, taking the change from him and walking away, but fully intending to keep doing otherwise. How else will she continue to afford her lunches and her lipstick, those rebels against her melancholy. ∎

THE ZIMA CATASTROPHE

I attempt to serve a Bay Breeze (vodka, cranberry juice, and pineapple juice) to a young woman sitting with her friend at one of the two-seaters in the front. As I set it down on the table, I lightly hit her almost-empty bottle of Zima with the back of my hand. It topples over, and wouldn't you just know it, with the neck of the bottle facing her. Luckily, it doesn't break, but its remaining contents gain speed, and, in a matter of seconds, take the plunge into her lap.

"Oh my god did that get you?!" I utter as I rush to wipe off the table—it had all happened so fast. In an instant I am truly sorry, and quite embarrassed, but in that same instant I really doubt she'll think it's a big deal: a few drops of a clear, harmless liquid—so what? So I look at her, waiting for her response. And so she looks back at me, quite seriously. And then she answers me.

"*Yes*, it DID!!!" she hisses, thoroughly disgusted. She is a scowl in full force.

I guess I was wrong. ■

MOVING ON

"So, Beth," I say one early evening in late August, as I sit down across from her in the back booth of the smoking section (closest to the kitchen), where we employees eat, do side work, and hang out when the booth isn't needed for customers, "I heard that you were leaving in a couple of weeks." She is cutting lemons.

"Yeah, I am," she says happily, laying down the shiny knife on the wooden cutting board, and sitting back comfortably in the booth. "Now that I'm a proud Pitt graduate"—she winks—"I got a job at Carnegie Mellon, working in the computer and systems administration department."

"Awesome!" I say, truly excited for her. "It's such a prestigious university to be associated with. Plus, it's pretty close to your apartment—you can walk to work when the weather's nice!"

"Oh, I know," she responds. "I'm just so thrilled. But you know what the best part is? They'll even help pay for me to get a master's degree there…"

I pause for a moment—eyes wide—quite taken with her success. "No way!…Wow, Beth, that's really amazing. Good for you."

"Thanks!" She smiles, a picture of elegant confidence. "And how about you, Jenna? What are your plans next? Do you think you'll keep working here during the fall? It seems like you'd be ready to work the night shift now."

I take a deep breath. But she is right. I am ready. The fear that I felt two months ago has turned into an eagerness and assurance that I could handle the evening shift quite well.

"I think that I will stay, Beth, although I hadn't planned to whenever I started working here. I had just been looking for a summer job, but, when I think about it, I could definitely use the money. I know that it will be difficult with all of my classes and the dorm desk job that I'm going to have, but I really don't want to be loaded down with too many loans whenever I get out of college."

"Hey, I know what you mean," Beth says, shaking her head. "That's why I feel so fortunate that I'll be working at Carnegie Mellon. But, you know, you can count on making pretty good money working the evening shifts here."

"Oh, that's good to hear… How much usually? Around fifty dollars or so?" I conjecture.

"Maybe on a bad night. The average for me has been around seventy."

"What?!!!" I answer, my eyes widening once again. I really had no idea that you could make that much in one night as a waitress. And, at this point in my life, seventy dollars seems like a whole lot of money.

"Yeah, there's really a big difference between the two shifts. How much do you average during the day—about twenty to thirty dollars, give or take?"

I nod.

"Well, some nights, if you have a really good night, you can even make a hundred. In fact…" she says, thinking, "the most I made in one night was around one hundred twenty."

"What?!" I exclaim, laughing, completely shocked. "If I would've known that I could make that much, I may have switched to the night shift much sooner!"

"Well," she says, grabbing a handful of the just-cut wedges of lemon and dropping them into a white plastic container, "now's your chance."

So it is. And I'll take it. ∎

OUT OF CHARACTER

"Two Budweisers and a fuzzy navel, please!" I call out, just about out of breath. I have five tables going at once, and I really need to get these drinks to the table that was last sat. They've been looking at me all thirsty and irritated for the past ten minutes.

I watch Curt—he's at the cash register punching in an order. But he doesn't acknowledge me. I usually get a nod of the head, or an index finger up in the air, or something. Well, I mustn't be loud enough again. I love Madonna's music (and "Borderline" is one of my favorites), but I really wish she would pipe down a bit.

"Two Budweisers and a fuzzy navel, please!" I call out again, but this time with a little more gusto. I wait patiently at the end of the bar, holding my tray tightly, and take a deep breath, determined to make myself relax a bit. Certainly he heard me this time. But—if that's the case— why is he reaching in the cooler for a couple of Heinekens?

"TWO BUDWEISERS AND A FUZZY NAVEL!!!" I yell once more—almost not knowing what's gotten into me—this time leaving out the formality, this time being quite pushy, and this time giving it all my effort, so much so that my voice cracks a bit.

(And I thought that the third try was supposed to be a charm.)

He doesn't even look at me, but he shoves the corkscrew into a bottle of merlot—the veins maddening in his forearms—and he twists it…and then he twists it again…and then he twists it even more—tense, acute shavings of cork escaping helplessly. And while he performs this procedure, his head shakes in utter disbelief, and upon his face explodes a wry, exasperated, ironic, intensity-ridden smile. *That* smile that tells me he's heard me…and all along.

Dumbfounded, extremely uncomfortable, mind racing. Yes, those are all of me as I stand at the end of the bar, bombarded with uncertainty, the surrounding movement and noise just a constant, numbing blur.

Why didn't I realize before that he's simply had too many orders to fill and hasn't gotten to mine yet? I ask myself, shaking my head as well. Why didn't I call out the order *once* and then go about doing other things until my drinks appeared in good time at the end of the bar, ready and waiting? It *is* a madhouse in here, Jenna. I mean, just look around at all the customers he has. He has so much pressure on him, making not only *his* customers' drinks, but yours and Bianca's as well.

But wait a minute! I yell back at myself, my mind U-turning on me, my embarrassment and self-doubt transforming into anger. Why couldn't he just have nodded to me or told me to be patient? I mean, how much effort does that take?! I already knew, of course, that he's more of a day-shift kind of bartender (he usually works only one night shift per week), but I never expected this.

"Hey, waitress!!!" It's so *freakin'* loud in here, but for some reason I can hear this generic appellation booming at me out of the jumble of people and chatter in the front. "We're trying to make it to the nine o'clock, and we haven't even gotten our drinks yet!"

I didn't know that my face could turn any redder, but here it goes. Yes, my ego's crushed, I feel like I've been stomped on, slapped, driven over, and run through the wringer, and I'd like to hit someone (he's *never* treated me this way before), but I'll learn…I guess. It is, after all, only my second week of working the night shift—an entirely different beast from the day shift, I'm quickly (and painfully) finding out. ■

JACK

There's just so much he gets lost in.

Unbearably sensual poetry. Candles flickering in his dark, disheveled bedroom. Light brown hair that ripples down his back. Having his back lightly scratched. Hot, enveloping hugs. Iffy and Cassandra—his roommates' cats—who love him more. Cigarettes. A Rolling Rock and a shot of Grand Marnier to accent the cigarettes. Hanging out at The Cage, the bar-and-grill around the corner. His family. Earl Grey. Chamomile. Cooking. His kitchen. The regulars he waits on. Computers and searching the Internet. The Beatles. Tori Amos. E. E. Cummings. Doc Martens. Long walks, especially to the co-op, to pick up fresh carrot juice. Deep, all-out kisses. Strong, defined calf muscles, which he's so proud of. And my blue eyes, which he tells me *pierce* him.

******

ON MONDAY AND TUESDAY evenings, I work with Jack. He's a good guy. Instead of us taking turns, he consistently lets me work in the nonsmoking section, which is great for me, since that section is usually busier overall and, therefore, more lucrative (if you'll allow me to call it that). Besides, he works five days a week and two of the busiest shifts, the Saturday- and Sunday-evening ones, so he is always happy to have a bit of a break.

We get along very well. He is fun and easy to work with, and is always willing to help me out when I get extremely busy. Plus, I like the reassurance of working with someone who has been here for a while.

And to tell you the truth, I am quite attracted to him, which never hurts—most of the time, anyway. He has this not-so-rough, biker-like appearance about him—the bangless, wavy hair loosely tied in a ponytail; the sexy mustache; the long legs; the filled-out, generous body; the narrow, penetrating eyes—yet at the same time he has such a soft and gentle personality, with his innocent, unassuming laugh; his warm, inviting hands; his stretching, interesting fingers, with his nails that are longer than necessary. And I couldn't help but notice how intriguing he looked that autumn night he came in for a drink, dressed in jeans and a red flannel shirt, smelling of Jovan Musk, his body slightly curving over the bar as he rested his elbows on it and took a sensual drag on his cigarette.

But you know what? He's really not my type. I'm in college pursuing a degree and he is not (he dropped out after giving it a semester's try, deciding that it "wasn't for him"), and he had a run-in with the police a few months ago and isn't permitted to drive for a year or so. In addition, he smokes and drinks *a lot*. And even more important than all that—the drinking, the smoking, the not being in college, the occurrence with the police—my best friend, Teeli, told me a few weeks ago that she's interested in him, really thinks he's just great. So when it comes down to it, there's obviously no reason for anything to happen between us.

Or at least that's what I keep telling myself. ∎

A WARNING

His face bright and happy, he gently places a perspiring draft of Rolling Rock on my small, round tray. This is the second evening I've worked with him, the start of working together on Thursday and Friday evenings for many months to come. "You are *so* easy to work with, Jenna. I mean, you never get mad about anything or lose your temper or your cool," he tells me. "It makes my life so much easier, especially when it's so busy like this. Keep it up…"

"Thanks, Nick. That's really nice of you to say," I reply, as I proceed to quickly walk around the bar toward the front of the restaurant, passing my coworker Bianca on the way. I feel great. I swear, however, that I catch a glimpse of her eyes rolling around in her head.

A few hours later, when there is finally a slight lull in business, I sit down at the ancillary bar, hoping to give my aching feet a rest. Bianca is sitting there also, facing the wall, glancing at the front page of the *Pittsburgh Post-Gazette*.

"Hey, Bianca. How's it going? And what's happening of interest in Pittsburgh these days?" I say, motioning toward the paper.

"Oh, the usual. You know. Discussions about tearing down Three Rivers and all that," she responds, not even looking at me.

"Oh yeah, that's really depressing," I say, waiting for her

to say something else, wondering if she is upset about the thought of the stadium being torn down or if something else is bothering her. "Bianca… Hey… Is everything okay? You…you just seem a bit unhappy tonight…kind of quiet."

"Oh yeah?" She immediately pushes the paper aside and quickly turns to face me, sitting on the edge of her seat. "Well, if you really want to know…the thing is, Jenna," she begins, her voice soft but intense, "I overheard Nick complimenting you earlier. You know, about how easy you are to work with, and—"

"Yeah, *I* was surprised by that myself. He's been so nice to me… Really, Bianca, I'm not sure why everyone complains about him," I say, shrugging my shoulders.

"Oh, you're not?" she replies, raising her eyebrows and laughing, her laughing so deep and saturated with wryness (and bitterness) that it's almost scary. "Well, he was nice to me at first also…but look…all I'm trying to say is…don't get too used to it, because the truth of the matter is, Jenna…he just hasn't chosen to pick on you yet."

She finishes with a defiant look and then walks away. ∎

THE METEOR HITS

Mel is a white-haired, short, wide, hunched-over man in his early seventies, I'd say, who constantly wears a ball cap, baggy pants, and an expression on his face like Dopey's. He drinks way too much, and he talks way too much. Except, in the midst of all the mumbling, I can never figure out what it is he's saying. Of course, maybe he can't either.

Other than that, I don't know much about him… But then again, there is one more thing: He likes Remmy, the new waitress.

How do I know?

Well, not just because he chatters at her all the time, and not just because he follows her around while she works—but because of what happened last week.

I was getting two bottles of Killian's Red from the cooler—grooving a bit to "It's Only Rock 'n' Roll" as I did so—and Remmy walked quickly past me, laughing, and said (while Mel trailed behind her), "He *goosed* me! Can you believe *that?*"

Actually, I really almost couldn't. Who knew he had it in him? I surely didn't.

But when I glanced up at him in his quest after her, he wasn't looking down at the floor—for once—but was focused on her, eyes ablaze.

It all proved to be way too much for him, however.

Instead of following Remmy to the front of the restaurant, where she had fled (she was really way too far in the lead), he changed his course (not voluntarily, I suspect) and scuttled into the narrow, short corridor that leads to the front exit.

But he didn't quite make it out.

He had been traveling rather crookedly and unsteadily, brushing the walls with his shoulders, when BOOM!: The entire right side of his body, led by his right shoulder, hit the interior wall—which is made up of milky-colored glass squares connected by fashionably smoothed-out cement— securely and squarely.

I swear I felt the whole place shake. But nobody felt it more than the couple who was sitting at the table that lines the other side of this wall. And you know what? I was so lucky to be the one serving them two fresh beers at just that moment, as chunks of plaster and concrete toppled onto their Cajun chicken salad and bacon cheeseburger.

Yes, the meteor had hit—but I was about to experience the fallout. ■

MARIANO

I can't believe I've found someone like him. He's sensitive and sweet; intelligent and honest.

He lives in a two-floor apartment on hilly, cobblestoned Ludwick Street in Squirrel Hill (I get lost within the turns and hills every time I drive there), with mounds of unopened mail thrown in a corner ("I'll attend to that one of these days," he says, his eyebrows rising); multiple bookshelves exploding with knowledge; a large, tempting, black-and-white picture of puckering-up Marilyn Monroe; a colorful photograph of himself, his best friend (Marlon), Nancy, Luis, and me—after our Latin dance performance on the Gateway Clipper Ship—with the beautiful Pittsburgh skyline behind us; and a squiggly bottle full of mercury that, when you hold it, bubbles and rises— sometimes feverishly…sometimes not. As *I* hold it, he tells me that it tests your tenderness level, and when I believe him—delighted—he just laughs at me admiringly.

The best thing about his apartment is the wall at the bottom of the stairs and to the left as you enter the front door, on which he has neatly taped a gigantic, glossy, white slab of thick paper. This blank slate has sporadically and abstractly (in various horizontal, diagonal, and vertical patterns) been covered by Mariano with his favorite quotes, in his fancy, stylish hand. There is also his signature figure—a cat with a round head, a round body, pointy ears, and a curlicue tail—which I've seen before on all the birthday cards he has given me.

He grew up in Lima. As a child, he was afflicted with chronic asthma, which confined him to bed and prevented him from going outside and spending time with other children. But this didn't stop him from going on adventures and making friends of his own. His books became his friends, and he spent countless, wonderful hours with them.

Magically, as he grew into late childhood, the asthma left him. So one day, naturally, he decided to leave his books at home and ventured outside to play. Out of nowhere, around noon, a major earthquake hit, and the city was devastated. Mariano, however, was feeling more alive than ever. Instead of running home, he walked around the crumbled city for hours, enthralled by all the changes the buildings had suffered—while his poor mother suffered at home.

Years later, as a young man, he lived in Chile, relishing the delicious food, the wonderful coast, and the culture— and finding two loves: the love of a woman and of the woman's little girl. But the yearning to come to America and to pursue his long-desired business dream was too strong to be denied. When the woman wouldn't leave the country she loved and pursue his goals with him, he was forced to leave his two loves behind.

Catastrophically, the business venture failed, and he lost all his hard-earned savings. It took him quite a while to get over it, of course, but it didn't damage him. There's just too much life in him for that to have happened, a fact so apparent to me from the very start.

We met one perfect almost-spring evening at Rosebud, a dance hall in the Strip District. He asked me to salsa. "You must have been Latin in a previous life!" he said after about two minutes, his genuine face beaming. "Why haven't I seen you here before?" And he led me into an underarm turn.

"Believe me," I replied, as I spun around twice, "I would've been here if I could've, but I just turned twenty-one a few days ago!"

Ah, that evening of fate. It was such an effortless beginning, and it's been so effortless ever since.

We relax on his porch in the cool summer evenings, savoring extra-strong coffee; sip fiery Pisco as we lounge on his enveloping couch and watch tapes of *Riverdance*, *The King and I*, and topless African samba dancers; sit around his table eating just-grilled steaks and baked potatoes, with a side of shockingly hot jalapeños, while we sip merlot, chat about books and movies, and listen to the romantic Plácido Domingo.

He comes into The Grill at least once a week to eat—sometimes two or three times—and he always sits in my section. He *loves* dark beer and eats his hot wings and celery with a fork and a knife (although I've told him various times that it's not necessary), and he always requests an extra scallion jutting out of the side of his Cajun chicken salad, even though he can never remember what it's called. There's no need to, anyway, because I always know what he wants.

Some nights he waits for me until my shift is over, and we sit at a tiny two-seater under the dimmed lights, with two fancy glasses of thick, glistening, sweet, amber-colored Disaronno Amaretto, looking at each other and talking intently. It's always so intimate, no matter how many people are around.

He recommends countless books to me, including *The Lover* by Marguerite Duras, *Paula* by Isabel Allende, and *The Unbearable Lightness of Being* by Milan Kundera. The first book is sensuous, about the love affair between a twenty-seven-year-old Chinese man and a young French girl; the second book I have yet to read (I'm having trouble finding an English translation); and the last book—well, I'm not quite sure how I feel about that one. Mariano tells me it's one of his favorites. He's read it again and says that it brings home to him what he's been feeling lately: that if only he were chronologically twenty years younger…

We go to the movies together a lot also, seeing films such as *Il Postino, Twelve Monkeys*, and *Toy Story*, the last of which is the most fun. We're free to see it because my classes and his appointments at the business school are canceled due to the huge snowstorm that hit the night before. Mariano eagerly trudges in the snow all the way from his apartment to mine, and then we walk together to The Manor Theatre, among snowy-dressed trees. After the movie, we go nearby to the 61C coffeehouse and drink hot cappuccinos, protected within mist-covered windows, savoring each other's company.

And then there are the many restaurants we enjoy. We frequent The Elbow Room on Ellsworth Avenue in Shadyside (Mariano *loves* going there), where we are free to be childlike and creative and draw in crayon on a paper-covered table while we wait for our food; Gullifty's on Murray Avenue in Squirrel Hill, well-known for its wonderful desserts, where after an evening movie we enjoy a thick piece of decadent cheesecake with fresh strawberries and whipped cream, two steaming coffees, and intelligent conversation; Harris Grill, also on Ellsworth, where we sit on the patio under colorful umbrellas shielding us from the hot summer sun, and relish large hot wings, Greek salads, the balmy breeze, and a discussion about how relationships between men and women differ in Latin America and the United States.

Often, he wakes up at four in the morning and can't go back to sleep. It's not such a terrible thing, though, he says, because his books on UFOs, aliens, and the world wars, in which he's so interested, fill the time perfectly. On Saturdays in the summer when this happens, he reads until it's a decent hour, then he picks up the phone and calls me, asking if I want to spend the day at the outside market in the Strip District. Of course I do, remembering what fun I had the first time he took me there, as we walked by all of the vendor stands and enjoyed the sights and smells of the fresh olives, fruits, cheeses, meats, and fish, and as we sat under an umbrella on a concrete deck overlooking the main, thriving street, with an enormous pot of steaming, garlic-covered mussels and two icy mugs of beer on the table in front of us. Also in the summer, one early evening we take a trip to Sandcastle, a water park in the suburb of West Homestead, and enjoy the large, refreshing pool, the relaxing, spacious hot tubs, and the various kinds of seafood being steamed all around us over outdoor, open fires, including king crab legs dipped in butter, and raw oysters covered with fresh lemon and cocktail sauce.

As dance partners in the Latin American Cultural Union, an organization devoted to disseminating the culture and art of Latin American traditions and life, we perform on a Three Rivers Stadium dugout during a Pittsburgh Pirates game, at various festivals, and at The Andy Warhol Museum on All Saints' Day. Afterward, we walk around the museum together, discussing and observing multiple versions of Mao Zedong and Marilyn Monroe. We *try* to perform at a festival in Erie, PA, but things don't go as planned. First of all, we're late getting to the car rental agency at the airport, so we miss the van that is taking the other dancers to the event. Mariano decides to drive the two of us there instead, but he eventually realizes that he hasn't brought the directions to the festival location with him. What's more, he can't even remember the exact name of the place. It's absolutely freezing outside, so we end up stopping at a hospital and sitting in its lobby for at least an hour and a half, perusing the phone book for any leads, wearing out the payphones, and asking anyone or everyone who walks through the door if they can help, but no one has a clue. We can't even remember the cell phone numbers of any of the other performers, and neither one of us owns a cell phone anyway. At long last, when we've tried everything, we give up and decide to go to dinner. We have a much easier time finding a very nice restaurant called Pufferbelly, where we both have beautiful salads and huge plates of flavorful chicken marsala, even huger glasses of merlot, and lots of satisfying conversation, as always. In the end, with our stomachs full and our heads much lighter, we decide, after all, that the long trip was worth it.

He's the kind of person who gives up an extremely well-paying, six-figure, full-time job for a very modest-paying, part-time job that supports him emotionally and gives him time to breathe, to read the paper, and to drink an espresso outside on a sunny Monday afternoon. He's the kind of person who will dance at a friend's party until four a.m., no matter what time he has to get up the next day. He's the kind of person you can go downtown to the China Inn with, and after a spicy meal and three glasses of white zinfandel, have no fear picking up the microphone on the karaoke machine and singing eighties "tongue-twister songs" (as he calls them), such as *Whip It*, even though you thoroughly detest public speaking. He's the kind of person you can go to Barnes & Noble or the Heads Together book and video store with and browse for hours, without feeling the least bit uncomfortable. He's the kind of person you can enjoy dim sum and jasmine tea with on a late Sunday morning at the Peking Gourmet on Murray Avenue, and when his fortune cookie directs him to kiss the person seated to his left, you're glad that you're the only other person at the table. He's the kind of person who gives you *The Little Prince* for Christmas, with "May the joy of Dance and Music be always part of your life" written inside. And he's the kind of person who gives you a light brown alpaca scarf that was handmade in Peru, which perfectly matches your coat and your long hair, and which you'll treasure forever.

One evening, when I'm sick and feeling down, he makes me a dish called ceviche, something I've never heard of before, let alone tried. We sit behind his apartment on his concrete patio around a little metal table as the sun goes down, and from the first bite I absolutely love the pungent, lime-drenched, meaty fish adorned with loads of garlic, onion, and slices of tomato. I can't believe that the lime actually "cooked" the fish, but he assures me that it has.

What *he* can't believe is that I've never seen *Casablanca*, and he says that we'll have to remedy that very soon. The following weekend we rent it from West Coast Video on Murray Avenue and watch it at his place. It's romantic and heartbreaking, just as he said, and I'm so glad that I saw it for the first time with him. When he drives me home later that evening, he looks over at me thoughtfully, almost sadly, and says, "Well, Jenna... We'll always have Pittsburgh."

Mariano... So good for me. Encourages me to dance, to write, to be happy—to live. Has complete faith in what I can do. Tells me, sincerely, after hours of salsa dancing, that he can't believe I'm still so "fresh like a lettuce," which always makes me laugh...it's just so original. Tells me how important it is to find your calling in life. But most of all, appreciates me completely and reminds me often, saying that if I were to bottle my kindness and sell it, I'd become a millionaire.

Mariano… My soul mate, undoubtedly. My confidant, friend, encourager. Older, but understands me better than anyone—is younger and more childlike than anyone I know. Dance, literature, passion, family, music, language, food, cappuccinos in a mug, art, intimacy, and Amaretto, walks in just-fallen snow.

His loves are mine. ■

NICK

A magician of liquid, he swiftly grabs a tall, dark green bottle from the top shelf on the left, then seizes an elaborate black one from the bottom shelf on the right, quickly and simultaneously pouring their altering contents into the thin glass full of ice in front of him, but stopping the flow of one bottle a few seconds before the other, releasing just the correct amounts of each, designing the perfect-tasting cocktail. He does this over and over again, and night after night, often making three or four drinks at once, relying upon the bank of information stored in his head, remembering all of the varying combinations of substances that come together in unique ways to create countless types of happiness. The authority here on the subject, he answers any questions I have. "What goes in a Singapore Sling, Nick?" or "What's a Grasshopper made of?" and he instantly rattles off the components. A couple of times he does have to think for a second or two before he responds, such as when I ask him about some obscure drink hardly anyone ever orders, or when someone older requests a concoction with an unusual name that was in fashion back in "their day," as they tell me. But almost always he replies as if the specific ingredients are written on his tongue. Only once do I see him refer to the cheat sheet that is yellowing in its place under the register. ■

ROLANDA

Invariably, whenever I walk through the door, there she is: an attractive, spectacle-wearing, African American woman in her mid-fifties, sitting at the leftmost end of the bar, next to the wall; sipping a scotch and water with a lemon twist; delicately smoking her sleek, long, brown cigarette; and playing the slot machine—her chin tilted slightly up, a discerning look in her eyes.

Rolanda is her name—or Lanny, as most are comfortable calling her. Sometimes, in the evening or on a weekend, I'll see her in a fancy pantsuit, sitting there contentedly—but, most of the time, she is simply in her blue post office uniform, her hair pinned loosely at the back of her head, a curl or two escaping on her cheek, her tiny gold-hooped earrings catching the dimmed light.

She's an employee of the Squirrel Hill Post Office, and has been so for quite a long time now. The post office is located just a few doors down from The Grill, on the corner of Murray and Darlington. Thus, The Grill, given its closeness and affordability, is the perfect place for her to go during her lunch break. Every day, she stops in for a bite to eat and a game on the slot machine—sometimes two or three, depending upon whether she has an entire hour or just half of one.

She enjoys trying the lunch specials and homemade soups, and she's particularly taken a liking to the various types of chicken sandwiches—the Cajun chicken, the bleu chicken, the bacon and cheddar chicken, the chicken au naturel—always requesting an extra mini plastic cup of mayo on the side. However, Curt, who gives her extra-special attention, consistently remembers the extra mayo before she even has to ask, one of the best things about being a regular here.

Lunch for her is usually from noon to twelve thirty or one, and then she's gone for the afternoon. But not more than ten minutes after five, she walks through the door again and takes her spot at the bar, which is more often, than not, vacant, as if everyone in the restaurant follows the unspoken rule that it is reserved for only her. She then takes a sip of her scotch and water through the thin plastic stirrer lying slantwise in the ice—the cocktail had been placed in front of her as she sat down.

Besides playing the slot machine, enjoying an after-work drink, and chatting with her crazy coworker Marcy—who giggles louder and talks louder with each beer she enjoys, and who tells a few off-color stories, if she can get away with it—Rolanda loves to read. There is often, lying on the bar beside her glass and skinny pack of cigarettes, an inviting, thick, paperback book. Among various others over the years, *My Ántonia* is one of the novels that is given that privileged spot.

"*My Ántonia*… Hmm… How is it, Rolanda?" I ask one early evening before business starts to pick up. I notice the book as I'm returning an empty wineglass to the bar. I run my fingers lightly over the lettering.

"Oh… Well," Rolanda answers, her eyes landing on the book and studying the cover, "I'm really enjoying it…yes, I really am…and I do have to say that I'm learning quite a lot from it too. It's set during the late eighteen hundreds in America and tells about the movement west and the deep relationship that develops between a young boy and girl."

"Sounds very interesting…although…yeah, I really don't remember having read anything by Willa Cather before, and, to tell you the truth, I really don't know that much about her either," I admit.

"Me neither, honey," Rolanda replies, shaking her head, "except it says in the preface that she lived in one of the beautiful houses on Murray Hill Avenue in—when was it exactly?—from 1901 to 1906, I believe… To be honest, that's one of the reasons I picked up the book in the first place," Rolanda says, smiling.

"*Really*? She actually *lived* on Murray Hill Avenue?"

I find this so intriguing because I am a student working toward an English degree at Chatham College—a gorgeous women's college nestled between Squirrel Hill and Shadyside—and Murray Hill Avenue is the cobblestoned, hilly road, lined with expensive and lavish homes, that runs just outside of, and parallel to, the college. I've walked and driven up and down that avenue many times—my car bumping along, my teeth vibrating—and a few of my professors live along it, including my French professor and one of my English professors, who is also my tutorial adviser. In addition, I'm very interested in learning anything I can about writers—especially writers of the classics—such as finding out about where they lived and worked, how where they lived and worked influenced their writing, how they had become writers, and what kind of temperament they had. I suppose, too, since I've seriously been thinking about becoming a writer—in the midst of all my other artistic pursuits!—that in the back of my mind I consider it a rather good omen that such a famous writer lived so close to where I am attending college.

I pause, as all of this zips through my mind, an expectant look in my eyes, I'm sure, but then I finally say,

"Rolanda, would you mind if I borrowed that when you're finished?"

"Of course not, honey. I'm about halfway through it, so I should be able to get it to you before too long."

******

IT'S NEARING DUSK on a Saturday, and the streetlights have just made their welcome appearance. I gaze at the busy street for a moment through the large, front windows of my favorite coffeehouse, the 61C, as a lime-green pot of Earl Grey steeps and steams on the little square table where I'm sitting, a miniature orange and red lamp providing a small area of light and warmth. REM fills the room with their unique sound, but, unbelievably, I hardly hear the music as I pick up Rolanda's book and study the cover—the elaborate letters that fit so well together, the picture foretelling, but maybe not, what is going to be told inside. I slowly open it up, perusing the copyright page, then the title page—these are both important for me to take in—then I read the introductory material about Willa Cather's life, as has Rolanda. I then slowly turn the page and read the opening sentence—"I first heard of Ántonia on what seemed to me an interminable journey across the great midland plain of North America"—and, for this moment at least—unlike so many others in my life—the restlessness has vanished.

******

SO EAGER TO LET HER KNOW what I thought of it, I return Miss Cather's best-seller to its owner. What I encounter, however, completely makes me forget all about my original intentions. You see, a dog-eared, paperback Stephen King novel is resting comfortably in the place of honor.

"Oh! You mean—*you* like Stephen King?" I ask, my face accentuating the tone in my voice, as usual. "That's *definitely* a switch from Willa Cather."

"Oh yeah, I *know*," Rolanda replies, laughing, apparently humored by my puzzled expression. "I really like mysteries and science fiction—better than anything, actually," she continues, "and even a good horror story every now and then. I mean, I had picked up *My Ántonia* for a change and, like I mentioned, I was interested since I had heard that Cather had lived for a few years in Pittsburgh."

To be honest, I'm not interested in those genres—science fiction and mystery a *tiny, little* bit maybe, but *certainly* not horror—so I'm not going to ask her to borrow the novel. Plus, I've always heard rather frightening, gruesome stuff about Stephen King's novels and am not yet ready to give them a try. One of these days. *Maybe*. But now? No. *Forget it*. I think I'll stick to my Hawthorne, and maybe some Poe. True, some of their stuff is really dark, creepy, and chill-inspiring, too, but in an entirely different way.

Well, at least I think so. But, then again, maybe they are more similar than I think. One of these days I'll just have to find out.

Just then, Remmy—with her short, blonde hair, attractive face, and energetic spirit—walks by. But then she just as quickly turns back around.

"*Carrie*, Lanny? Get out! That was an *awesome* book! Are you liking it?"

I look at both of them in confused, dilapidated wonder.

"Well, it's been giving me quite a thrill, to say the least," Rolanda replies.

"It surely will do that—no kidding. After having read that one, though, I've been meaning to read the rest of his books, but, unfortunately, I just haven't had the chance yet."

At this comment, Rolanda's eyebrows rise, and the corners of her mouth turn up intriguingly. "Well…kiddo," she replies, and then pauses for a moment, "this just may be your lucky day." She pulls down the handle of the slot machine with a great deal of gusto.

******

ROLANDA SLOWLY WALKS IN with an old cardboard box, books piled to the top, partially obstructing her view—and my view of her. She eventually puts the box down on top of the bar with a heavy sigh, but with also a smile, as always. And then she lets us in on the story.

It turns out that a month or two ago an old friend of hers gave her the books when he moved out of town. "If it were me, however, I wouldn't have given all the books away like that—no way," she continues, shrugging, "but oh well…*I'm* certainly enjoying them. I mean, there's a smattering of everything in there!" Yes, there are some Steels and a few Koontzes and one or two Tolkiens and even some Dickens (the guy had quite an eclectic taste, I'd say), but, at this moment, these don't really much matter—to Remmy, at least. To her utter amazement, and delight, the complete Stephen King collection is scattered among them.

And I can only imagine how freaked out she's gonna be by the end of this.

******

"HEY, LANNY! I'm ready for the next one!"

"*What?* Are you serious?" Rolanda replies, her eyes wide. "That was really quick!"

"Well, you know, when something catches your int—"

Rolanda gently puts up her hand. "You don't have to say anything more, sweetheart. I know *exactly* what you mean. Just a second, and I'll ask Bobby to get the box out of his office."

******

IT'S EVEN MORE FUN coming to work nowadays, getting to see Remmy and Rolanda rummage through that treasure trove, deciding which adventure Remmy will go on next. They don't even care if I eavesdrop and learn about King's plots and his style of writing, as they wonder how he could have ever come up with such bizarre, terrifying stuff, but are evidently so deliciously glad that he did. And, quite tickled myself, I can't help but think, again and again (even beginning to seriously consider picking up a Stephen King novel myself—God forbid): Who would've known it? This place I work, this deceptively simple bar-and-grill, has turned into a meeting-of-the-minds haven.

And all because of Rolanda.

******

EACH EVENING, around seven or eight, sometimes later, she'll say, "Well, it's about that time, Nick... Would you mind calling me a cab?"

"Sure thing, Rolanda." And Nick will happily do so.

"Did they say how long he'd be?" she'll ask, as Nick hangs up the phone.

"Ah...probably around ten to fifteen minutes...at the most."

"Oh!—well then," she'll say, sitting back down on the edge of the stool, with one foot on the rung and the other on the floor, her coat on but her mind still with her friends relaxing around the bar, "Why don't you give me one more..." ■

ATTACKED

"**Y**OU NEED TO CALL THE DRINK ORDERS OUT TO ME *LOUDER!*" he's begun to yell at me often, a disturbing gleam in his eye. Never mind that when he usually says this he is at the other end of the bar, retrieving a glass from a shelf beneath it, which just happens to be next to the noisy electronic poker machine and one of the speakers for the music system.

"Just walk over here and I'll tell you again, jackass," I mumble to myself later after work as I sit fuming in front of my TV—poor David Letterman being pummeled with all of my anger—replaying the incident in my mind, knowing that *I* couldn't walk behind the bar to get closer to *him* because I had been yelled at for doing that also, for *getting in his way*. "We can't *both* be back here at the same time!" he had shouted, that unhealthy gleam present then too.

But when Nick speaks that way to me—no matter how many times he's done it—I just stand there meekly, with a dumbfounded look on my face, trying to hide my hurt. I've never been spoken to that way before, and it always comes as a shock, particularly because I know I don't deserve it.

I've wanted to talk back to him so many times, to put him in his place, but in all honesty, my body won't allow me to get the words out. ∎

IRWIN

"You're different from most, you know."

I am reaching and stretching, upon my tiptoes, for the large plastic container, full of colorful hard candy, that sits on the ledge above the register.

"Oh yeah, how's that?" I answer, looking furtively over my shoulder as I place a yellow Jolly Rancher and a red cinnamon treat on top of the check that rests on the black plastic holder in my hand.

"I can just tell. From the way you work. Your attitude about every little thing… You know—you're serious. You have a very good work ethic."

I turn around slowly and smile, then walk a bit closer…

So he *has* been watching me, I think to myself, as I've thought—and sensed—so many times before. The way I move from table to table. The way my thin fingers rest upon the bar as black, fizzy Pepsi shoots from the gun into the ice-filled pint glass. The way a piece of soft hair lies astray upon my long, bare neck as I punch an order into the machine.

"That's very sweet of you to say, Irwin," I answer, looking thoughtfully at him, at his black, plentiful shock of hair, and at his black, thick-framed, thick-lensed glasses, as he sits at the bar having a beer. "And it's even nicer of you to notice."

"Oh, it wasn't hard," he quickly replies, chuckling in his innocent—yet-trying-to-appear-tough—way. "Not too hard at all."

******

EVERYBODY LOVES IRWIN—or "Bubba," as most are used to calling him, an oxymoron without a doubt—especially Curt and Nick and Mary Ellen (the kitchen manager and main evening-shift cook), who, in an instant, would lay down their lives for his. I'm not sure how or why or when or where they met—probably here at The Grill, where so many lifelong relationships have sprung and been nourished—but they are just about as close as people can get.

Frequently he arrives in the evenings when either Curt or Nick is bartending, all stocky-but-lean, five-foot-four of him strutting in—or *attempting* to strut in—like John Travolta dressed in too-blue blue jeans; a white, decaled, overly long T-shirt; and clunky, tired, open-laced high-tops. He then coolly pulls out a bar stool and sits "casually" upon it, one foot on the lower rung, the other placed firmly on the floor, legs spread wide, the empowering mound of gold and silver metal from West Penn Hospital—where he works as a receptionist—lying haphazardly on the bar. Next he orders a beer, in the most masculine voice he can find, and then takes a sip of it, slowly tapping his fingers on the bar and grooving his head up and down to the music, his chin in the lead.

After about an hour or two, when he gets up to leave, it's obvious that he didn't really come in for the beer—there is usually at least a quarter, sometimes more, of the liquid left in the only bottle he ordered. Rather, it was the friendship and the chatting that he was after, and—depending on who was working—the observing and the watching.

Some nights he arrives especially late, and just for Mary Ellen, who has called him in desperation. Either the sink is relentlessly clogged (with various scraps of food), the faucet is leaking all over the place, or some essential parts are getting rusty and old. So many times—and just in time—he appears in the kitchen through the back door, his glasses fogged up, but his mighty, experienced, red toolbox right beside him. Down on his knees he goes, flat on his back he lies, no dirt or wetness fazing him, his tools fitting perfectly in the grooves of his hands, like familiar friends. And in no time at all, and with a magical skill, the problem is gone. The sink drains effortlessly, the faucet is done crying, the parts glisten shiny and new. It hasn't taken me long to realize that working at the hospital is his day job, but plumbing—it is his art.

When Irwin isn't actually physically at The Grill, he is here over the phone, calling up Curt, again and again, for help on the *Pittsburgh Post-Gazette* daily crossword puzzle, which he loves to challenge himself with (to make up for the challenge he apparently isn't getting at the hospital). And he is right—Curt is the person to ask. He is *especially* good at the puzzles, doing them every now and then when he has the chance. I hear him dishing out answer after answer to Irwin—*Barton...mardi...Cook...Waters...*—while I imagine Irwin eagerly filling in square after square, using a number two pencil, making thick, deliberate letters. Every now and then I even get to participate, like the time Curt handed the phone to me, saying, "You'd better handle this one." I picked up the phone, said hello, and there was Irwin, talking in a serious, earnest voice, like he was getting ready to operate: "Okay, you're ready?... This has five letters, ending with an *a*. And here is what it says... Ready?... Okay... *Af-ri-can dance...name means...'to rub navels together.'* Have any—"

"Oh, oh!" I replied, cutting him off, so proud to know the answer. "It's *samba!* The answer is *samba!*"

A few seconds of silence followed this outburst, but then Irwin responded with one of his own.

"Right!… Oh yeah, right! I think you're *right!…* I would've never gotten that one!… That's great! Thanks for your help! Now I should be able to get the rest of them!"

Sometimes, when he hasn't had the chance to call during the day, he even brings the unfinished crossword puzzle in with him after work, interrogating anyone who seems interested—a raised eyebrow or a wrinkled forehead giving them away—passing the paper from person to person until each mystery is solved. "I think I know it, Irwin" or "Give me a second to think" are the kinds of expressions that are soon flying around the place, accompanied by hands scratching heads and shoulders hunched forward eagerly. When an answer is finally found, especially one that has taken an extra amount of time and effort, you would think that the Steelers just won the Super Bowl! The clapping, the yahooing, the smiling, the noise— there is just so much of it.

What a simple thing it is, this Irwin-inspired detective game, but how happy and involved—and connected—it makes all of us feel. ∎

BIANCA

I've always thought that she has the name of a movie star. Just pronouncing it—*Bianca Blume*—sounds beautiful and rich.

To most people, coworkers and customers alike, she's known as Bea or Bianc, but I almost always hear Curt call her Bianca—maybe his right by having once been her love.

She's certainly beautiful—just like her name—with her soft face and light blue eyes, and is particularly bewitching with her hair down, which is long, blondish, and loosely curled. After finishing her shift and changing out of her work clothes, she walks from the restroom toward the bar, in her worn blue jeans that perfectly fit, with her hair free and flowing, as if tiny jets of air are hidden beneath it. And then there's her stride, which at the same time is carefree and confident and, because it is both of these, sexy.

It's obvious that many eyes, particularly male eyes, are upon her as she pulls up a bar stool and orders a shot and a beer—usually a Jack Daniel's or a tequila and lime and a Budweiser—grabs her basket full of tips from behind the bar, and counts her hard-earned money. When she speaks and laughs, you can actually feel the happiness in her voice and laughter—or at least her effort to be happy—which is always accentuated at this time of night by her big, knowing smile. ◼

AN IMPROMPTU CHA-CHA

The Carnegie Mellon University Ballroom Dance Club elite…

What an appearance they make.

There's Drew, the president—brainy, stocky, and continually bald-headed (a condition he was born with)—sipping another Pepsi that I've just refilled. Liza, the vice president—a student in the School of Design; unabashedly frank and sexual—swishing around the stirrer in her gin and tonic. Pam, the secretary—blonde, friendly, and confident—taking another gulp of her beer. And Pat (short for Patrick), the treasurer—tall, nice-looking, and masculinely feminine—licking the salt off his margarita.

It's quiet tonight, and except for my dance friends—and Rolanda, who is sitting at the bar feeding the electronic slot machine—the place is empty. And I have no clue why, but there's something like elevator music playing on the sound system. So when Pam gets up and heads toward the wall jukebox, I'm not a bit surprised. What I am surprised about is that it took her this long.

She flips through the cards that list the selections, studies them for a moment, then pops in a few quarters and takes her pick.

DA! da da DA! da da DA! da da da DA! DA! DA!
DA! da da DA! da da DA! DA! DA! … Uh!!!
Oye Como Va…

Tito Puente's catchy tune begins.

Pam sits back down, but her heart just isn't in it. She looks knowingly at each of her friends, and without a word they stand up in unison, move the tables to the side, and break off into pairs. Rolanda turns around to watch, and Nick—can this really be happening? He dims the dome-covered, hanging lights.

As she rock-steps back on her right leg, Pam sexily juts her hip to the side, and Pat steps confidently toward her, the connection apparent between them. Liza shoots her arm high up into the air, with a curling flourish of her wrist and fingers, while Drew spins around two times. Pam then spins around too, falling into Pat's arms as he lowers her to the ground and as she lifts her right foot to her left knee and her chin to the sky. Liza and Drew flick their heads backward at the same time, Liza's reddish-brown hair snapping in the air. The couples pass each other in horizontal and vertical patterns, even switching partners every now and then, in some kind of ordered disorder. And the barely perceptible headlights of the cars, as well as the interested eyes of the passersby, glimpse through the window at the mystery of the moving figures within.

As for me, I stand off to the side, completely engrossed in it all, involuntarily doing a few cha-cha-chas of my own. ■

COLLISIONS

ute. If I were asked to describe Shane in a word, that would be it. He is five-foot-threeish/fourish, about my height; is thin, but not too thin, a bit of a belly apparent above his belt; and has blue eyes and pretty, shiny, straight, silky, golden-blond hair. He always looks comfortable and casual in his light blue button-up shirt and too-long khaki shorts; white tube socks scrunched down around his ankles; and preppy, black, large-soled shoes. Every time he finishes taking an order, he quickly and adeptly places his pen behind his right ear, a movement that seems so natural to him, which frees his right hand to punch the order into the computer.

Not only is Shane cute in appearance, but he has a "cute" personality as well. He is friendly, soft-spoken, and fun-loving; is quite bubbly most of the time; has a sweet and innocent air; and is super easy to joke around with. He is especially fun to be around when he drinks. He becomes extremely silly, relaxed, and giggly, releasing his hair from the gum band that holds it in a low ponytail behind his neck while he's on the clock.

Take one night after work about a month ago, for example. Shane and I and quite a few coworkers and regulars were sitting around the bar having a few drinks— let me clarify: *I* was having a few drinks; Shane was having *many*. He was sitting on the bar stool beside me, to my right.

Due to the amount of beer he was drinking, he was often making trips to the men's room, which is down the hall on the left, right before the kitchen. He'd slide off his stool, hesitantly placing his right, then left, foot on the ground. Slowly, he'd start walking, but he was never able to walk straight ahead. This was a problem, because the hallway is fairly narrow, not more than four feet wide. Lining the hallway to the right are a few booths. And to the left there is a dividing wall, which separates the smoking section from the slightly elevated nonsmoking section. The solid part of the wall is only a few feet tall itself, because the top part of it is "cut out." In essence, it is a lengthy, glass-free window. Customers in the nonsmoking section can see down into the smoking section, and vice versa. It gives the small restaurant, which is much longer than it is wide, a nice, open feeling.

Walking down that hall isn't any big deal if you haven't been drinking (God knows I've carried countless trays of food and drinks up and down it, often passing others— trays and people—on the way!), but it doesn't leave much room for error if you have been. So, when Shane would start walking toward the bathroom, he'd veer too far to the right, almost at a diagonal, and…WHACK! He'd hit the first booth with the lower part of his right hip, and with enough force to send him in the opposite direction, his body involuntarily curved in a sideways U… CRASH! Then he'd hit the dividing wall with his left shoulder, again with enough force to send him back where he came from, his body curved the other way, flyaway hair and unruly hands trailing behind him. Poor Shane! This would keep happening until he had christened every booth in the section—thank God there are only three! Everyone at the bar would watch and laugh, some so hard that they could barely catch their breath, as he bounced from booth to wall, then wall to booth, his body becoming less whole every second.

Upon returning to the bar from one of these bumpy rides to the bathroom, Shane looked particularly tired out. There were beads of sweat on his forehead, and his shirt was half tucked in, half tucked out. Even though I was chatting with Bianca, it was difficult not to notice him trying to climb back up on the stool. To tell you the truth, he was approaching it like he was a mountain climber, preparing himself for a risky and daring undertaking. On his first attempt, his foot slipped off the bottom rung, while his hands gripped the top of the stool, his knuckles the color of fire. I intently looked at him, my eyebrows raised. "Are you okay, Shane?" I asked.

"Yoooouuuuu betcha!" he replied, and rather exuberantly for someone who looked so worn out, as he somehow turned himself around and planted his butt squarely on the stool, sighing deeply and with much satisfaction. I don't know why I hadn't seen the resemblance before, but he reminded me of David Spade in the midst of one of his crazy comedy routines.

Shortly, he resumed doing what most of the other people at the bar were doing: drinking and smoking. He picked up the large draft in front of him and swallowed a generous mouthful, then took a luxurious drag on his cigarette; and again he picked up the large draft in front of him and swallowed a generous mouthful, then took a luxurious drag on his cigarette. He did this repeatedly, amid the chatter and laughs. Each time he set the tall, funnel-shaped glass back down, it wobbled unsteadily, and a bit of the auburn Penn Pilsner ran down the side of the glass and onto the top of the bar. It was almost as if the well-known ritual of drinking, smoking, drinking, laughing, smoking, talking, drinking, laughing, smoking had a hypnotic effect on him, because it wasn't too long before he sat still, glassily staring straight ahead, his eyes focused on nothing in particular, his shoulders hunched forward a bit, and his arms motionless, hanging at his sides. "Shane, *really*, are you sure you're okay?" I asked. But it was too late. He was in no position to answer—literally. He began to tip sideways, and, in approximately two seconds flat, that's when his head landed…BOOM!

…in my lap.

I was sitting on the bar stool, Shane's beautiful blond head in my lap. ∎

TEELI

Every time she walks in—a bit unsteadily—with that big, black, book-laden leather satchel hanging over her left shoulder (I swear it's a permanent fixture there), holding—in her left hand—her metal, Chatham-insigniaed container of coffee (she must drink at least ten to twelve containers-full a day), I'm so happy to see her. Some days she'll sit in my section and order a skinny glass of cranberry juice, the sun-dried tomato pesto pasta, and a side salad (which I always cut up for her) with blue cheese dressing; other days she'll sit at the bar and de-stress with a cigarette and a seven and seven and chat with Curt, whom she can't say enough good things about. But no matter where she's sitting, she takes out her books and works, whether writing poetry (which is always so interesting) for her creative writing class, or working on her tutorial about the massacre of the American Indians—her forehead furrowed. And whenever I get the chance, I'll sit down for a while and visit with her. Somehow, no matter my mood or outlook, this always makes me feel wonderful.

Not only do we spend a lot of time enjoying each other's company at The Grill, but our absolute favorite thing to do together is to hang out at the coffeehouses in Squirrel Hill and Shadyside—there are just so many to choose from. I relish going to them at any time and with anyone, or alone, but I have the best time when I'm enjoying these magical, eclectic, inspiring, comforting, cozy, noisy-but-quiet havens with Teeli, because she "gets" them just as much as I do. On any given day we'll make an appearance at one, and on special occasions, sometimes two or three, including the Arabica and the Coffee Tree Roasters on Forbes; the 61C on Murray; the Greenhouse on Ivy (the building really does look like a greenhouse, solar windows and all); the Coffee Beanery on Walnut (there's a cute Thai American guy who works there, whom Teeli has become rather friendly with); the Beehive on Pitt's campus (you just have to check it out, if you don't fear passing out from all the smoke); and the Kiva Han on Craig (they have a neat loft area if you want some privacy). She prefers the Coffee Tree Roasters, while I adore the 61C, but this doesn't cause any trouble—we always have an easy time compromising. What we're really after anyway is the environment and the chance to be together amid our books, the music, the luscious aromas, and the tea and coffee, studying one moment, and chatting and guy-scoping the other.

We also love going out to eat together, and especially for Thai food. The food at the Thai House on Bellefonte Street in Shadyside is delicious (they actually have a dish made of hard, dried noodles that form a basket, filled with fresh, crisp, sautéed vegetables), but the place we like best is the Lemongrass House, which is located above a men's clothing store in Squirrel Hill. We sit by the curving glass wall and enjoy looking at busy Forbes Avenue below and at the enchanting, mystical statues of Thai goddesses within. We start out with delectable Thai iced teas (if you've never had one, you're missing out!), made with the perfect mixture of rich, orange-colored Thai tea and sweet, heavy cream. I nurse mine for as long as I can, but Teeli usually downs hers rather quickly and then requests a Thai iced coffee.

Next, we order. One evening we'll have tom yum soup (lemongrass-heavy broth with succulent shrimp and tender-but-firm mushrooms) and fish cakes to start, then spicy tofu in a black bean sauce (for her) and green curry with chicken (for me). The next time, we share everything, enjoying corn cakes for the appetizer, a shrimp salad drenched in lime juice, chilies, and garlic for the main course, and, for dessert, sweet sticky rice. And we eat all of it with their beautiful, copper-colored, majestic cutlery with the curlicue flourish at the end of the long stems. But watch out! Their food is *hot!* (As in *spicy hot.*) I can eat hot food—don't get me wrong—but the level of hotness contained in some of the dishes is just plain amazing (on a scale of one to ten, I've finally learned to order a three). Teeli, however…talk about amazing. She's an order-a-ten-consistently type of girl. And there's never any wincing. No downing all the water in her goblet. No taking a break for a few minutes to catch her breath. All I can figure is that the Thai blood running through her veins must have something to do with it.

It's kind of surprising we get along so well, though. We're very different young women, with very different looks and very different backgrounds. She has dark features, and mine are light; she's agnostic or Buddhist (or something in between), and I'm Catholic; and she had a rather difficult childhood, and mine was, for the most part, carefree and happy. But that day, in February of 1992, when we met on the winding staircase in beautiful Fickes Hall, on our way to becoming freshman roommates, I had a feeling our relationship would be something special.

Rooming with her in that big, fancy dorm room *did* take a little getting used to, however. First of all, she stayed up until three or four in the morning studying, lying on her stomach and hiding within her covers (innocent eyes peeping out), books spread all over her bed, and her desk lamp (also on her bed, quite precariously) shining like a veritable spotlight. After a few weeks of enduring this (and not sleeping much), hiding within my covers as well (my head completely covered, though), I tried to talk to her about it, but I didn't press her when she said that she studied best at night—"It's always been that way"—and hated to be downstairs in the library or living room alone, it just made her too nervous. Secondly, she set her alarm clock to the heavy metal station—and never forgot to turn the volume up high. Therefore, each morning I'd be awakened by silence-thrashing Metallica, Ratt, or Mötley Crüe (take your pick!), which never failed to jump-start my heart. And thirdly, after taking a shower down the hall in the communal bathroom, she'd come back to our room and nonchalantly walk around naked as she decided what she was going to wear—in front of *me*, who hates to undress in front of even my mother.

But the more I've thought about it, I could live with those minor things, especially because the person who did them has such a heart of gold, and has done—and does— so many other things that truly do matter. Like when she never forgets to give Edward, the kind homeless man who sits on the short brick wall that's adjacent to the bagel shop—just a couple of doors down from The Grill—a steaming, fresh cup of coffee, particularly when it's freezing outside. Like when she tries to cheer me up by giving me "happy gifts," as she coins them, such as a pretty, V-necked, button-up cotton top in a shade of yellow—my favorite color—or *Trial by Fire*, the just-released CD of Journey, my absolute favorite band. Like when I'm suffering in my dorm room with tonsillitis, and she brings me a plate stacked with food, even though it's hard for her to carry it all the way from the dining hall with a brace on her leg and the use of only one hand. Or, like when it's my birthday and she writes the sweetest, most earnest note to me, even though it's so difficult for her mind to form the sentences sometimes.

But that Teeli, she's a fighter. She grew up without her mother. She's been through multiple surgeries. She goes to a reputable, four-year women's college even though she was told not to. She continues going to this college, even though, again, many advise her to transfer. Plus, she works the graveyard shift at Eat'n Park as a hostess, and then walks all the way back to campus in the morning as the sun rises.

Whenever I can, I give her a ride to wherever she needs to go, in my yellow Dodge Shadow (and she always offers me gas money). I braid her long, wavy, beautiful black hair before she goes to work—and adjust and brush her short, straight, black wig when she goes through radiation and chemotherapy. Every once in a while I butter her toast in the dining hall. I edit her papers and help her to form ideas and transitions. And whenever she misplaces something, I try to find it.

But Teeli, she does so much for me, too—but it's much more important stuff, I know. When I work as a live-in nanny for a wealthy doctor and his wife, the summer before my sophomore year, she keeps me sane. When I'm aching inside with a broken heart, she listens to me and comforts me when I think there's no comfort.

Unfortunately, we do have our problems, though. For a couple of months she's thoroughly mad at me and won't say two words to my face. One day during this time she comes into The Grill with Amanda, my ex-roommate and a "friend" of ours from Chatham, and passes me coming out of the bathroom. "Teeli, what's *wrong*?" I ask, desperate, but she hardly acknowledges me. Later that evening I call her and leave a message (she lives across campus in Woodland Hall), but she never returns my call. I can't, even though I think and think about it, figure out what is wrong. All I know is that she's not happy (to put it mildly) about my new love interest, and I just bet that Amanda is putting some weird ideas into her head.

Eventually, after a lot of heartache and unanswered questions, she comes cautiously into The Grill one evening—without Amanda, for once—her large, round, brown eyes welling up with tears. I give her a ride back to campus later, and she apologizes profusely, admitting that she doesn't know what got into her. "I'm *so* sorry, Jenna. I was just so worried about you being with Joey—I was so scared for you," she says. "Plus, Amanda was saying all of these mean things…about you…and for some reason I started to believe her, even though I knew in my heart that they were in no way true… But, finally, it all dawned on me that the only reason she wanted to hang out with me so much was because she had found a bank in me… I'm so sorry, Jenna. I'm so sorry… And I love you—you know that…don't you?"

If someone truly wrongs me, I can never seem to completely get over it, and it is tucked within me forever. But with her, after she says those words to me, it's never again an issue. The slightest tinge of anger or resentment against her vanishes forever.

Maybe it's because she's such a good soul, maybe it's because she tries so hard, maybe it's because she has so much to fight against…but I think it's because she loves me, and because she tells me so—tells me so, more than anyone I know.

Originally, I hadn't even planned to go to Pittsburgh for college. After a tumultuous two weeks at a college in Ohio, plus a few more months of embarrassment, shame, despair, and indecision, Chatham became my second college try. And Teeli, upon receiving the rejection letter from Juniata College in Huntingdon, PA—where she had longed to go—she was forced to go to number two on her list. Thus, it seems that somehow, at this raw, wonderful, explosive time of our lives, we are destined to be here—in Pittsburgh, at Chatham, hanging out at The Grill—together. And not just for the serious, heart-wrenching, scary, earth-shattering aspects of living, but for the fun, easy, simple, crazy, and utterly enjoyable stuff, too, which, in the end, turns out to be just as memorable and life-changing—if not more. ■

THE HARVEY WALLBUNKER WOMAN

She's here again—that woman—who wears the multicolored, striped toboggan over her short, orangish-blonde hair; who wears the pointy black dress shoe that cramps her bare, left foot; who wears only the fuzzy green sock on her right foot, which won't stop moving at the end of her crossed legs; who wears the tight, gray, beaded sweat suit; who wears the small, round-framed glasses; who sits sideways on her bar stool, her left forearm resting on the bar while her right hand lazily and richly allows her lips to take a puff of her skinny, brown cigarette; who comes in so late at night.

She must think she's a movie star. Well, at least that's the rumor.

"I'll have a Harvey—hiccup!—Wall-bunker… pleeaaaaaassse," she slurs as she surveys the entire place, her head bobbing softly up and down.

I'm standing at the waitstaff register, at the end of the bar, and my friend Mariano is sitting in the middle two-seater against the dividing wall in the nonsmoking section, his favorite spot. Both of us have stopped for a moment—cautiously—glancing back and forth at one another, our eyes tacitly focused on the bar.

And Nick, who is counting the money in his register, hasn't even turned around to face the woman, but I know that he heard her. I can see his eyes rolling around in his head, and the irritation spreading like a hot flash all over his face.

"Harvey *Wall*-bunker, I said!!!" the woman suddenly exclaims, making most of us at or near the bar flinch, as she smothers her cigarette in the ashtray in front of her and stares intently at Nick's back, her cool demeanor vanishing.

Amazingly, Nick turns around slowly, but I wouldn't be surprised if a bunch of rockets took off through the top of his head.

"*Listen*, lady," he begins, walking toward her and looking intently back at her, "you've had way too much to drink already. And I'm *certainly* not going to serve someone who can't even get the name of the damn drink right. So…I'm going to turn back around and continue what I was doing, and when I'm finished, you *better* not be sitting there anymore."

"What *nerve!*" the woman remarks as Nick turns back around. She slams her stretched hands on top of the bar and looks wild-eyed at anyone who will acknowledge her. "*Well*…I…I…I…" She seems beside herself about what to do, but she eventually sits abruptly back in her stool and lights another cigarette.

Like he said he would, Nick continues tallying up the money, and I continue working as usual, retrieving a credit card from the regulars from Barnes & Noble who are sitting in the front and have been drinking and laughing for the past couple of hours. I think to myself, as I run the credit card through the machine that is on the wall above my register, that Nick is being especially tolerant tonight, allowing the woman to sit there quietly even though he told her that she had to leave. But then—interrupt that thought—I sense that something isn't right, so I look over my shoulder and glance behind me.

"Nick!" I yell, trying not to make a scene, but it's of no use, for every single person in the place has stopped what he or she was doing and is staring at the bar, including Mariano, who has gotten about halfway out of his seat, his attention diverted from *The Sorrows of Young Werther*. Thank goodness there are only a handful of people here to see it, though, to see the Budweiser tap and the Sierra Nevada Pale Ale tap at full throttle, the streams of fresh beer—one light, one dark—flowing uninhibited and heedlessly into the draining receptacle below.

"All right, lady, you are *really* pushing it," Nick says as he hurriedly snaps the taps into the off position, and just stands there, his hands on his hips. I swear he must be using every ounce of composure he has, must have dipped into a reserve somewhere. "One more trick like that and I'll escort you out of here myself."

"Oh *will* ya?" she says, taunting him, pulling the toboggan off her head and frantically running her hands through her hair, her eyes not leaving him for a second. "Well, what would you do if I did *this*?" She picks up an ashtray, which holds her smoldering cigarette and a pile of ashes, leans over the bar a bit, turns on one of the taps, fills the ashtray with the beer, raises it to her lips…and…and drinks it!…ashes and all!…her eyes glimmering endlessly.

Nick watches the whole thing. The whole thing! But once she takes that drink—once she hangs herself—he walks abruptly around the bar and is about to grab her arm. But then, just as abruptly, he puts his hand down. "Better yet…" he says, thinking aloud, and returns to his station behind the bar.

He picks up the phone.

Shortly (it's odd how quickly, in fact), the car pulls up outside, and two of them walk in, standing on each side of her, surrounding her and saying "You have the right to remain silent…"—these two towering men in ominous blue.

"Hey, Nick, how's it going?" they say next, and I get the impression that they've been here before, and because of Nick's beckoning.

"Oh, it wasn't going so bad…that is, not until this one showed up," Nick replies, gesturing in her direction.

"Well, you know, we've seen this one before too. But—don't worry—a night in the slammer usually straightens her up…for a while, at least," one of them says, laughing.

"I felt bad about calling, but she was just getting way too out of hand," Nick replies, shaking his head.

And I stare at him, trying to figure out if he really does feel bad, but I do have to admit that I see a touch of regret in his eyes.

I know that I feel bad, watching her as she clings, nails scratching, to the edge of the bar as they try to tear her away from it, her toboggan brushed aside in the struggle and falling limply to the floor, her face stressed and miserable, her words "I don't *want* to go!" childlike and intense.

She must give up eventually, though. Must submit to the metal constraints they SNAP! around her wrists. Must calmly and respectably walk out the door with their hands clasped around her, and get into their car.

I don't think she'll be back. ∎

ADAM AND ANTHONY

A silver snake curls around his right ring finger. Lines from Williams' *27 Wagons Full of Cotton* rush through his mind. Hot, steaming coffee in a white mug—placed in front of him on the edge of the bar while he works—warms him when he is feeling fine; cinnamon and apple spice tea—I *love* the smell of it—when he isn't, as he gently dunks the red, shiny tea bag up and down, in rhythm with his steps as he approaches the bar from the kitchen. Generous squirt upon squirt of Tabasco sauce— which he aggressively grabs from the disheveled condiment assortment on the ledge nearby—on his chicken sandwiches, burgers, and buffalo wings during his lunch break; generous amounts of cigarettes, shots, and beer after work… An actor.

******

DEEP BLACK, SOFT, feathery hair adorns his already Italian, undeniable good looks. Wonderful pasta dishes with white wine, made especially for me, increase even more my high opinion of his cooking ability. Papers and business plans in need of writing destroy his after-work drinking plans every so often—when he allows them to. Sense of humor and tender personality make me laugh and smile… A Philly boy.

******

IT'S TEN THIRTY on another cold but sunny Saturday morning, and I push open the old, clunky, wooden screen door that leads to the kitchen (the heavier door has already been propped open). There stands Anthony—in his white T-shirt, gray sweatpants, full-length apron, and heavy, black, steel-toe shoes—busily chopping up onions with a large, sharp knife, on a white, plastic cutting board.

The door thumps behind me, and I glance up, and when we lock eyes I instantly know what is coming.

"JENNANA BANANAAAAAAAAAA!!!!!!!!!!!!!!!!!!!!!!!"

The expression slides easily and exuberantly off his tongue, as it has so many times before and will so many times again, like a small child shooting down a steep waterslide; but at the same time, it sounds full-bodied, rotund, and larger-than-life, reverberating throughout the entire restaurant, through the walls, and into the Squirrel Hill atmosphere.

"Here you go," he says, as he hands me a perfect, golden, ripe banana that was waiting on the shelf beside him. "I stopped at Giant Eagle on the way here."

"You *never* disappoint me, do you?" I reply, taking the banana and beginning to peel it.

"I try not to," he answers, smiling—his deep, brown eyes shiny—and returns his attention to the onions.

******

I'M BEHIND THE BAR, wetting a rag, when I hear the lock in the front door turn. It's almost ten to eleven.

In walks Adam—well, at least he *tries* to walk in; his dirt bike is caught sideways in the doorway.

"Holy *hell*," he grunts. But, as usual, he isn't frowning.

"Tough night once again?" I ask, lightly covering my mouth with my hand.

He has just finally gotten through the door and is

practically leaning on his bike. His brown, wavy, thick hair is sticking up in every direction, sweat is lightly running down both sides of his face and into the stubble above his lip and on his chin, and his tight, white pullover and baggy jeans are lightly clinging to his stocky body.

He sighs. "Yeah, well, I guess it's pretty amusing, isn't it? Me looking like this every Saturday morning?"

"Well, *you* know," I reply.

"Yeah, I *do* know," he answers, smiling gently, and looks at me with red eyes. "Yeah…you guessed it…it was another night of raucous snowboarding…and drinking," he says, really to no one at all, as he pushes his bike toward the back of the restaurant and then disappears into the basement.

And, as I giggle to myself, I can't help thinking, as I've done so many times already, that he looks like he has just snowboarded down the mountain, rather than the night before.

******

MUCH TO MY SATISFACTION, that's what—or should I say *whom*—I have to look forward to when I wake up on Saturday mornings: Adam and Anthony, my two good-looking, good-natured, easy-to-get-along-with (and not to mention terribly sexy) male coworkers. *God must be looking out for me* I whisper over and over again, being able to see Anthony every time I walk into the kitchen, and Adam every time I walk out of it; being teased by them and being able to tease them back—obviously some divine recompense for my having ended up attending a women's college. ■

MARY ELLEN

Working the day shift, I heard through the grapevine about the infamous Mary Ellen, the kitchen manager and evening-shift cook. But what was possibly hinted at more fearfully than she herself was her temper. Yes, that's right—her *temper.* From what everyone told me, I eventually began to think that it was an otherworldly entity that floated about and covered the walls of the small, cramped—but nonetheless, cozy—kitchen of The Grill on Murray Avenue.

I used to wonder, however, what in the hell everyone was talking about. I would see Mary Ellen for a few minutes here and there, when I was ending my shift around five and she was just arriving to prepare for the evening. She'd lazily but proudly walk through the front door, half a smile on her face—which was usually flushed from the heat—a white headband placed securely in her short, but full, red hair. She'd be wearing a large, white, baggy T-shirt, either white shorts or white sweatpants, and white, well-worn tennis shoes, and she'd carry a small knapsack over her shoulder. She was always friendly enough to me, usually casually saying, "Hi how are ya doin' tonight?" and then she'd continue on her way, saying hello to others, which took a while at that time of day (during happy hour), when a lot of the regulars came in to hang out. Finally, though, she'd make it back to the kitchen to begin her preparatory work. I did notice that she became irritated every now and then, like everybody does, but it was not nearly to the extent that I had heard rumored.

Well…

How many times have you been told that you really don't know someone until you live with them? The same goes for working with someone, at least as far as I'm concerned. Oh yeah, now that I've been working the evening shift, my mind has been changed…and quite completely. That otherworldly entity is for real. "*MORE SAUCE*!!! What do you mean *MORE SAUCE*??!! If he wants any more than this, you're going to have to charge him for it! Do you hear me??!!" And then ten minutes later: "Too *BLAND*! Is that what she said? That's how I always serve it, and everyone *loves* it!… These damn, fuckin' customers—I've had about enough!!!"

Mary Ellen, Mary Ellen. I've never met someone who is so not afraid to speak her opinion and to tell you *exactly* what she is thinking—in a clear, forthright, utterly bold voice too. As I just conveyed, she is especially vocal whenever a customer complains about a meal that she has prepared, whether the complaint is "This isn't hot enough," "This is too tough," "This has no flavor," etcetera, etcetera, etcetera… Anyone who has ever had the pleasure of working in the food-service industry is undoubtedly well aware of not only the varying and large number of complaints that exist, but also of the sheer asininity of a lot of them. And, in Mary Ellen's view, almost all of the complaints are asinine, whether they are merited or not, and particularly when she is in an even feistier mood than usual. In fact, whenever any of us waiters and waitresses arrive for the evening, one of the first things we find out, besides what the soup of the day is and which section we are scheduled to work in, is the "Mary Ellen

Daily Report": "What kind of mood is she in today?" we secretly whisper to each other (like a bunch of worker bees), trying to discover her current temper level, wanting to know whether it is somewhat in control or flowing with full force.

Once in a while, whenever a customer complains, I can assuage him or her and fix the problem myself, which I always try to do. Most of the time, though, I have to consult Mary Ellen. It's not as if I can walk back into the kitchen ("her" kitchen, as she calls it) and dip out more sauce, or throw a steak on the grill to cook it a bit more, without her permission (unless, of course, she has stepped out of the kitchen for a few moments and I can surreptitiously and quickly do it!). For me, it is often a test of personal fortitude to relay a complaint or a request to her. First, I have to build up the nerve to walk back there; second, I have to actually open up my mouth and force the words out; and third, I have to brace myself for her reaction, which I can never predict. A lot of times she completely surprises me with her calmness, giving me exactly what I need with no confrontation at all: "Okay, no problem, Jenna; here you go," she'll say as she hands me a few more carrots for the vegetable tray or another scallion for the grilled chicken salad. But some nights, be on guard!—especially when it is really busy. The last thing that we waiters and waitresses want to be is the messenger of bad news to Mary on a chaotic Friday or Saturday night. The unspoken motto seems to be: "Prepare yourself for flying cookware!" No, but really, I've never seen her *aim* at anybody; she *will* at least yell "WATCH OUT!!!!!" before she flings a hot, steaming pot across the kitchen and into the overflowing sink, as either Richard (one of our dishwashers who occasionally cooks) or Anthony ducks out of the way.

"Oh, that's nothing," Marty, her friendly, good-natured husband, told me, when I was joking with him one night at the bar, talking about the pot-throwing incidents. He had just finished his shift at the Gulf Station nearby and was enjoying a few Buds, as he often does. "She's really mellowed compared to a few years ago," he said. "In fact, a while back, some *major* dynamite had exploded in that kitchen," he added, chuckling.

"I don't doubt it," I replied, laughing also, and imagining what kitchen havoc she had wreaked.

But you know what? The more I work with Mary Ellen, the less I am intimidated by her, and the more I like and understand her. Her explosive reactions are honestly quite amusing now (most of the time, anyway) and make some otherwise mundane evenings a lot of fun. And I've begun to learn what kind of things she is amenable to (even though she complains the entire time she is doing them), and what kind of things she will completely refuse to do without even a second thought. Which reminds me of a game we play whenever a customer requests something completely bizarre, irrational, or unexpected. It all started the night a customer asked me if we could do him a small favor. He would like to order the penne with marinara sauce, he began, but with a slight change. Could we divide his bowl of penne (you know, the usual amount) into four smaller sections, topping one with marinara, another with alfredo, the third with sun-dried tomato pesto, and the last with olive oil and garlic only? (No, I'm not making this up.) I really think I stared at him for a moment, quite unintentionally, but I was rather amazed that he thought we could be so accommodating, and I knew, from experience, that Mary might fall over dead if I asked her, or, if not do that, let loose *all* the pots and pans from their hooks, and maybe (God forbid) even a few knives. So, to put up a good front and please the customer, I replied, in my sweetest voice, "Well, I'm not sure about that, but let me ask the cook for you and see what she says…okay?" I walked back to the kitchen, got Mary Ellen's attention, and said to her, in the bluntest, most convincing, most there-can-be-no-other-answer tone, "Mare, just tell me no." She looked squarely back at me, seemed to instantly understand me, and without a glint of hesitation said no. From then on, it's been a game of ours, but it works so well. Anytime a customer requests something ludicrous, infuriating, or downright insulting, something I know that Mare will answer with, "Are you *SERIOUS*? There's *NO WAY*!" I simply save the time and energy of both of us and play "The 'Tell Me No' Game." And, most importantly, the customer at least thinks that I'm giving his or her request my best effort.

Given this friendliness that's grown between us, and the increase in my relaxation on the job, I'm really beginning to understand Mary Ellen and the motives behind her fiery reactions. In all honesty, I was at first seriously taken aback by how she reacted to many situations. Isn't "the customer is always right" the motto that employees of the service industry are supposed to follow? Personally, I am much more laid back and try not to get so bent out of shape when someone complains (well, at least on the outside I don't). But, the more I've thought about it and tried to understand, I've realized that I'm not the person who prepares the meals that the people are complaining about—I "just" serve them. To Mary Ellen, these dishes are her creations, her designs, her trophies, her dance steps, the results of her heart, mind, and hands. She is utterly proud of her cooking, a proudness that, I would venture to say, borders on cockiness. It is almost as if her knowing blue eyes and her attitude collectively say, "No one in this city cooks better than I do—no one," even though she has never come right out and said that. She probably feels this way because although there are complaints, as there are with anyone and anything, the majority of the time the customers are extremely happy with her cooking. They even wander back to the kitchen and tell her so: "That steak was done just perfect, Mary Ellen" or "Those chicken breasts were juicy and tasty, the best I've eaten." To tell you the truth, I don't know how many times I've waited on customers and, before I've taken their order, they've asked, "Mary Ellen's cooking tonight, isn't she?" I've really gotten the feeling that many of the customers come to The Grill on the evenings when they know Mary will be working. It's no wonder that she has such confidence in herself.

She is also a stickler for presentation, cleanliness, and freshness. The dishes she sends out are totally attractive. I often see her use a clean white cloth to wipe off a bit of oil, mayo, or grease that has fallen from a sandwich and has marred the appearance of the clean ceramic plate it is sitting upon. She also wipes off any extra oil that has splattered on the edge of the large white pasta dishes that have just been filled with hearty pasta. And, after the kitchen closes each night, she makes sure (even if she doesn't do it all herself) that the many utensils, knives, dishes, and pots are cleaned and neatly put away, and that the grill, counters, and kitchen floor are scrubbed and shiny. She gives any leftover soup to me or to any of the other employees who want to take it home (but there often isn't too much remaining!), or prepares a Styrofoam cupful for her friend Irwin, whom she loves. She then drains the hot water from the metal bins that keep the soup hot during the evening, and wipes them down until they are glistening.

In fact, Mary Ellen enjoys preparing fresh, new soups

each day, such as her flavorful, cold gazpacho or her well-loved chicken noodle soup, full of big pieces of juicy chicken and vegetables. Many times I see her standing over a steaming pot of chicken stock, as she stirs the liquid with a big wooden spoon and inhales the delicious aroma. There is also my favorite, her thick, delicious cream of mushroom, to which she always adds a touch of Burgundy (I often bring back a glass of Burgundy from the bar for her when she is making it). She knows that I love this soup, so she always makes sure that I get a cup to take home if there is any left over. On the nights when this soup is available and I ladle out a cup or bowl of the mixture full of juicy, whole mushrooms for a customer, my mouth waters and I can't wait for the end of the evening so that I can enjoy a bowl. Of course, some nights I end up being disappointed because we run out of the soup, which is certainly great for business, but not so great for me! And then, as everyone knows, accidents happen. I vividly remember the night that there was half of a large container of the cream of mushroom soup left—business had been extremely slow. "Wow, Mare!" I said, lifting the soup container's metal lid and peering inside. "There sure is a lot of soup left!"

"Yeah, I know..." she responded, from her usual position near the grill. "Would you like to take it home with you? I know that you really like this kind."

"That would be great! I'd really love that."

I was truly happy about it, because I knew that the soup would supply a few lunches for me. It is so filling and creamy that a bowl of it practically fills me up.

Mary Ellen came over and proceeded to lift the plastic container filled with the soup out of the water-filled metal bin that it was kept in to keep it hot. As she did so, with her other hand she removed the metal bin's lift-off top, which was equipped with two, rimmed openings that kept the container of soup and a container of pesto sauce (which she had previously removed) in place. "Okay, well, here you—" she began to say, and then…

SPLASH!!!

The container had slipped out of Mary's cloth-protected hand, fell into the bin of water, and tipped over, causing all of the soup to spill and liquefy. It quickly no longer looked like cream of mushroom soup but "mushrooms swimming for their lives" soup.

"Shit!" Mary yelled. "Well, there goes that…holy *shit!*… I'm really sorry about that, Jenna. I guess you won't be taking any home now!" she said, trying to lighten the situation.

"Oh well—that's okay," I replied quietly. I was disappointed, but what more could I say? I would just have to wait until the next time.

One dinner specialty that Mary Ellen prepares that I've never gotten to take home are her barbecue ribs, because we invariably run out of them a few hours before closing. It was last summer that she and Bobby first introduced The Grill's "Backyard BBQ Night," which took place every Thursday. Well, it was so popular that they're having it again this coming summer. Brightly colored sheets advertise the specials, which we hand out in addition to the regular menu. Clear, black text is printed upon pages of deep red, green, orange, and yellow, which definitely grab the customers' attention. The main specials are a rack of ribs; a half rack of ribs with a boneless breast of barbecue-glazed chicken; and a Polish sausage sandwich. Each special comes with coleslaw, potato salad, and a thick, juicy piece of watermelon—oh!, and we mustn't forget, a small plastic container of rich barbecue sauce for dipping. Many customers return Thursday after Thursday for the flavorful and extremely tender ribs, which makes Mary even more proud of her ribs than she already is. "It's my secret method of cooking the ribs that makes them so tender," she says, without actually letting anyone in on what that method is. She even goes so far as to claim that they are "the best ribs in all of Pittsburgh."

What do I think about them? Well, I haven't made it a habit to go around to all of the restaurants in Pittsburgh that offer ribs on their menu, and to try them and compare them, but I'll have to say that Mary Ellen's are excellent and fall right off the bone. The few samples that she's given me to taste were delicious, and I enjoyed them thoroughly. The thing I don't enjoy, however (since we are on the subject), is carrying those specials out on the trays! One order of ribs completely covers one large plate, and then there are all of the individual side dishes as well. To serve a table of four is quite challenging! I often have to make several trips back to the kitchen to serve a table this size, when usually with other meals I have to make only one or two! It's true that this theme night does bring in a lot of business, but we waiters and waitresses definitely work for any extra money that we make because of it. It tickles Mary pink, though (literally), and she takes off her apron and often walks right out to the tables (almost swankily, if you can imagine someone being swanky in shorts and an old T-shirt) and asks the customers how they are enjoying her ribs. They gloat over them—naturally—and she nods and smiles just as confidently as ever.

Not only is Mare a wonderful cook, but she's a wonderful mother figure as well. You would think that an independent, fiery, fly-off-the-handle type (such as she is) would have no use for the little ones. But that is the furthest thing from the truth. She *loves* children. Never having any of her own (for what reason, I don't have a clue), she treats other people's with great kindness and love, especially Nick and Cathy's boys, Nick Junior and Billy. She adores those kids, and she watches them and takes care of them whenever she is needed, or even when she's not. She even goes to watch Little Nick's ball games, rooting for him with a mother's intensity.

She is also so kind to these two precious, big-eyed, dark-haired, utterly beautiful little girls who come in to eat quite often with their mom, dad, and uncle. The dad and uncle come in first, sit in the nonsmoking section in the booth farthest from the bar, and order a dozen barbecue wings as their appetizer, and draft beers and Johnny Walker Reds on the rocks to drink. Believe it or not, the dad's name is Glen Campbell. "Look at what his name is, Curt!" I said one early evening as I held his credit card up to Curt's face.

"Yeah, I know—aren't you lucky? You're waiting on someone famous," Curt joked with me, grinning.

The uncle, who is tall and thin and always comes into the bar wearing a ball cap, is very shy and reticent, but very, very kind and gentle. He has sort of a stutter, and it is really quite an effort for him to get his words out, although he never relies on anyone to order for him. "Joh—John—Jo—Johnny Walker—Red—on—th—the—the—rocks, pl—pl—please," he'll say (or some variation of that), looking straight at me with his brown, unassuming, innocent eyes, always thanking me when I return with his drink and as I proceed to place a small, square bar napkin in front of him and then place the rocks glass full of red scotch down on top of it.

About half an hour to forty-five minutes later, the attractive, thin, dark-haired, professional-looking mother with glasses arrives with the two little girls, one on each side of her, holding each one's hand. It is never too long before I see and hear the girls lightly pawing their mother and whispering, "Can we now, Mommy—can we?"

"Well, you should really wait until you are finished with your dinner, but I guess you can go ahead," she replies.

The two little girls slide off of the booth and slowly and hesitantly walk down the steps and in the direction of the kitchen. The older girl, who is five, clasps her hands behind her back and nods her head slightly forward, but raises her eyes upward, as she walks. The younger three-and-a-half-year-old runs her small hand along the dividing wall in the center of the restaurant, as if she is looking for moral support. Once they reach the edge of the entranceway to the kitchen, however, together they yell "Mary!" as loud as they can, which actually comes out like a whisper because they are so tiny, sweet, and shy. Then they wait patiently, and expectantly.

"Oh, hello there, you two sweeties," Mary says in her softest voice when she notices them standing there. "How are you today?"

"Fine," they say in unison, rocking back and forth.

"Well, just wait one minute. I just think there may be something waiting downstairs for you."

The two little angels look wide-eyed at each other, wondering what is coming.

In a few minutes, Mary returns, holding a few packs of candy in her hands, sometimes gummy bears or jelly beans, other times lollipops. She offers the treats to the children, and they take them slowly, almost uncertain that they should be doing it, even though this scenario has been repeated so many times before. The fact is, they are disciplined, good kids, and I think that's what Mary likes so much about them. Even though they are so young, they don't assume that they should get a gift no matter what, but seem to really appreciate and look forward to these special moments.

Mary deliberately brings in the candy from home for them. There's been once or twice when she hasn't had anything to give them—"Oh, I *completely* forgot," she said in one instance, after they had walked away empty-handed, the distress apparent in her face. "I feel *so, so* bad about this…" But most of the time she always has something fun and yummy to give them.

"Thanks, Mary," they say, a glow on their adorable faces. Then they turn around happily, and quickly walk back to their seats, studying their new treasures on the way. "Look, Daddy and Mommy; look what Mary gave us! Can we open it?"

Mary walks out a few minutes later, and she peers over the dividing wall into the nonsmoking section. She leans against the wall and relaxes her arms and hands on the wall's ledge. She smiles and says hello to the grownups and chats about the two little girls, praising them for their manners, saying how well-behaved and respectful they are.

This ritual of brightening the children's day, connecting with them on their level—she is so proud of it. It is a high that appears to surpass even the high she gets from her cooking. And I can see why. Out of all of her talents for making one delicious meal after another, managing a kitchen, being funny, and being a good friend, I am the most impressed with her talent for making the sweet little girls smile. ▪

TOMMY D.

He has taken such a liking to me that you would think I was Marilyn Monroe, and he, Joe DiMaggio.

Tommy is his name. He is an attractive, stocky, fifty-something man who is naughtier than the naughtiest. Believe it or not, every time he appears in the doorway and locates me, the googly eyes and seductively humorous facial expressions and contortions begin. On his way to where I am, he has this habit of pushing his lips together quickly, luxuriously, and in succession, like he is puckering up repeatedly and endlessly, as his eyebrows reach up and down and his eyes widen under the shadow of his ball cap, their devilishness never forsaking me. Then he either hugs me, kisses me on the cheek, or places a hot hand on my shoulder, or—if I'm extra lucky—does all three.

His well-known excessive flirting and joke-telling follow next.

"A Jew and a Catholic walk into a bar…" he begins one moment. "Did you hear the story of the three mice and the toad?" he asks next. "There was once a woman so beautiful that even the…" he adds later. "The sex was so good that the husband couldn't believe…" he says, licking his lips.

Obviously, he *loves* to tell jokes with a lusty passion—short jokes, long jokes, simple jokes, complicated jokes, and—oh yeah…*dirty* jokes. He specializes in those. And, really, I have no idea where he comes up with all of them. It's as if he's pulling them out of a hat somewhere, one after another. Of course, I could relate the entirety of some of them to you right now, but I really don't want to offend anyone. Because I do have to admit that, at first, his flirtatious ways and off-color comments made me somewhat wary of him. But ever since I began to realize what a friendly, good-natured person he is, I haven't minded him a bit. So when he tells me a joke now, I simply blush a tad (or *a lot*—as I tend to do), shyly giggle, say "Oh, Tommy!" with a fond slap on his shoulder, and walk away smiling. ■

TOMMY B.

Yes—there's another one.
And boy is he naughty too.
It must be the name...
Do you know what he said the other night?

He and Mary Ellen were cooking together, and I had just slid into the kitchen to pick up my order, the special of the day: pasta marinara with a generous helping of mussels.

"Wow! They look *delicious*!" I remarked, eyeing the steaming bowl of pasta covered with the thick red sauce and with the just-opened, shiny black shells protecting the succulent-looking, various-shaped delicacies.

"Delicious?!" Tommy replied, grinning, as I reached for the large white bowl and moved it onto my tray. "Delicious, you say? Well, if you want my opinion, what they *really* look like is—"

"TOMMY!!!" Mary Ellen and I yelled in unison as she slapped him on the shoulder and as my eyes almost popped right out of their sockets, and as Tommy broke into a mischievous laugh.

But it was too late, for the image was in all our heads now. And I couldn't help but be embarrassed (and amused) for the rest of the night.

******

IT'S TRUE—just like Tommy D., he has no trouble saying

what is on his mind, especially if it's of a sexual nature. Which, really, although it's a bit shocking sometimes, is not such a bad thing. Not everyone can be as reserved and inhibited as I am, after all. If they were, just think how hard it'd be to get to know anyone, or to learn anything, especially of a delicate nature.

His comments in the kitchen, therefore, about me having a Black woman's butt—"You know, like a table or a rack…it's abundant and projects out far enough that you could set something on it" (as he demonstrates); about the pluses and minuses of having sex with a woman, *or* a man (and he doesn't leave out the details); about the wild nights—and people—at the dance club downtown called Pegasus; about the man who was rushed to the hospital because he got a hamster stuck in his… (His WHAT? I still can't *quite* fathom that one); and about how cute I looked in the khaki shorts I wore to work the other day (What *was* I thinking? Hadn't I realized how short they were?) are sincerely welcome. In fact, I'm almost eager for them. Because, with him, my questions are answered without me even having to ask. And because, with him, it's safe.

He's from a large, extended family in the Midwest—in Indiana—and he loves his mama. He's tall (almost six-two), lean, nice-looking, long-legged, and sweet, and his skin is as unblemished and silky smooth as powder, though nowhere near the color. He knows how to dress when he's going out on the town, and always leaves me wrapped in a heady scent after he hugs me, either from the front or the back. And I can't believe how filthy and greasy his lightweight, wire-rimmed glasses get when he works, until he finally can't stand it anymore and wipes them on the apron completely covering his overly short sweatshorts, joking that he's no longer able to read the order slips. He doesn't drink or smoke much either—not at all, really—

says that he's never had any interest in that stuff.

Sometimes, when he's cooking, it takes a long time for people to get their orders. And sometimes, when he's cooking, the chicken breasts don't get cooked through quite enough and have to be sent back. But I suppose these things happen mainly because he gets bored with the job every now and then.

Maybe, now that I think about it, that's one of the reasons why he entertains—and informs—me. Do my shocked eyes and giggles and blushes and soft rebukes, but recurring interest, seem out of the ordinary to him, and as a result, intrigue and inspire? Am I so far on the other side of the realm that he feels I need to learn otherwise? Is there other work to be done than his daily routine of preparing food? The work of preparing me further for the world that now is, and making me more tolerant of it by putting a face, and words, and feelings on and in it?

Oh, maybe I think too much of myself. Maybe I'm being too philosophical. Maybe he does this with everyone: jokes and "tells all" and shocks. But that's okay, because I can't believe what I'm hearing sometimes, because my head is swimming with all kinds of unbelievable stuff I hadn't even dared to think of, because I'm being educated, and because, most of all, it's obvious he's genuine.

He couldn't be so open if he weren't. ∎

WHAT IT'S ALL ABOUT

It's Saturday afternoon, and I move hurriedly from table to table, taking one order after another, separating each with a thick blue line on my tiny pad of paper (I don't dare leave anything to memory—too much room for error). Call out any alcohol orders to Adam (or even any juice or soft drink orders, which he'll happily prepare for me if he has the time) while I quickly punch the food orders into the machine by the bar.

Okay—two bleu burgers my mind tells me as my eyes begin at the top of my notepad, and as I press the tiny, square button—not much larger than the tip of my index finger—that has the words BLEU BURGER printed on it in little block letters. Then I press it again. *Richety richety* the machine responds as the white roll of paper inside it advances and registers a copy of what I am ordering. *FF* and *CS* are what my eyes see next on my notepad, as my finger presses the 7 square twice, then ENTER *(richety richety)*, then the 7 square again, followed immediately by the 8 square, then ENTER *(richety richety)* (77 is the PLU number for french fries; 78 for coleslaw). Don't forget the Pepsi (PEP)—*richety richety*—and the ginger ale (GING)— *Where is it?—richety richety.* Slide a sturdy, rectangular, thick-but-not-too-thick receipt, made just for the machine, securely into the printing slot, and press SEND. *Richety richety richety richety richety* the machine then says again and again and for as long as it takes the order to be simultaneously printed on the receipt and on a slip of paper that emerges from the diminutive printer in the kitchen. Put the receipt-cum-bill quickly in my apron pocket with the other ones, and start again. (Lucky for me, my receipt contains not only the food that I ordered, which is the only info that the kitchen's receipt contains, but the drinks also, as well as the corresponding prices for each item, the tax amount, and the total price. Whoever invented it—thank you very much! When I first started here, we had to write out the orders by hand and do all of the math in our head.)

Next, deliver the drinks, which Adam has placed neatly at the end of the bar. Seat the couple who just walked in. Pick up the food, from the kitchen, that's already done (Anthony doesn't mess around). Say "Hi!" to Harold, a gray-haired regular in his sixties who regularly drinks beer, and who always shows up dressed in his work clothes, covered with specks upon specks of paint. Walk casually past the tables to make sure that everybody is taken care of and doesn't need anything—more ketchup, cutup lemons for their iced tea, another Pepsi, a piece of apple pie for dessert, maybe?—without bothering them or being a pest. Clear away their plates. Pour two decafs out of the just-brewed pot. Deliver the bill upon a little, black plastic tray—it's more professional this way—and don't forget the after-dinner mints. Chat for a while with crazy Marcy, a post-office employee who likes to sip a tall drink with a large straw, play the poker machines, and laugh, laugh, laugh…constantly and exuberantly. Get change for the gentleman sitting in booth number six. Say, in all sincerity, "Nice to see you again and please come back…"

Busy, challenging, overwhelming, dizzying sometimes. But methodical, empowering, exhilarating, and satisfying most of the time—definitely not confining.

I'm happy.

******

TODAY'S A DIFFERENT KIND of Saturday. It's slow and calm, laid-back and easy, customers floating in every half an hour or so, or longer. I take my time with them as they decide what to order, explaining in detail an item on the menu that they've asked about, glad to respond to their inquisitiveness or curiosity, telling them as much as they want to know. Being more thorough and conscientious than usual with every aspect of serving them—simply enjoying what it means to be a waitress. Taking it slow (but not too slow, of course) while punching in the orders, avoiding making the types of mistakes that occur because of haste. Enjoying the smell and look of the freshly brewed coffee and the smile and gratitude upon an elderly gentleman's face as I pour it into his empty cup. Noticing the pretty way that Anth arranges the food on the plates, or the skill with which he slices the mushrooms. Chatting with my customers, learning that the two elderly women in the first smoking booth, exhibiting long fingernails, glittery scarves, and gold jewelry, are tourists from New York City, visiting Pittsburgh for the first time. That the good-looking middle-aged man with glasses who is sitting at table eleven and intrigued by the book *Conversations with God* went through a divorce about a year ago and is still searching for some healing, because he hasn't found any yet and wonders if he ever will. That the couple sitting in the front, holding hands across the table, had been in to eat a few months ago and are thrilled to be back. Or that my Indian friend Vankat, with the gentle demeanor, who is a PhD student at Pitt, is coming along well on his thesis.

Meeting new people. Being surrounded by familiar faces. Observing and feeling the happiness and sadness that is carried into and out of this place. The relationships that are formed here—and broken. Cheering someone up by giving them service fit for a king or just by refilling their soda before they have to ask. Being cheered up by a customer telling me that I'm her favorite waitress…

That's what working here is all about, and these semi-busy Saturdays always give me more time to delight in all of it. They may not be as lucrative, but they're certainly just as rewarding. ■

MY DANCE PARTNER

I seat a well-known local TV news reporter and her gentleman friend in booth seven, the second booth in the nonsmoking section. Right after that I grab the check and money from the elderly couple sitting in booth six, ask Adam to make change for me, and then return it to them.

Now this isn't just any elderly couple—it is an elderly couple who comes in often to eat and whom I've waited on many, many times before. And they are quite intriguing. They walk in together very carefully, the tall, thin, white-haired, practically blind man shuffling across the floor like the well-loved Tim Conway *Carol Burnett Show* character, his attractive, classy, black-haired, somewhat-younger wife walking behind him with her right hand clasped around his right arm, her left hand clasped around his left arm, peeping around him to guide the way. Earlier, when they arrived, they ventured up the two steps into the nonsmoking section (they usually sit in booth thirteen, the first booth in the smoking section, which is much easier to get to). "I'm…feeling…eager today!" Albert commented, his voice patterns reflecting the way he walks.

When they finally sat down, I handed a menu to Gretta only—Albert always already knows what he wants, the same thing every time. "I'll have…a…burger, well-done…it…*has*…to be…well-done," he emphasized to me in a gruff voice, with a pointed, crooked index finger shaking in the air. (I've heard this a hundred times before, but he always insists on re-enlightening me.) "Just the…burger, though. Roll lightly…toasted…and put on…a separate…plate… And *don't* forget the pickle!" he added, which reverberated like a cymbal in my ears.

He never has any trouble with that pickle part. He *loves* those juicy, flavorful, dill pickles. And thanks to him, I've learned quite a bit about them, because he just had to know who made them so he could get some for himself.

"They're the Boar's Head brand," I told him, after having searched, shivering, all over the walk-in freezer in the basement one afternoon, looking and looking for a container of them so that I could read the label. (I had never thought to notice before. Anytime I need them, they are already sliced and placed within the multi-dish plastic container in the kitchen, along with the sliced onions, mushrooms, tomatoes, olives, and scallions.) "But, you know what?" I continued, regretfully. "The general public isn't able to buy them in the grocery stores." (Mary Ellen told me this.) "They usually only sell in bulk, you know, to restaurants and businesses."

A cloud covered his face but, just as quickly, a smile reappeared. "Well!" he began. "That just…means…the wife and I will have…to…come…here more often!"

And Gretta just sat there gazing at him, the fingers of her right hand gently grasping the classy, silver cat frames, with the shiny silver chain, that always adorn her beautiful, contoured face.

Albert particularly enjoys asking me about my dancing, and is especially curious about all of the clubs I frequent on the weekends (and sometimes during the week!). He sits there relaxing as I talk about the places I've been, the people I've met, the dances I dance, looking not at me, but straight ahead, his hands folded and resting on the table. Still, there is no doubt he is giving me his complete attention. Try as it might, the glaucoma invader hasn't completely won, has failed to hide the clear blue sparkle of wonder and happiness—of younger, easier, freer dancing days. Glenn Miller, blaring trumpets, fancy suits and bow ties, sophisticated ladies, flirting, unbearable attraction: It is all there…on fire…magnetic. As I talk, he feels…and dances. Waltzes across the floor. Holds in his arms a beautiful young thing who smells of lilacs. Jitterbugs and sweats. Moves his hips and spins around.

When I finish talking, he says in response, almost completely to himself, a melancholy smile approaching his face, a longing not entirely hidden in his voice, "Yeah…I am…I mean I was…quite the…rug cutter…in my…day…as well." And then he sits there quietly for a few seconds, the look on his face saying that he is not yet ready to leave that place again, that wonderful, fabulous, carefree place.

But when he returns, he says (obviously making an effort to lighten things up a bit), "Yeah, maybe…after you get…off of work tonight, we can meet up…and…tear…up…the floor together!"

And I laugh in response, saying that I just can't w—

"WAITRESS!"

I'm not even able to finish my sentence.

"There *are* other people waiting to be served, you know!"

Who else could it be but the TV reporter, glaring at me, completely turned around in her seat, shooting me all kinds of nastiness. Reality has not only hit my elderly friend, but me as well.

How dare *you be so rude!* I can't help thinking, as my head jerks in her direction. But I manage to say, and as evenly as possible, "I'll be right there."

Part of me does understand, after all, where she is coming from. I *have* been talking to my friends for quite a few minutes now, and I had noticed her glancing restlessly at me. But the other part of me is furious, furious at her for not recognizing the importance of allowing me to complete the ritual, the reminiscing, the comforting.

"I think I better go now," I mouth to my friends, who don't say anything but just look down and nod.

Before going to the reporter's table, however, I place my hand on my friend's shoulder, bend down a bit, and whisper in his ear, "Don't you worry yourself a bit, okay? Things were cut a little short today, but we'll definitely dance again together next time…"

And we do—countless times—again and again and again. ∎

PRETENDING

I walk in late, maybe fifteen or twenty minutes late…tops. Besides, it's Saturday morning.

But there's no escaping. Anthony—and his all-too-familiar mischievous look—is intent on me.

"Yep, yeah, we see what's going on," he begins, not allowing me to head toward the front of the restaurant, but wasting no time cornering me—my back up against the metal soup-tureen bins—all the while slapping the square blade of a large, metal spatula into the palm of his hand, his lips pursed and his head moving from side to side. "You had *way* too much to drink again last night, *didn't* ya? You just couldn't make yourself go home after your shift, *could* ya? Dancing on the bar, seductively unbuttoning your shirt, flirting with all of the guys… I heard all about it."

Adam then appears out of nowhere, also closing me in, leaning his body against the wall adjacent to the bins. "Yeah, here you are coming into work again—all red-eyed and sluggish—and late," he says, "the smell still on your breath. I'm serious, Jenna. I'm gonna tell Bobby if this keeps up much longer. It's getting way too out of—"

"Oh yeah, you guys have really got my number," I cut in, looking seriously at one, then at the other. "Jack Daniel's, margaritas, countless beers, pieces of clothing flying this way and that, my hair loose and all over the place," I disclose (as I illustrate all of this with my hands), "giving my number out to whoever wanted it—there was *just* no stopping me."

For a while, this give-and-take goes on…and on…and on, but any week I'm late, and the more we get to know each other, the wilder and more explicit my exploits become.

We eventually stop, however, each of us deciding on our own that we should save some of my adventures for next time. So we just stand there, cautiously, attentively, looking at one another. And then we wait for it. And wait. And wait. And wait…

And then I laugh (I'm always first). And so does Anth. And so does Adam.

The idea of it is just too crazy for all of us to keep it up for too long, but it sure is fun pretending. ■

KINDRED SOULS

It's so unnaturally easy for me to open up to him—to this much older, married man. Is it because he's part Italian and Catholic (as I am), a Catholic who takes his faith seriously, a Catholic who couldn't separate himself from being so even if he tried with all his might? I so admire that he wears a scapular around his neck. "I never take it off," he says when I notice the dark brown string peeking out from under his T-shirt, at the neckline. "I wear it when I sleep…in the shower…everywhere." I too wear a symbol of my faith around my neck, a Miraculous Medal that my parents gave me for Christmas a year ago. It hangs beautifully on a dainty, yet sturdy, glistening gold chain. It continually gives me a sense of security and calm, no matter how anxious or uncertain I am feeling. And I know that Tommy feels the same.

Maybe another reason it is so easy for me to talk to Tommy is because he is so unabashedly frank. And particularly about sex, if you want to know the truth. No one has ever been quite this way with me before, not even my friend Teeli, who isn't the least bit shy, and not even Tommy B., although he has prepared me well, I must admit. But *my* Tommy—he isn't embarrassed *at all* when it comes to talking about it, which therefore, in some twisted, crazy way, makes me feel less inhibited—*me*, who keeps everything inside like I'm a safe wrapped with duct tape.

With him, though, almost from the very beginning, I just knew that he wouldn't judge me on what I told him, so why not tell him what I'm thinking and doing? We all need someone to completely release ourselves to, after all, without fear of damaged expectations and disappointed looks.

Besides, it's not as if the two of us are so extremely explicit or constantly go into all the private details that are involved (although there have been a couple of times that I've turned the color of the Burgundy wine that I serve). Instead, we talk about the wonder and the necessity of it— and not the physical necessity, but that spiritual, otherworldly need that draws you to another person in the first place. I love the fact that he recognizes—and still believes, at this stage of his life—what a crucial role intimacy plays in a relationship and in a meaningful life, particularly because the whole idea of sex and all the mystery that surrounds it is so new, fresh, confusing, and exciting to me. ■

A HOLIDAY TREAT (times two)

I walk in, draped in a winter coat, mittens, and my furry, rebellious brown hat, with its tattered strings peeking out everywhere (my mom hates it when I wear it), and Bianca hands me an envelope with "Jenna" written on it in fancy, perfect letters. "What's this?" I ask, surprised.

"Just a little something for the holidays," Bianca replies in a soft voice, touching me lightly on the arm.

I've come to the bar in search of a nightcap—a rum and eggnog with whipped cream and a sprinkle of nutmeg adorning the top—and a bit of holiday music and chitchat.

"Oh, is this from Bobby?" I wonder aloud, as I tear off my mittens, open the envelope, and take out a thick piece of paper. I look it over for a moment, and I am happy to find that it's a gift certificate—worth fifteen dollars—for the National Record Mart, the music store around the corner on Forbes Avenue.

"Well, actually, it's from Curt," Bianca whispers, glancing around.

"Really?"

"Yes. He's giving all of us who work here one, and he's also giving one to many of the regulars too, like Rolanda."

"Wow! That must be expensive for him—but it's so sweet!… And my name," I continue, running my fingers over it, "it's written so beautifully."

"Oh, well…that's all of Curt's calligraphy training when

he was a child," Bea explains.

"*Calligraphy* training... Are you serious? I've never met anyone who's gone through *that*."

"Yeah—that's what happens when you're raised by your grandmother," she says, laughing.

"Oh, I didn't know that...did...did his parents leave him or something?" I whisper, trying to be gentle.

"Well, actually...it's really terrible, but...when he was four years old, his parents got killed in a car accident."

"Oh my god!" I say, as much under my breath as possible. "Poor Curt!... I had no idea."

"Yeah, well, that's how he is, you know. He sort of likes to keep that kind of stuff to himself. I mean," she says, changing the subject, "take these gift certificates, for example. He does nice stuff like this but never wants to be fussed over. He's trying not to make a big deal out of it. He doesn't even want me to tell people who the gift certificate is from when I hand them out—thus the reason why he's not handing them out himself—but of course I'm letting everyone in on it," she says, grinning, and pausing for a moment. But then she begins again, almost dreamily, a faraway look in her eyes (and I'm amazed at how much she's opening up to me tonight—it must be the topic of conversation). "Yes, you know, when we were a couple, living together—you do know that we used to be together, don't you?"

"Well, I wasn't quite sure, but that's sort of what I figured," I reply. (I thought there was something going on in the way that they familiarly engaged with each other now and again: a slight touch of the hand here, a lingering look there.)

"Oh—yeah—we were together for about five years, in fact... But... Well... Anyway... For my birthday and for Christmas—it never failed—he'd blindfold me and then lead me into the living room, slowly take the blindfold off, and then say, 'Surprise, honey!' And there they were, time and again. Gifts upon gifts stacked upon each other, wrapped in the most beautiful, shiny, colorful, glittering wrapping paper and bows—god were they beautiful!—and there'd be a desk one year, a computer another year, a TV the next, and the most stylish clothes and wonderfully smelling perfumes always…. Yeah, that Curt," she says, pausing, shaking her head, "when he wants to, he certainly knows how to make you feel good."

As she tells me this story, it makes such an impression on me, but not just the part about the lavishness with which he treated her, but most importantly the part about the wrapping and the bows. Because I've always thought—maybe because of some painful experiences I've had—that you can judge the character of a person by observing such particulars, although simple and seemingly mundane, like whether he takes the time to wrap up your presents, or just throws them in a bag (paper or plastic: in this case, it doesn't much matter) and forgets to remove the price tag, and casually says, "I'm really sorry, but I didn't have time to wrap them." To me, it shows a deeper level of caring and concern if he takes the extra time to beautify something he is giving you, to show you how special and beautiful he thinks you are.

"Are you okay, Jenna?" Bianca eventually asks, looking at me inquisitively.

"Oh sure, Bea…sure… I was just thinking about what you were saying… But, anyway, thanks so much for giving this to me!" I say, holding up the gift certificate for a moment, and then lightly squeezing her hand.

"Sure, honey, my pleasure," she says, adding that she really should get to table three and take their order. "You have a good night."

Watching her hurry away, I take off my hat and coat, and place them on the back of a bar stool, the only one free in the place. Then I plop down on it and order my new favorite drink from Curt. And while he makes it, I decide that I have to—just have to—thank him for the gift. It was such a thoughtful thing to do.

"Really, Jenna, it was no big deal," he says in response, as he places a goblet filled with the thick, rich deliciousness in front of me, then turns around and busies himself with opening up the cash register and making change.

So I let it go at that. It's obvious he doesn't need any overt recognition for his kindness, because he knows in his heart, already, what he has done. ■

THE SINGING MUSE

Could it get any slower…
With no other choice, I've spent most of my time today doing side work, and then extra: cutting lemons; preparing salads, covering them with plastic wrap, and storing them one on top of the other in the refrigerator till they resemble the Leaning Tower of Pisa; using a clean, white cloth and window spray to wipe off the fingerprints and grime that have accosted the glass refrigerator door; brewing iced tea and coffee; stocking the plastic storage containers with straws and tea bags, and the shelves with napkins and just-washed, tiny tin teapots, which are deliciously hot to the touch; assembling a large stack of place settings; and refolding and arranging the menus, and inserting a colorful "Specials" sheet into each.

Honestly, though, there's only so much stocking you can do, and only so much space to put all of it. But don't worry—Adam and I always find a way to entertain ourselves, whether it is watching *Talk Soup* on the dusty, old TV that sits high upon the beer cooler behind the bar, or using the remote to flip through the channels with Walter—one of our Saturday bar regulars—trying to decide what movie to watch, the changing picture flashing like a disco bulb.

This afternoon, however, Adam and I have decided to write a goofy, nonsensical song together, for no other reason than that it sounds like fun.

"You start," I say, daring him, as I slide my stool closer.

"You got it," Adam responds, not one to back down from a challenge.

He grabs a little notepad and immediately begins writing the first line, following it with three deliberate dots.

I just stare at him, surprised by his sudden inspiration.

"So, are you going to let me in on it or not?"

"Patience, my dear, is a virtue," he says, grinning.

"Adam…"

"Okay, okay, Jenna…" He clears his throat. "Here we go… 'There was a girl who wore lots of pearls…'"

I smile. "'She put them on every morning…'" The line just comes to me.

Adam nods approvingly and writes it down. He then thinks for a moment. "'They hung about her neck in various swirls…'"

"'You…you…you…you would've thought she was performing…'" I announce.

He jots it down.

"'She wore so… One day she…'"—he shakes his head. "Okay, okay, now I got it… 'One day she wore so many, she could not see…'"

"Good one," I say, laughing. "Okay, then…" But I sit there for a few minutes, tapping my fingers on the top of the bar.

"It *is* your turn, you know, Jenna," Adam points out, shooting me quite an ornery look.

"Oh, I am quite aware of that," I say, shooting him the same look back. I sit there for a few more minutes, though, feeling the same way I feel when I am sitting in front of my word processor in my tiny dorm room, trying to come up with an ingenious conclusion for one of my Shakespeare papers. "Oh, oh, I've got it, Adam!" I eventually say, spastically jumping up from my seat as if the answer to "What is the meaning of life?" has just hit me. "'They ravaged her like a bunch of fleas!'"

Adam looks down, about to write, but then he looks up, his forehead wrinkled. "What!!! Are you *serious*!? That doesn't make sense!"

But I just laugh again, my head falling on my hands, the tears swelling up in my eyes.

After about twenty minutes of "hard" work, though, we finish our lyrics, and Adam embellishes them (who really knows why) with a drawing that is, well, *distinct* (a Rambo-look-alike woman with a scary face, her entire body inundated with an unlikely mixture of pearls and fleas). So we alternately sit and stand there for a while, taking turns serenading each other with our creation, each time in a different rhythm and melody:

There was a girl who wore lots of pearls...
She put them on every morning...
They hung about her neck in various swirls...
You would've thought she was performing...
One day she wore so many, she could not see...
They ravaged her like a bunch of fleas...
She tore them all off and flung them away...
And boy does she regret it—she regrets it to this day.

But thank God no one is around to hear us. Adam is a tragic actor, inspired by Melpomene. I am a dancer, blessed by Terpsichore. But Aoide, the muse of song—she must have been absent the days we were born. ■

DIANA

When I first met Diana, boy was she reserved. Not yet an employee of The Grill, she would often come in to have a few drinks or a bite to eat with her boyfriend, Ace, when he got off of work. A dishwasher and assistant cook here at The Grill, Ace was an alternative-music-loving, earring-wearing type of guy who was rather quiet, but friendly, and had a raspy, but nonetheless attractive, voice. Diana seemed to be very nice too. Each time I waited on her she was polite and friendly, but she never said much. She would just sit there in the booth, sipping her tall draft beer, with her long brown hair flowing over her shoulders, and her big brown eyes keeping to herself. She almost seemed uncomfortable.

A few months later, Bobby hired Diana, and I helped train her. She followed me around attentively, listened well, and was extremely respectful, apparently very happy to have the job, and eager to do the job right. And during the first few months, she always worked hard and retained her shy, quiet, and introverted manner.

I'm not sure what's happened, but given that she's been on the job for a while now, a new Diana has emerged. She jokes around with everyone, is feisty and strong-tongued—telling exactly what she thinks to anyone who asks (and many times to anyone who doesn't, for that matter)—and has cut her hair to just above her shoulders, as if signaling that she has broken out of the last bit of her shell.

I am particularly amused by Diana's method for filling drink orders. Whenever she has a large drink order to take care of (two Pepsi's, two waters, and a ginger ale, let's say), she hastily and perfunctorily fills five pint glasses with ice, filling each one in turn by irreverently plunging the metal scooper into the ice bin at the end of the bar with her right hand, scooping up the ice, tossing it into the glass that she holds in her left hand, and then placing the glass on the end of the bar. Next, she grips the bar gun mercilessly, using her thumb to press the various little, white identifying buttons that sit atop the gun, allowing the liquid to escape. Filling the glasses with water is the most frustrating for her; there is almost no water pressure when you press the blank button, and the water meekly trickles out. But the Pepsi button, marked with a black capital P, shoots forth the Pepsi with more force, but apparently not enough for Diana. If she is going to fill two glasses, instead of pausing for a second after she finishes filling the first glass, she passes the gun from the one glass to the other (which she has placed side by side so that they are touching), without relieving the pressure she has placed on the Pepsi button. She's become particularly good at this, never spilling much liquid on the bar at all. What is most humorous to me, however, is that while she fills the glasses, she simultaneously growls under her breath, taps her foot, presses *extremely* hard on the buttons (with twice as much pressure as is necessary), and stares intently at the liquid filling the glasses, like a witch commanding an object to move with her eyes, and as if doing all of these things is going to make the liquid magically come out faster.

On top of all this, she smokes a lot, drinks a lot (*a lot* as far as I'm concerned—I'm amazed at how much she can put away without it affecting her), and curses a lot (every now and then). *"Fuckin'* guy!! What did he think he was *fuckin'* doing!! Of all the stupid, damn, shitty, *fuckin'* dumb things to do!!"* I remember hearing her saying this as we were sitting at the bar having a few drinks one evening after work. In fact, I don't even remember who she was talking about; I was just so amazed at how many curse words she fit into a few short statements. Apparently my good friend Mariano—who is nothing but a perfect gentleman—was too. He was sitting to my right, at the end of the bar, and Diana was in full view and within earshot of him. Each and every time she forcefully blurt out a curse word (which was *five* times in that *one* instance), his head jerked slightly back, and his face scrunched together, as if he were being punched again and again.

Mind you, I don't want to give you the wrong impression. Diana isn't always so abrasive and free with her language—it happens particularly when she's had too much to drink. But, then again, I do often hear some interesting comments flying around under her breath when a customer gives her a hard time, things that she would've never said when she first started working here. In fact, the innocence I first noticed in her has turned into a lusty passion for everything. Often, when she finishes working the early shift, she sits in the booth that is designated for employees—which is the last booth on the right before you reach the waitstaff station and then the kitchen—eagerly waiting for the meal that she has asked the cook to make for her. When the food arrives, she devours it with a voraciousness I've never seen before (well, at least in a woman; my younger brother, Lee, has always eaten like that, ever since he was a little baby sucking on his bottle, my mom tells me). If the treasure is a juicy, thick burger, she firmly picks it up with both hands and takes a large bite, sauce dripping everywhere. If it is a medium-rare New

York strip steak, she quickly cuts a large piece, chews it, and then swallows it, hardly pausing between bites. I pass by her on my way out of the kitchen to deliver food, and when I return just a few minutes later, she is finished. Pushing her empty plate away from her, she leans back, puts her hand on her stomach, and softly closes her eyes, obviously completely satisfied. "Mmmmboy that was good," she says, again and again and again.

Believe it or not, there is a period of time when Diana completely swears off eating red meat of any kind, for some reason or another regarding being humane to animals. "It's been two weeks, Jenna," she says after she finishes one of her shifts, holding up her index finger and middle finger prominently to emphasize the fact. "*Two weeks*... I'm having a hell of a time, but I haven't given in yet."

"More power to you," I say, utterly amazed.

About a week later, however, I pass by the back booth and there she is, on the attack once again.

"Diana! What happened?... I thought you gave that stuff up."

"I did. I had... Oh, I just couldn't do it, Jenna," she says, shaking her head. "The cravings were just too strong."

"No kidding... And no judgment here. Because believe me, I understand. I wouldn't be able to do it either," I reply.

So she offers me a bite. ■

NOT ENOUGH

"Jenna," he begins, slowly. (I am mixing a gin and tonic at the corner of the bar.) "Have you seen *The Nutcracker* yet this year?"

I look up, my hands frozen for a moment. "No, Irwin; actually, I haven't," I reply, as I manage to put the dark green bottle of gin back in its place on the shelf.

"Well, I was…uh…sort of thinking about maybe going to see it, and…uh…uh…"

He pauses for quite a while, apparently having a hard time getting his words out.

"Yeah, you know…since you like to dance so much and everything, I thought that maybe…that maybe…you'd like for me to take you…"

What redness in his cheeks! What expectation in his eyes! And what a grip he has on his beer bottle!

"Oh, wow, Irwin…I…well sure…I mean, I'd love to go, Irwin. That really sounds wonderful," I reply, quickly thinking to myself that it would be fun and that there could be no harm in it, despite whatever feelings are there—or not.

"Great," he replies, involuntarily sighing—obviously very happy and relieved, but also obviously trying to be calm, cool, and masculine, as he is always trying to be. "And don't you worry about anything. I'll take care of it all. The tickets. The transportation. All of it. You just bring your pretty self."

"Okay, Irwin," I say, laughing, placing the drink on a tray. "You got it… And I'm really looking forward to it."

******

I OPEN THE DOOR, and he's already arrived, sitting at the bar. He's wearing a black suit, a bow tie, and extra-shiny black shoes, his hair behaving more than usual. He looks particularly nice…

I'm wearing my off-white outfit that I wore to my homecoming dance my junior year in high school. I love wearing it now just as much as I loved wearing it then, with its above-the-knee, stretchy skirt and its baby-doll top with the square-cut, pearl-heavy neckline. I especially love my off-white, innocent-but-sexy lace stockings, which perfectly match the lacy, flowery print of the outfit itself. My hair is long and curled, and my feet look stylish in black suede. I feel particularly pretty…

I pause in the entranceway for a moment, take a deep breath, and then begin to walk. I pull out a stool and sit next to him—and as I do so, he just looks at me, and looks at me, and says nothing, but helps me out of my long, black coat.

There are a few customers sitting at the bar, and an elderly gentleman is eating and reading in one of the booths. And Mary Ellen has just appeared from the kitchen, apparently aware that we were going to be here. But it is quiet, peaceful, and warm, with soft jazz filling the air, and bright sunshine flowing in through the front window.

When Curt places a fancy glass mug of eggnog, rum, cinnamon, and whipped cream beside Irwin's Iron City, some words finally arrive, and we sit there for the next hour, chatting and enjoying each other's company and the company of our friends.

Irwin borrowed Curt's car for the evening, which he has conveniently parked at a meter across the street, in front of the large, inviting, book-lined window of Barnes & Noble. And although the radio doesn't work and the driver's-side window will go only three-quarters of the way up, it is still much better, as he puts it—before he shuts my door—than his "cluttered, junky pickup, which is in no way decent for an evening out at the ballet."

On the way downtown, we talk more, first about general stuff, like our friends at The Grill, and the regular customers, but then the conversation becomes much more intimate and serious. "Do you remember, Jenna, the night of the Christmas party?" he eventually asks, shyly glancing at me out of the corner of his eye.

Of course I remember it. I had such a wonderful time that evening, feeling even more than usual like a member of an exclusive club, the sign on The Grill's door announcing: "Closed for the evening. Private party." Bobby and all of the employees—Curt, Nick, Mary Ellen, Shane, Adam, Jack, Bianca, Diana, Nina, Tommy, Anthony—and many of the family-like regulars—Rolanda, Marcy, Joe Fish, Firpo, Zeech, Ken, Marty, Walter—sitting and standing there, talking and laughing. Globy bartending (taking a night off from The Decade), getting anyone and everyone anything and any amount they wanted to drink, all on Bobby. Trays upon trays of food—mini egg rolls, lasagna, vegetables and dip, dumplings—covering the booths in the nonsmoking section. Nick, sentimental and serious, freed by the alcohol—almost to the point of breaking down—standing above us on the steps leading into the nonsmoking section, a drink raised in his right hand, toasting and praising Bobby, "The best boss anyone could ever have…and I really, really love him…" Me both participating in it all and observing it all, wearing my ribbed, U-necked, fuzzy gray sweater; purple, stretchy, cotton pants; black stockings; and black Naturalizer pumps; my hair uninhibited and free. Probably one of the first times, or maybe the first time, they all saw me looking that way.

"Well," Irwin continues, "I must confess that I thought you looked beautiful that night…really feminine, you know…and I really wanted to walk up and talk to you—Curt and Nick kept *egging* and *egging* me on—but I just couldn't get up the nerve to do it," he admits, shaking his head.

I remember—and remember sensing—that too. I was sitting at the main bar, drinking and eating, and he was leaning against the ancillary bar, a few feet behind me, and to my right. I kept thinking and feeling all evening that he might approach me, but when the doors locked for good for the night at two a.m., all that had been said was a quick hi and nothing more.

"That's okay, Irwin," I respond, glancing back at him. "We're taking care of that now."

Our conversation continues from there, and takes an even more serious turn, focusing on the age-old conflict of leaving or staying, of exploring further or being satisfied with where you are now. How it's so difficult, when growing up, to leave your home, family, and roots and to go away. But how it's even more difficult not to explore—not to leave your home, family, and roots in search of making your own new life. The mistake of denying that necessity inside of you. The cruciality of breaking away—however painful—from the people and surroundings that are your comfort and support, and to test and give a chance to the ideas, hopes, and desires that would consume you if you didn't.

I learn now, sitting beside Irwin on our way to the ballet, that he did just that. Traveled out West. Left Pittsburgh—his home—for many years. Followed the need to get away and to be on his own, going where the work in plumbing was plentiful and where he'd be paid well for it. Met new people, lived in new places, and learned new ways of life.

"Yes, it was a *very* big change at first. But it definitely was good for me and made it clear to me what I really wanted out of life." He says this as he pulls into a parking garage near the theater and grabs a ticket from the automatic dispenser.

"Hey, you know what, though? Let's definitely talk more about this later," he says. "I think we're getting a bit too serious. Now's the time to be carefree and to go and enjoy the beautiful show."

He smiles and winks at me sweetly.

******

AS I EXPECTED, the performance is lovely and very inspiring, and the music and the settings put me in the perfect mood for the season. But what puts me in an even better mood is how wonderfully Irwin treats me all evening. During the show he is a perfect gentleman, nonetheless letting me know of his affection for me, his leg subtly and gently brushing against mine every now and then.

Later that evening, we sit in a secluded corner of a cozy, dimly lit, downtown tavern, pretty lights dangling above us—the perfect spot for a first date and an after-show drink.

"Yes, I was away for quite a while, but then, yes I did…I came back to Pittsburgh," Irwin tells me, continuing our conversation from earlier. He's drinking a Heineken, and I'm relishing a spicy Bloody Mary with olives and a fancy, tiny umbrella—and he's talking to *me*, looking me straight in the eye, and making me feel so important. "So don't worry, Jenna…you'll figure it all out. I know that you've become really attached to Pittsburgh, and that it's like a second home to you now…but if you feel that once you graduate you can't pursue all of your dreams here, go wherever you can to make them happen… And so what if you get wherever you go and it's not all you wanted or thought it'd be, and things don't work out the way you planned?... You can always come back. But suppose if they *do* work out?... And besides, why stay here and forever wonder?"

I sit there looking at him, running my fingers through my hair, and sipping my cocktail, as everything suddenly becomes so clear. *You're exactly right, Irwin, exactly right,* I tell him with my eyes. *I just needed to hear someone say it.*

******

AFTER OUR DRINKS at the tavern, we decide to go to The Decade and hang out, where Curt and Globy are bartending for the night. Before we do that, however, Irwin suggests that we change into something more comfortable.

We head to his place first, a large, white, many-floor old home that he bought a few years ago in Greenfield, a crowded, hilly, welcoming area just outside of Squirrel Hill, where Nick and Cathy, and Mary Ellen and Marty, also live. When we pull into the driveway, I can't help but notice the multiple pieces of lumber piled on top of each other and strung in the yard amid the snow—"For the deck that he was going to build a year and a half ago!" Nick later tells me, laughing mischievously—and inside, the countless hammers, tool chests, pieces of plywood, scissors, measuring tapes, boxes of nails, and stacks upon stacks of blueprints and papers, detailed with instructions, that are completely covering the counters in the kitchen and the furniture in the living room, and waiting patiently in the corners of the house. "Yeah, as you can see, I'm working on many home-improvement projects at once," Irwin comments, chuckling, when he returns from upstairs, where he quickly changed into jeans and a flannel shirt.

We then go to the Chatham College apartment where I'm staying for the two weeks between the end of the fall semester and the beginning of the interim term, during which time the main residence halls are closed. The apartment is in Berry Hall, a beautiful, stately building that sits to the right of Woodland Road as you enter the campus from Wilkins Avenue. And the apartment is beautiful, too, and very spacious—as opposed to the postage stamp of a room I've been inhabiting in Fickes Hall—with high ceilings, a nonworking fireplace with a mantel, white walls, sky-blue molding and detailing, my very own bathroom and shower, a large closet, and two single beds. During the year, this apartment is used for hosting guests, whether they be event speakers, visiting professors, or prospective students and their families. But since the college was basically closing down for a short period of time and I needed a place to stay near my job, I was the lucky one to be handed the keys.

Yes—my very own apartment for two weeks. Feeling carefree and responsible. Feeling independent and grown-up. No homework to do but just a job to go to and money to make. Everything I want and love.

And now I have an older man—at least ten years older—in the apartment as well, just him and me, all alone.

"Why don't you just watch a bit of TV, Irwin, while I go and change," I suggest, closing the bathroom door behind me, jeans and a low-cut, button-up, striped top with ruffled edges in my arms. "I'll just be a minute."

******

SPENDING THE LAST few hours of our date at The Decade is perfect. Curt and Globy are smiling and laughing, busily and excitedly ding!-ing the cowbell every time they throw a tip into the metal bucket hanging above their heads, every time they easily pour a shot of tequila. Craig Brockle is carding people and collecting money at the door, his friendly smile never leaving his face. Walter is savoring his liquor on his lips, as usual, in his nonchalant, unassuming, natural way. And Bruce Springsteen and his sexy, rough voice are enhancing it all.

And then there is Irwin—sitting next to me, close. But this time there is no alter Irwin. No affectation, no efforts—however unknowing—to appear tough, or manly, or masculine, or other than he is. Just Irwin, just being himself. Just the simple, honest, caring, intelligent, tender, lovable guy who took me to *The Nutcracker*.

******

IN THE WEEKS FOLLOWING, we spend more time together, first among friends at a Super Bowl party at his house, where, after a conversation with Curt and Nick about the new movies he has added to his collection, he takes me aside and tells me about a great flick he has just seen, whispering in my ear that there were some very amorous parts in it, so we'll just have to watch it together sometime when we are alone, me utterly not knowing how to respond. Next, at Eat'n Park, where we go for a cup of tea and a late-night snack one Friday after my shift has ended around one a.m. Abruptly and unexpectedly we are interrupted midway by the sudden appearance of a fuming, highly agitated, red-faced, laser-eyed Nick, who has been searching for Irwin for at least an hour. "*YOU PARKED ME IN BEHIND THE GRILL, IRWIN!!!*" he explodes, which summarily ends, as you might have expected, our little get-together.

There is also the time that he gives me a ride home to Chatham after work—it is just too freezing to walk, and my car is in the shop. We head toward his pickup, which Marty let him park for free in the Gulf Station's small parking lot (his habit of parking in the driveway behind The Grill has been, I think, finally broken). The Gulf Station is closed by this time of the night, and Irwin's pickup is the lone vehicle in the lot. It is also rather dark out, except for the rays of the streetlights, which are just almost making it to the truck. I climb into the vehicle, Irwin closing the door behind me, and try to find a spot for my feet among the collection of tools, spark plugs, batteries, and paraphernalia that seems to be growing by the second. And then Irwin hops in, puts the key in the ignition, and starts her up. "Damn *cold*, isn't it?" he says, thrusting his hands into his pockets, waiting for the vehicle to get warm, "The Thrill Is Gone" seductively playing on the radio.

"You've…got…that right!" I reply, shivering profusely and looking straight ahead, as I quickly rub my hands together and make an honest attempt to stop my chattering teeth.

But then it happens… Out of nowhere… But is it *really*? Certainly I have seen it coming all along.

The shocking coldness of his lips, but the even more shocking hotness of his tongue. The lingering, and the earnestness, and the sweetness.

What have I done?

******

HE WARNED ME—my older brother—practically avowed that a man and a woman (in most cases, at least) couldn't be *just* friends, that the attraction and the wanting, especially on the man's part, would always get in the way. That a man would tolerate the friends-only status for a while, but it was always in the hopes that more intimacy would follow. Otherwise, really, why would he bother in the first place?

"But, *no*, John," I protested, so convinced that I was right. "Look at my ballroom dance partner and me. We spend tons of time together and we're just friends; nothing more has ever happened between us and probably never will. And I think he's perfectly happy with all of that."

"Oh *yeah*," John replied, his eyebrows raised, and his tone of voice so confident. "Slap a kiss on him unexpectedly one day, and *then* see what happens…"

******

I THOUGHT, at the beginning of our relationship, that maybe I would grow to want to be with him, that the attraction would become stronger and stronger until one day I'd wonder what had taken me so long to desire him. How often does bang-on-the-head attraction and desire arrest you the first time you meet someone anyway (someone who is actually available, that is)? I can remember it happening to me only once (okay, *twice*), and it hit me *hard*. But the *former* situation—it's happened to me often…almost too often, in fact. The more time I've spent with someone, the more we've talked, the more we've discussed our likes and dislikes, the more I've wanted him.

With Irwin, however, it never got to that point—that point of longing, craziness, aching. That point where he invades your thoughts and, frighteningly, your decisions. But the friendship we built together, I truly valued it, and I began to think—*hope*—that maybe he could be satisfied with it, too, with the talking, the sharing, the hanging out, the learning from each other, the rewarding exchange of thoughts and words.

But, as I've quickly learned, he couldn't. And I've begun to wonder, and regret. Was I too selfish and too frivolous with his feelings? Knowing how he felt from the beginning (and how *I* felt from the beginning), should I have backed off, stopped hanging out with him, never have accepted his offer to go out in the first place?

In his own way, he's answered me. And much, much too quickly. The penetrating looks and the partiality have ended, the easiness and the familiarity are gone. The stares and interest that were mine are now given to another—Remmy—a cute, intelligent blonde just-arrived from Cape Cod, who wanted to "get away and try some place different."

No more late-night cups of coffee, rides home from work, meaningful conversations.

So now I stand watching, in the distance, knowing that it is probably for the best, but also knowing that I'll never be looked at quite that way again. For in Irwin's world, without that exchange of passion, or at least the possibility of it, there is nothing else left. ■

THE BURGUNDY INCIDENTS

"Hey, Bea, how's it going?"

I walk through the front door, ready for the Saturday day shift, and there's Bianca— at least I think it's her—hunching down behind the bar, attaching a fresh keg of Rolling Rock to one of the taps.

"Oh, not too bad. I can't complain," she says, throwing her hand up in the air.

"You're working for Adam today?" I ask, peering over the bar.

"Yep, that's the plan," she answers, glancing up at me and smiling.

"Oh, that's good. Saturdays are always— Oh, but you know what? I was wondering…how was last night? Was it busy?"

"Boy, I'd say it was," she responds with a heavy sigh, standing up and wiping her hands on her apron. "There were so many people in here that I don't think I had a break until after ten."

"Really? Well, that's the way it's been lately. It's great for the pocketbook, though…but, oh god! How—how did Shane handle it?"

"Well, for his first Friday night…" she replies, as she lifts her eyebrows and a hint of a smile forms at the corners of her mouth. "Well, you know, things weren't going too bad until the incident with the Burgundy."

"The incident with the *what*? Oh, don't tell me that he—"

"Oh yeah. All over the guy sitting in the two-seater near the window. He got his hair, his white cotton shirt. Didn't miss a spot, in fact…"

"You're *kidding*???" I reply, my eyes getting bigger, the corners of my mouth beginning to turn upward as well (I haven't even taken my coat and hat off yet). "I bet Nick was *pissed*," I whisper, looking around to make sure no one can hear me say this terrible word, even though Bea and I are the only two in the place.

"Yeah, well, *that's* an understatement… But I'll tell you. It's really too bad that that wasn't the end of it."

"Ah, *come on*."

"I'm not joking. After Shane apologized over and over again, wiping as much of the wine out of the guy's hair as he could, dipping a cloth in soda water and trying to get the stains out of the guy's shirt—oh god, Jenna, it was such a spectacle—he went back up to the bar again and ordered another Burgundy from Nick."

"Okay."

"No, it really wasn't okay. After he put the glass on the tray, he was rushing, like we all know he does, and he spun around way too fast. So—"

"Oh, please don't tell me—"

"So the wineglass tipped over, and the wine spilled all over the floor. And, to top it all off, the glass rolled off the tray, too, and you can just guess what happened to *it*."

I try my best, for at *least* ten seconds, but it is of no use. I can't hold it in any longer, and neither can Bianca. We start laughing like crazy, the tears flooding our cheeks.

"I bet Shane never covers a Friday night for me again!" I exclaim, wiping my face with my gloves.

"*Covers* for you? Are you serious? How about if he ever *talks* to you again?" Bea points out, and we just laugh even harder. ∎

PARADISE LOST

"Yep—she was a pretty one, that wife of mine," Tommy says, laughing sweetly. "Long, blonde hair; big, dark brown eyes; a beautiful, shapely body. And—you know me!—boy did I ever try and try with her, forever and again, for a couple of years, in fact. Can you believe that? But she would have nothing to do with it, other than some snuggling and kissing every now and then. Nope. She was the purest, most headstrong person I think I've ever met. Nothing at all until the vows were said and sealed. So much fortitude, I could hardly understand it. But, boy…I tell you what…when they tell you it is worth the wait…believe you me…they were in no way kidding," he says, sighing, his eyes shining with pride despite himself.

"Now, however," he says dryly, a shadow suddenly passing over his entire demeanor, he almost seeming to be a different person altogether, "I feel like we're back to that pre-marriage status. I mean…it was fine then…I could wait. But all these years later… I've sincerely tried to get the fire going again—God knows I still have it within me— but when I approach her, she's never interested. Nope— day in and day out… How has it come to this?… All she does now is sit around with her hands entwined in that rosary…" ∎

THE FORSAKEN

The entrance in the back of The Grill sees a lot of action. It is through this gateway that the men of Sysco deliver all of the restaurant's essentials. While working, we employees often have to watch out for overstuffed boxes and crates full of heads of lettuce and various vegetables (you can every once in a while see a radish or a carrot peeking out), large, plastic containers of dressing (Russian, French, raspberry vinaigrette, pepper parmesan, chunky blue cheese, buttermilk ranch), and large, glass jars of Boar's Head pickles making their way through the tiny, crowded kitchen, down the worn, cracked, wooden steps, past Bobby's small, paper-ridden, photograph-laden, and newspaper article–covered office, and across the hot, stuffy basement to the walk-in cooler.

Of course, this secluded doorway isn't nearly as aesthetic as the front entryway: The road along it isn't paved (which can be quite muddy when it is raining, and really slippery when it is icy), many garbage cans are located on either side of it, and there is a short concrete wall facing it (behind which a row of thick, tall bushes live, obstructing any kind of view). We employees can take a load off and relax on this wall (and escape from the customers!) when we desire a few minutes of peace and quiet or a breath of fresh air (if you can call the air *fresh*)—or a cigarette (Shane and Diana sit together out there in the twenty-degree weather, no coats on but the orange tips of their cigarettes giving away their presence in the darkness, and their puffing and the rising smoke providing some warmth, making them forget about shivering). But despite the cigarette butts lying here and there, the garbage cans (and their occasional nasty odor), and the inconvenient mud and ice, I feel special to know about this private entrance and experience a surge of pride as I enter The Grill this way, like a royal member of the court.

That's not the end of it, though. You know what really interests me and makes me think as I stand in this doorway or pass in and out of it? It's what it allows me to see next door. Not more than a few feet away, in fact, is the Squirrel Hill Flower Shop. As would be expected, the area outside its back entrance is also used as a garbage-storing area. The flower shop's garbage isn't always garbage, however. Over and over again, I witness boxes upon boxes overflowing with bundles of flowers, sometimes red roses, other times yellow and orange tulips, still other times orchids, apparently tossed because they were no longer in "perfect" selling condition. Sure, there are instances when the flowers are completely dead or dried up, but most of the time they are a tad bit wilted and the edges are just beginning to turn brown, but they are still pretty, and valuable—definitely good enough for my dorm room.

Obviously Mary Ellen feels the same way. Every once in a while I'll walk through the back entrance and she'll be standing there working, a glass vase beside her containing a white daisy or a pink carnation, keeping her company. ∎

A FAMILY OF SIX

Mom, dad, grandmother, baby girl, and two little boys…

The front of the restaurant is empty, so I decide to put them there. As they wait, eyes upon me, the baby wriggling in the mother's arms, I move the four-seater to the center of the space (it usually sits fairly close to the wall that lines the entranceway), and then add to it the two-seater that is normally next to the window. As I hurry to the back of the restaurant to retrieve the wooden high chair that is hiding in the space behind the booth closest to the kitchen, the family has already started to move in, and without my signal (as happens often). I carry the high chair to the front as fast as I can (although a bit unwieldily), and then try to push it into place beside the mother, although as soon as I do that she gets up and moves to the other side of the table as one of the dark-headed boys keeps imploring "I want chicken fingers and french fries," and as the baby tugs fiercely at the winter hat that has fallen down over her eyes. I then grab menus from the ancillary bar and try to pass them out individually but fail to get anyone's attention. Adam is glancing at me from behind the bar as he draws a beer, a look of concern in his eyes, but it's obvious that he is just too busy to help, a full, active bar surrounding him.

I rush to the back of the restaurant to check on the two

parties that have already been served, hoping that I haven't neglected them for too long. Then I fly into the kitchen, warning Anthony that a large order will be making its way back in a few minutes.

Next, I ask the family what they would like to drink. This, which is usually the easiest part, is a struggle in itself. *Root beer or Sprite?* the father inquires (over and over again), but the little boys just can't seem to decide, their changing minds reflected in their wide eyes. My notepad is full of strikeout lines.

Having finally gotten their drink order, I rush around to fill it. Soon I head back to their table, carrying their drinks on a small round tray: one root beer and one Sprite (each in a small cardboard cup, with a lid and a straw, as requested by the mother), a Fuzzy Navel, a bottle of Iron City, and a strawberry wine cooler with a glass of ice, plus three pint glasses full of ice water. I steady the loaded tray in the palm of my left hand, my long, thin fingers spread out underneath as far as they will go, and I deliver the drinks with my right as I move slowly around the table. Still, after all of this time, it amazes me that I can do this, this balancing act, this feat of coordination, this cardhouse that could weaken and shatter in an instant—yet somehow, at the same time, I lack no confidence.

They give me their food order. A Cajun chicken salad with pepper-parmesan dressing, *on the side, please.* A cheeseburger and potato salad, with cheddar, lettuce, tomato, pickle, and raw onion—*make sure it's well-done, though…thanks.* An order of buffalo wings, with celery and blue cheese, *and plenty of extra napkins.* A side of apple sauce, *for the baby.* A child's order of chicken fingers and french fries (surprise, surprise), and a child's order of spaghetti with marinara sauce, *but not too much sauce.*

I head to my register to punch in the order, but I'm

stopped on the way by two sets of couples who have just appeared in the doorway. Instantly, *Holy hell!* flashes across my mind, but, calmly, *Two for lunch? Smoking or non?* proceeds from my lips.

After seating both couples, I manage to make it to my register without interruption, wishing that I had been able to put in the family's order a few minutes earlier, knowing that it takes at least twenty-five to thirty minutes to grill a well-done burger.

The next half hour passes by quickly, filled with taking orders, refilling drinks, making change, and preparing desserts, although I feel the stares and irritation emanating from the front. I realize then that I should've told them that a well-done burger takes quite a while to cook, especially since it's a generous serving. I usually do this, but somehow it slipped my mind today. I avoid catching any of their eyes, too busy to deal with their impatience, when the ring of the bell finally releases me.

I race back to the kitchen, telling Anthony that I'll take half of the order out first (as I load it onto a medium-sized rectangular tray), and then come back for the rest. "No problem at all," he answers, in his usual, good-natured way. Actually, though, I'm supposed to carry the entire order out at once on one of the extra-large, oval trays (you know how it goes: Set up the folding support-gizmo ahead of time and then set the large tray on top of it and deliver all of the food in one trip. It's more professional to do it this way, and half the party won't have to wait to eat their food out of respect for the other half who haven't received theirs yet). But I fear doing this. (Where'd that confidence go?) To begin with, there's a really good chance that I could knock the side of the tray against the wall as I exit the kitchen, given that the corridor is unbelievably narrow, which could result in the avalanche and crashing of plate upon plate (and food upon someone's head). Most of all, however, I just don't have the upper body strength to do it: first, to heave those pounds up on my right shoulder; second, to carry all that weight to the front of the restaurant (even though it's really not *that* far); and third, to crouch down and set the tray upon the support (which really isn't very high) without tipping it too far one way or the other. Luckily, in the evenings when I work with Diana, she's always very willing to carry these large orders out for me (tell a caring person your weakness, and they'll usually compensate for you). But on Saturday afternoons like this one, I'm on my own.

I deliver the Cajun chicken salad (the large glass bowl takes up half the tray itself!), the wings, the applesauce, and a stack of napkins (not the good ones, but the square, thinner type). "I'll be right back with the rest," I tell them, smiling, and then return to the kitchen quickly, the tray hanging by my side. There sit the two dishes for the children, but the burger and potato salad are nowhere in sight. I don't think too much about it, sure that the burger is hidden behind Anth, who is standing over the charcoal grill with a spatula in his hand, his back facing me. I stand there for a moment, but then, unable to wait any longer, I ask, "Is that burger just about ready, Anth?" I hope I don't sound like a pest.

He turns around quickly, a confused and shocked look on his face. "Burger? Did you order a burger?" he asks quickly as he grabs the receipt that he had placed under the bowl of spaghetti, which is usually a signal that he has finished preparing an order. I glance at the grill, and all I can see on it are a few chicken breasts... My heart sinks.

"Oh my *god* did I for—" he begins, but before he can finish, he looks up from the receipt and tells me the bad news. "There's no burger on this order, Jenna." He hands it to me gently.

I examine it, maybe three or four times, in utter disbelief. "Oh my *god*! You mean *I* forgot to order the burger?" I mumble, still staring at the receipt. "How could I do such a thing? Especially with something that takes so long to cook? I never miss—"

But Anthony, thank goodness, interrupts me. "Jenna— these dishes are gonna get cold. Why don't you take these out now and I'll get started on that burger? Okay?"

"Oh…oh yeah…yeah…okay," I say, nodding, but I load the dishes onto the tray slowly, trying to think. "He wants it well-done, though, Anthony."

"Okay, no problem; I'll take care of it," he answers.

Somehow I make it to the table, and as I approach it, there everyone sits staidly (except for the baby, her pretty blue eyes observing me), the food untouched. "Here you go," I say to the two little boys as I place their food in front of them, which, like a magical potion, energizes them completely. But then, as if I'm trying to force down two tablespoons of the worst-tasting cough syrup you can imagine, I make eye contact with the man and say the words. "Sir, I'm terribly, terribly sorry, but your burger isn't quite ready yet. It's actually a rather thick burger, a quarter pound, and it takes around thirty minutes to cook. It shouldn't take too—"

"But it's already *been* thirty minutes," he answers abruptly. His wife and the grandmother are now staring at me too. (The boys, however—they could care less. They are in taste-bud heaven. And the little, curly-haired blonde baby…even though I'm totally stressed, I can't help thinking that she's just about one of the cutest things ever.)

"Like I said, I'm terribly sorry. It really shouldn't take too much longer," I assure him, trying to look confident, although I'm really lying (but not about the being-terribly-sorry part).

I rush back to the kitchen (boy, are my legs tired!), glancing at my other customers on the way to make sure there aren't any crises occurring there.

"Anth!" I say, practically sliding into him. "Is there any way at all you can speed up the cooking of that burger? That guy is *really* not too happy."

"Well, I did start it out in the microwave—and *please* don't tell anybody about that, Jenna, especially Mary Ellen—but I just can't cook the entire thing in there… I just can't do it," he confesses, shaking his head. "It's supposed to be a char-grilled burger after all. And it just wouldn't taste the same."

Good ol' Anthony. Anthony and his principles. That's why I dig him so much.

"Yeah, Anth…that's okay," I respond calmly, all of a sudden perfectly at ease. "I understand—completely."

******

EVENTUALLY, and thankfully, the infamous burger does get done, in about ten to fifteen minutes' time. Anthony's use of the microwave and his decision to cook the burger medium-well instead of well (it tastes much better that way anyway) really speeds up the process. During this waiting period, I have to deal with my own realization that I royally messed up, plus—despite my moment of acceptance in the kitchen—an incessant uneasiness that results from the dissatisfied gestures and drilling looks of the customers. There are moments when I feel as if I am in a straitjacket and can't get out.

It all works out fine, though. Despite the burger's lateness, I can tell that the gentleman really enjoys it, and everybody else seems pleased with their food as well. To my complete surprise, they even leave me a decent tip.

But that's not the last of it. Now there is the aftermath to deal with, not only on the tables but also on the floor: french fry fragments, countless spitballs (those ornery devils), smeared ketchup, scattered napkins, melting ice cubes, crumbs galore—and much grosser things I can't even begin to recognize.

I scrunch down under the tables—on my knees— broom in one hand, and waste bucket in the other. ■

THE SNOWSTORM

"Hey, Shane," Nick says, as he leans over the end of the bar and comfortably rests his forearms on top of it. "Are you the early-person-out tonight?"

Shane, busy doing his side work, stops with his hand buried inside a white plastic container of bright blue, yellow, and pink sugar and sweetener packets. He looks up expectantly. "Yeah, I sure am, Nick," he replies.

"Well, why don't you get going then? It's nine—a little early—but there's no use sticking around here any longer tonight."

No argument there. Within minutes, Shane puts the plastic container back on its shelf near the kitchen, grabs his coat and scarf, says a quick "See you guys later," and is out the door. As he passes by the front window, I can't help but admire his silky blond hair glistening in the prancing snowflakes.

About fifteen minutes later, Mary Ellen strides lazily out of the kitchen, her apron jumbled in her hand. "It's dead in here," she says, stopping with her knee bent and her hip jutted to the side, glancing at me as I sit on a stool at the bar, my head resting in my hands, and at Nick, as he counts a stack of money he has just taken out of the register. "There's no use keeping the kitchen open any longer for this...so...I'm closed," she says in her usual manner of matter-of-factness. With that, she turns back around and eventually disappears.

I resume staring out the window, thinking how refreshing it would be to take a walk in what really looks like the winter wonderland I had sung about so often as a child. Around seven o'clock, a deliberate but beautiful snow had started to fall, and fall, and fall…

"Jenna."

Startled, I quickly straighten up in my seat.

"Nick…oh…sorry…I was just looking—"

"Oh no, that's okay, Jenna. I was just going to tell you that you should probably get out of here too. I don't think we're going to get any more business tonight anyway, and if we do, I can handle it. Besides, the roads are getting pretty bad…so…as long as all of your closing duties are taken care of…"

"Oh yeah, Nick, I finished them a while ago," I reply, jumping down from my seat.

"Great… Well, go ahead and take off then."

"Thanks!" I say, smiling, as I proceed to walk toward the kitchen and then turn the corner to go down into the warm basement to pick up my coat, hat, gloves, and duffel bag.

Once I'm all bundled up, I climb up the cracked wooden stairs and remember to grab a Styrofoam cup of minestrone that Mary Ellen has left for me on the stainless-steel counter in the kitchen. As always, the surface of the counter is gently reflecting the small overhead night-light.

I pass by the bar on my way out, calling "Have a good night, Nick," who is now concentrating on doing the report for the credit card machine. But before I get to the door, he stops me.

"Jenna…" I turn around and look at him. Has he changed his mind?

"Yes, Nick," I answer.

"Do you have your car tonight?" he asks.

"Yeah…I do… But it's parked nearby, on the street in front of the Gulf Station," I say, pointing in that direction. "I can get there al—"

"Well, just hold on for a second, would ya?" he asks, and, without waiting for an answer, heads—in his usual focused, deliberate, and athletic manner—to where I've just come from. I can hear him jogging down the steps.

Soon, he reappears, but he is not alone. He is holding a broom in his right hand, the straw head resting on the ground.

"I just thought you could use some help cleaning your car off," he explains. "There must be at least three to five inches out there by now." As he says this, he motions for me to go in front of him.

"Oh…okay, okay," I reply. But for some damn reason I cannot move.

"Jenna?" he says, finally. "Everything okay? You seem a little—"

"Oh yeah, sure, Nick… Sorry, Nick… But, Nick…I was just… But don't…don't you want to put your coat on?" I ask, not sure what else to say, but then I immediately start laughing, realizing what a stupid question that is. Nick is wearing shorts, which he always does, whether the temperature is eighty-five or two. "Just forget I said that," I say, laughing again, and then I turn around—Nick right behind me. I seriously pray that I don't stumble or trip.

I take a few steps forward. I lift my hand. I place my hand on the door handle. I exert my force. I push the door open. I walk outside.

And then he does. And then he's beside me.

And suddenly, I can't believe how it all feels. Like a pool of cold water that doesn't stun but exhilarates. Little drops of life piercing our faces and our tongues, a thousand a second. Feathers under our feet and covering all of the buildings and streetlights—and covering us, as we walk—romanticizing everything.

"Is this it?" Nick asks. He once again awakes me from my reverie, pointing with the broom handle toward what looks nothing like a car.

"Well, uh," I say, glancing up and down the street. "That's where I parked it. And besides, there's nothing else like it on the street anyway."

"Yeah," Nick says, laughing, "I guess most people went home early, or didn't go out in the first place."

"Yeah, well, it's their loss, right?" I say, shrugging my shoulders and catching his eye through the falling snowflakes.

"Yes," he says, nodding, "it is quite beautiful, isn't it?"

And we just stand there for a moment, focused on each other. ∎

CONFRONTATIONS

Suddenly, she shoved the tray of drinks at me, liquid escaping everywhere—a disgusted look and nasty words escaping too. Just last week this happened, after I had finally gained the courage to approach her. But it was something that I had been wanting to do for such a long time.

Before I did it, though, she had confidently strolled up the steps to the nonsmoking section and begun taking her first drink order of the evening—and I had just stood against the ancillary bar and watched. She had then headed toward the main bar and started filling her drink order— and again I had just stood there and watched, as I had done countless, frustrating times before.

That night, however, as I caught that arrogant, carefree flicker in her eye, that glint of all the money she knew she would have a few hours later in her basket as she sat down for an after-work drink and as I continued to cocktail waitress for a few more hours until closing, something sparked within me. And somehow—with "One of Us" playing in the background—my feet led me to her, and my mouth spoke the words.

"*Bianca*...you know—it's *my turn* to work the nonsmoking section."

She looked at me quickly, releasing the pressure from one of the little round white buttons that cover the fountain gun, which was pointed in my direction. And her free hand—it went to her hip.

"What…what do you mean?… I've been working the nonsmoking section on Friday nights for as long as I can remember now."

"Yeah, well…that's…that's what I'm trying to say."

"Okay…so?"

I could see that this was going to be difficult.

"Well, you know, when I was working both Thursday and Friday nights, it worked out so well. You know, I worked the nonsmoking section on Thursday while you worked the smoking section, and then we switched the following night. But now—for the past few months, in fact, I've only been working Friday nights—because of my rehearsal commitments on Thursdays—"

"That's not my problem, Jen—"

"I *know* it's not, Bianca."

"Well, then, fine then."

"No, Bianca. For me to work the smoking section *every single* Friday night, which is almost *never* even close to being as busy as the nonsmoking section is…I'm just not making enough money, and I don't think it's fair—and especially since I have to stay here until closing, to top it all off. I mean, even with the money I make after you sign out, I bet I don't even come close to making *all night* what you make during just the rush hours."

She stared at me unbelievingly, took a deep, hindered breath, and shoved the gun into its receptacle. And her hands—now they were both on her hips.

"*Look*, Jenna. I've worked here for almost five years now, much longer than any of the servers here—and certainly much longer than *you*, so—*I* deserve to work in the nonsmoking section on Friday nights. I've done my time, and I've earned that right."

Then, with an audacity that was almost unimaginable to me, she looked down, placed her hands on the edge of the tray, and was ready to pick it up and be on her way. And unimaginably, again, I almost let her. But now that I had that sense of freedom bubbling, though still cautiously, in my blood, I couldn't abandon it again.

"Wait, Bianca."

"No—*you* wait. People are expecting these drinks, you know."

"Yes, I do know. And I completely understand everything you've said. But isn't it the accepted policy that all the servers here should switch sections each and every time they work with each other? I mean, if the section you got to work in was based on seniority, poor...poor Diana!—she'd *never* get to work the nonsmoking section, and she works about five days a week!"

And then, just at that moment—that's when the tray of drinks headed my way.

******

FOR THE FOLLOWING HOUR, I was so busy that I was feeling rather dizzy. But beyond my feet and hands going rather crazy, trying to keep up with everything, so was my mind, and not just on all of the orders I had to keep straight. I was experiencing that uncomfortable mix of pride, uneasiness, uncertainty, defensiveness, and guilt, knowing that I had done the right thing, but nonetheless still questioning myself if I should've done it and if there wasn't a better way that I could have gone about it. Essentially, I did have to work so closely with her, and she had made some valid points. Plus, she was nowhere in sight. Maybe I should have just left well enough alone, as I had done so many weeks before and in so many situations, let alone this one. In all honesty, isn't it better sometimes to just back down and go with the flow? I mean, if someone can't realize by herself that she's being unfair, is it worth the trouble and ensuing chaos to make her aware of it?

Well, maybe so…

I had finally gotten a moment to take a short break, and there she was, approaching me so nonchalantly. The usual prettiness—which had so quickly disappeared a short time ago—was back in her face. Yes, that is Bianca. Whether she is feeling confident or not, she almost always has some magical way of looking it.

"Jenna," she said, softly, very close to me. "You know, I took a while and thought about it—after all…I haven't been very busy!" she said, laughing freshly. "And I really want to apologize for the way I acted earlier. I guess it really would be a drag to work the smoking section week after week, especially when you have to be here so late and then be worried about closing up. I really should have been more aware of it. So…from now on…we'll switch, okay?"

I looked at her, smiled, and immediately felt better, so glad that, because of her apology, an *entire* night of tension was going to be avoided.

"Bianca, thanks so much for saying all of that. I really do appreciate it," I said, and I couldn't help but touch her arm. But I also couldn't help but feel satisfied and rewarded for what I accomplished that night. Not only did I conquer my fear of approaching Bianca—older, confident, experienced Bianca—but I also conquered my fear of confronting my feelings and myself, the greatest of them all. ∎

WANT SOME COFFEE?

It's two-thirty in the morning. Shane, Jack, Bianca, Nina (our main hostess), a crew of regulars, and I, after having had some beers and shots at The Grill, have walked over to Shane's apartment on Darlington Road, just about a block away, to hang out and talk. Shane lives there with his roommate, Doreen, a pretty, skinny, pale, reddish blonde, friendly, mild-mannered girl. She often comes to the bar with Shane on his days off, and they relax in one of the booths, talking and smoking, their eyes resting on each other. Two large, perspiring drafts sit in front of them. A thin, brown cigarette lies gently between the index and middle fingers of Doreen's right hand, floating in front of her face, her elbow against the table. A thicker, ordinary white cigarette is held more firmly between Shane's thumb and index finger, the rest of his fingers rounded downward, his forearm taking a break on the table.

They have a comfortable, roomy apartment. As you walk through the front door, you immediately enter a hallway. Two bedrooms line the hallway, to the right. At the end of the hallway there is a small kitchen, which contains a round, wooden table, with a few wooden chairs, not leaving much more space for anything else but the refrigerator. Off of the kitchen is the living room—a rather spacious room with a fireplace, a few overgrown plants, a worn-in couch, a couple of pictures on the wall (one of forest animals, and the other of a garden scene), and a bunch of large, cushy chairs placed in this and that corner, or wherever, which are now filled with talkative, happy, tipsy young people listening to The Police at one moment and Alice in Chains at another.

"This is an awesome place to hang out," I say to Jack, who is lounging on the furry, used-to-be-green carpet, as I'm practically swallowed up in a huge brown recliner, a tear or two quite evident but not marring its comfort at all.

He takes a gulp of his icy Rolling Rock. "Yeah, I've always enjoyed hanging out here. Shane and Doreen are great hosts," he replies, as he glances around at everyone.

A little later, with more and more empty beer bottles and over-full ashtrays collecting on the end tables, and with Sting making himself heard through the chatter every now and then, there's Nina—in her short black bob and a short black skirt—walking toward us, with what looks like a Captain Morgan and coke in her hand. "Hey, you two," she says. "A few of us are going to hang out in Shane's room for a few minutes," she continues, motioning in that direction with her head. "You want to join us?"

At first I have no clue what she's talking about. But when I see the spark in Jack's eyes, that quickly changes. I finally realize all too well why people have been in Shane's room off and on all night—with the door shut—and understand why I haven't been feeling myself, but much less inhibited, since I got here.

"Not me," I say, without a second thought. (Getting it secondhand has been quite enough. I don't need to venture any further.)

Jack is about ready to stand up, but then he glances at me and his expression changes. "I think I'll pass this time, Nin," he says, and digs in his pocket for another cigarette.

Nina shrugs her shoulders. "Okay. You got it." She

motions to Bianca, who is sitting on the couch with her new love interest, Vic, an attractive, ash-blond, long-haired, mustached guy who works at Heads Together, a really cool, eclectic underground bookstore, video store, gift shop, and card store on Murray Avenue. "You coming?"

"Yeah, I'm coming. I'll be there in just a minute," she says, as she leans over and gives Vic a kiss.

Just then, Doreen opens the refrigerator door, takes out an icy Iron City, holds it up in the air, and says, as she looks into the living room over her shoulder, "Anybody need another beer?" Before even one of us can answer, however, Shane plops down heavily in the middle of the living room—malleable as a piece of dough—his shoulder-length, golden blond hair loose and disheveled. I immediately glance at Jack, a questioning look in my eyes. But he doesn't look back at me. He is squinting, his forehead is wrinkled, and he's staring not just at Shane and the sly look he has on his face, but also at the backpack lying in Shane's lap, his focus alternating between the two. It's true that the backpack does look very, very odd—almost swollen, in fact.

We stare for a while longer, wondering what he's up to this time, but then he attempts to say something. It doesn't escape very easily, though, because he is giggling profusely, and apparently at nothing at all. But then he lets us have it.

"Forget the beer!" he exclaims, as he quickly unzips his backpack. "Anyone want a good cup of coffee?"

Tumbling forth, all over his lap and the floor, are small, shiny, silver packs upon packs of ground coffee, an avalanche of Java surrounding him.

"Shane!" Jack yells, and the entire room erupts in laughter.

There is no need for the purveyor himself or anyone else to explain where he has gotten that stash, for we all know its source. ∎

AN EXECUTIVE DECISION

He suddenly appears through the front door with a white cardboard coffee cup in his hand (*Coffee Tree Roasters* fancily written in green on the side), his heavy key ring jingling as we are preparing to open— Anthony chopping up vegetables, heating up the soups, and lightly cooking some pasta; Adam filling up the sinks behind the bar and wiping off the liquor bottles; me making iced tea and coffee and setting all of the tables with a paisley place mat, napkin, knife, and fork, writing *Soup du Jour* with an erasable marker on the lit board above the poker machine; some old movie playing on the TV. It is always a good feeling when he shows up, though—never a tensing of the shoulders or neck or an eerie feeling of doom. I mean, I'm sure he comes in to check up on things and make sure that we are arriving reasonably on time and doing our jobs properly. But Bobby is about the most easygoing boss you could ever get. No, I'm serious. Think about the nicest boss you've ever had and then multiply that by two—even three.

It's unusual for him to be here this early, however. Most Saturdays it is just the three of us—us young college students in our early twenties, effectively running the entire day-shift operation. This, certainly, is another reason why I love working here on this particular day of the week. And not because there is no authority figure around to keep us in line. Rather, I love it because Bobby has placed a huge amount of trust in us—put his pot of gold, his shiny diamond, his new car, in our hands. And not just once, either, but week after week, and month after month. So, in fact, we don't act negligently or take advantage of the absence of authority, as many might expect. We *become* the authority, get a true taste—continually—of the confidence, respect, and responsibility another's trust gives you.

"Who wants breakfast from Pamela's?" he asks, once he sees, with a few glances, that we have everything under control, and as he sits down at the bar to flip through the mail from the week before. "Eggs, banana pancakes, bacon, chocolate chip or strawberry pancakes…whatever you want…"

The three of us gather around him. Adam and Anthony give him their orders, which he quickly jots down on a small, rectangular pad of paper, identical to the ones I am so used to using.

Big surprise, but I can't decide what to get (I have a *horrific* time making decisions). Do I want the fluffy, homemade pancakes stuffed with juicy slices of banana and tender walnuts? A Belgian waffle topped with pretty strawberries and outlined in whipped cream? Or simply a fresh egg sunny-side up, with toast?

"Bobby, you know what," I tell him, after taking way too much time to think about it, Adam and Anthony shooting me many ornery, impatient glares, "I *really* can't decide between the banana pancakes and the eggs… Why don't you just order something for me?"

"You got it," he replies instantly (I like a man who doesn't hesitate). After securing his stack of mail with a rubber band and sliding it into the space between the bar's register and the wall, out the door he goes, on his way to the crowded, always-busy, small café around the corner on

Forbes Avenue (across from The Cage), which consistently has a folding chalkboard out front that highlights all of its specials, and is always packed with hungry, chatty, smiling, so-happy-it's-the-weekend-and-I'm-out-for-breakfast Pittsburghers.

About twenty minutes to half an hour later I see a sneaker jutting its way inside, as Bobby successfully opens The Grill's front door with the help of his foot, a stack of Styrofoam containers in his arms.

"Adam! Anth!" he calls. "Your breakfasts are here!" Then he turns his attention to me. "Where are those two? Making plans for later, I assume…as usual?" he asks, grinning and shaking his head.

"I think you're pretty well on the mark with that," I answer, secretly hoping that those plans include me.

"Well, Jenna. Enjoy." He walks toward me and places two large Styrofoam containers beside the tower of place settings (place mats cum napkins) I am constructing. I look up at him in surprise.

He laughs. "Well, since you had so much trouble deciding, you must really have wanted both. So, an important executive decision was in order." ∎

THE HENRY EFFECT

On my way to the bathroom to freshen up, pull my hair back, and put on my apron before my shift begins, I pass Diana sitting in the back booth. As usual, she's smoking; but not as usual, she's completely engrossed in a dense, paperback book. She doesn't even look up when I turn around and approach her. I almost feel guilty for disturbing her, but I'm just too curious.

"Hey, Diana," I say, nudging her softly on the shoulder. "What's that you're so interested in?"

"Oh, shit!" Startled, she looks up.

"Oh, god…sorry, Diana. I didn't mean to scare you."

"No, c'mon, that's okay." She pauses for a second, but then she turns the book's cover toward me. I move a little closer to be able to read the title better.

"What? *Tom Jones*! No way! By Henry…Henry…let me think…Henry Fielding, right? I read that not too long ago at Chatham—I think for my eighteenth-century English literature class. That's actually one of the books for class that I took the time to read word for word, even though it's around one thousand pages, isn't it?" I ask.

"Well, pretty close," she says, flipping to the end.

"I didn't know you liked to read, especially classic literature. I haven't found too many people in this place who have a passion for it quite like I do," I say.

"Well, you know, about six months ago I read the first

half of it in about a week or so—"

"Really?" I ask, utterly surprised (I've always been a very slow reader).

"Yeah, I guess I read pretty fast… But, anyway, like I said, I read the first half of it so quickly—I just couldn't put it down—but then we got so busy here at work and I picked up a few extra shifts, I just didn't have the time, or energy, for it. I felt bad for not reading, like something was missing, but what could I do? I've just been too damn tired… Well, last night I was clearing off my dresser—man, was it a fuckin' mess!—and I found the book lying under a bunch of unopened mail. I found the page that I had earmarked, and started reading where I had left off. I sat down on my bed, and the next thing I knew, it was two o'clock in the morning! And now here I am, reading it whenever I can get the chance."

"Yeah, that's how it is. Books will really do that to ya," I reply, smiling, shaking my head.

"Are you reading anything interesting right now?" Diana asks, putting down her cigarette and sliding a napkin between the pages of her book.

"Well, actually, I'm reading a book I borrowed from my friend Mariano—you've met him, haven't you? He comes in to eat quite often."

"Aaaah, yeah…let's see… Oh yeah! He's the nice, intelligent Latin American man who teaches at Pitt, right?"

"Yeah, that's right," I respond.

"Yeah, actually, I talked to him for quite a while up at the bar one time—I think you were working that night. Anyway, he's a really interesting guy, isn't he?"

"Oh, there's no doubt about that. And he absolutely loves to read too. We've gotten into the habit of recommending and lending books to each other and discussing them… Well, the book I'm reading now—

maybe you've read it—it's called *Tropic of Cancer*. It's by Henry Miller."

Diana's eyes light up.

"Oh, are you familiar with him?" I ask.

"Yeah, I am, although I haven't *read* anything by him, but I've read *Henry and June* and *The Diary of Anaïs Nin*," she responds.

"Anaïs Nin?"

"Yes. She was Henry Miller's lover for quite a while, but"—Diana leans closer to me and lowers her voice—"she actually was bisexual and had a woman lover as well, named June, who—get this—was also Henry's wife."

"Is that right...?" I say, my eyes widening. "Actually, it all sounds pretty racy, just like in the *Tropic of Cancer*."

"Oh yeah?" Diana seems thoroughly intrigued. She sits up straight, her slouch disappearing.

"Oh yeah, very much so. Henry Miller's certainly not afraid to talk about passion and sex and every little detail associated with it. I can't believe some of the stuff that I'm reading... He's actually really crude in many parts of the book, to tell you the truth. But, then again, it's really addicting, I must admit."

"I know *exactly* what you mean. You should read Anaïs Nin's diary if you really want to *read* something—I could bring the book in for you if you want," she says.

"Yeah? Well, that would be great! And I'm sure that Mariano wouldn't mind if you borrowed the *Tropic of Cancer*, if you'd like to. I'll mention it to him the next time I see him."

"That sounds like a plan, Jenna. I can't wait to read it," she says.

And so it begins, just like that: my and Diana's intimate, illicit book club.

What fun it will be. ■

GENEROSITY AND COFFEE

"**J**enna, would you mind coming over here for a second?"

It's Curt, calling to me from behind the bar.

"Sure," I reply, walking toward him. "What do you need?"

It's Saturday night around eight, Bob Dylan's "Like a Rolling Stone" is mixing in with the various conversations, and there is finally a bit of a lull in business, before the late crowd arrives. And instead of wearing my usual hat, I'm hostessing, picking up a few extra hours and a few extra dollars. I've been busy for the past two hours, asking customers which section they'd prefer to sit in, leading them to their seats, and handing them the menus. I've also helped bus tables and reset them, take drink orders and deliver them if Diana or Remmy was too busy, and carry food from the kitchen to the tables.

"Do you feel like going on a coffee run?" Curt asks, excitement in his voice.

"A *coffee run*? What exactly would *that* be?" I ask, smiling, really wondering what he means, because I'm certain there are plenty of coffee packets in the bin on the bottom shelf of the waitstaff station—I checked when I came in.

"Well, if you don't mind, please ask Diana and Remmy and everyone in the kitchen, plus the regulars—you know, like Rolanda, Marcy, and Walter—what they would like from the 61C, and use this money" (he hands me two twenties). "Okay?… And please make sure to get yourself something good—anything you want—and to give whoever makes the drinks a good tip too… So," he concludes, his deep, black eyes glistening, "what do ya think?"

"Well, sure, Curt," I reply. This seems very unusual—not for him, but for a work night—but it also sounds like fun. "I mean—who could say no to that? Besides, it'll be nice to take a short walk and get outside for a while."

I turn away from the bar, ready to do the rounds, but stop abruptly. "But wait, Curt," I say, glancing back at him. "Don't you want anything for yourself?"

"Oh yeah!" he replies, laughing. "Of course. I mean, the coffee here is good, but I'm in the mood for something stronger and richer, so…how about a tall iced caffè mocha?"

"Okay, Curt. You got it," I reply, nodding.

I make my way back to the kitchen, an eagerness in my step. "Anyone want a coffee drink from the 61C?" I ask. "Curt's treating."

Diana is slightly hunched over, preparing a side salad on the tan baker's table that sits to the right of the refrigerator. She turns to look at me, her eyes grow big, and she licks her lips and rubs her hands together. "Oh great!" she says, practically jumping up into the air. "What a good idea! I'll have an iced mocha, with the caffeine and the whole milk, and an extra shot of chocolate—everything!"

"Okay, Diana. I'll make sure of it!" I respond, giggling.

"Nothing for me, thanks," says Mary Ellen, her back to me as she places a chicken breast on top of the grill.

"Actually, I think I'll have an iced caramel macchiato," Richard says. He's standing over the sink, washing many heads of lettuce swimming in a big pool of water. "I've always wanted to try one of those."

"Okay, guys…sounds good… I'll be back soon."

I return to the bar and take a few more coffee orders. After a bit of indecision, Remmy decides upon an iced caffè latte (she is taking a break, chatting with Walter at the bar).

"I'm satisfied with the drinks I have in front of me, but thanks anyway," Walter chimes in, lifting up his CC on the rocks, tipping it toward me, and taking a mouth-watering gulp.

"Rolanda? Marcy? Care for anything?" I ask, going down the line.

"I'll have an iced mocha," Rolanda replies.

"That sounds good. Me too," Marcy agrees.

"Okay. So let's see," I say to myself, using my fingers as a guide. "One iced latte, four iced mochas—oh wait!—five iced mochas…one for myself, and, oh yeah, an extra shot of chocolate for one…and a caramel macchiato… Gee, I guess I better write this down." I take a small notepad out of my pocket and scribble the order down, making up new shorthand symbols as I go along. I'm used to taking orders, of course, but this is the first time I've taken an order such as this.

With my list in hand, I walk out the door into the warm summer evening, and it is just beginning to get dark. The heat feels so good on my skin, in contrast with the air conditioning of The Grill, which every now and then makes the little hairs on my arms stand up (that is, when the air is actually working). I feel a tinge of exhilaration shoot through me, at this concept of leaving right in the middle of work in search of decadent refreshment, and getting it from one of my most favorite places—the 61C— which has already given me so many great memories. I cross the street, and on the way to the coffeehouse I allow myself to pause and peer through the immense, inviting window that makes up the entire right section of the first floor of Barnes & Noble. What's a few more extra minutes anyway? I press my eyes to the window and examine the colorful, cushy, antique-looking chairs full of knowledge-seekers, and the bookcases displaying the classics in embossed, colorful leather (dark green, dark blue, and scarlet), with dainty, silky, bookmark ribbons peeping out at the tops, sides, or bottoms. There's *Leaves of Grass, Dr. Jekyll and Mr. Hyde*, and *The Hunchback of Notre-Dame* in clear view, and looking at them and imagining what's inside sends another unexplainable thrill through me, as does the anticipation of sitting upstairs in the bookstore's café—with a pot of Earl Grey—and finding out. I experience the same kind of pleasure as I walk a few doors down the street and gaze through the much-smaller window of William Penn Jewelers, the jewelry store to the left of the 61C. I love all of the jewelry that's on display there, in the shiny, protective, glass cases, but particularly the burnt yellow and burnt orange stones, in square and rectangular shapes that glitter, making their homes in gold rings or in dangly, silver earrings. And as I look, as I've done so many times before, I imagine walking in and purchasing one of them and placing it on my body, making me feel richer and sensuous and more alive. But I've never done it. In fact, I've never even gone in. I guess the wiser part of me realizes that sometimes it's more gratifying on the outside.

Just then, I hear the squealing of brakes, so I look over my right shoulder. A PAT bus, flashing "61C—McKeesport—Homestead—Pittsburgh via Oakland and Squirrel Hill" in bright, golden text above the front window, pulls up to the curb in front of the coffeehouse, and lets out a few of its passengers: two cute, stylish, Japanese girls, with open-toed, backless pumps on their feet, and compact, floral-design-covered purses over their wrists; a white-haired, somewhat-hunched-over elderly woman with a poodle and a wire-mesh carrier on wheels trailing behind her; and Bill—a friend of Teeli's—a rather tall, hard-not-to-notice guy with a generous beard, lots of untamable hair, and a laptop case flung over his shoulder, who is a PhD student at Pitt. Except for the elderly woman, who's on her way to the Giant Eagle, they all head for the coffeehouse. So I do the same. I follow them in through the large, glass doors and get in line.

"One iced latte, five iced mochas—one with an extra shot of chocolate—and a caramel macchiato, please," I tell the tall, interesting-looking guy with the shock of platinum hair and black eyebrows, when it's my turn. Atop the counter sit clear jars filled with biscotti, chocolate chip cookies, oatmeal raisin cookies, M&M cookies, and coconut and almond macaroons. The Beatles can be heard clearly through the speakers above.

He stares at me blankly for a moment. "Seriously?" he asks.

Apparently he's used to making only a couple of drinks at a time. Plus, by now, there are about four or five people waiting behind me.

"Yes. And sorry for such a huge order, especially when you're so busy. They're for a bunch of us over at The Grill."

"Oh, that's no problem, really. I was just surprised by the largeness of the order, that's all."

"Sarah!" he calls across the room. I look to my left and there's a girl with short, black, bobbed hair and glasses, wearing baggy jean overhauls and wiping off a table near the window. "Would you mind helping me out over here please?"

She appears behind the counter in no time at all, and with a concerted effort, they get to work. One prepares the drinks, pouring combinations of whole milk and chocolate syrup into large, pint-sized metal containers, while the other one steams the coffee and the milk.

While they work, I look around the place, always liking what I see. There are the luscious desserts waiting on the shelves below the counter, protected behind freshly cleaned glass: triple chocolate mousse cake, Bailey's Irish crème cheesecake, key lime pie, and Oreo cheesecake. On the wall behind the counter, fancy, golden-framed chalkboards of various sizes list what the coffeehouse offers, in eye-catching, intensely bright colors of chalk— pink, blue, green, yellow, and orange. One board lists the freshly squeezed juices: orange, grapefruit, carrot, apple, pear, pineapple, kiwi, and ginger. A second board lists the teas—beside a cute sketch of a teapot—such as Earl Grey, rose, Darjeeling, and Chinese oolong; the espresso drinks, such as americano and macchiato; and the brewed coffee, such as café au lait and shot in the dark. A third board lists the soy-milk drinks, including latte and caffè mocha. And the fourth board lists the specialty coffees and their prices, with such fancy names as Costa Rica, Guatemala, Sumatra, and Ethiopia, and such simple ones as House Blend.

"You want some cocoa powder sprinkled on top of these?" Sarah eventually asks me, a metal container— dotted with powdery holes—waiting in her hand. Knowing my friends at The Grill, I nod yes and look at her as if there could be no other answer.

While she's adding this final touch, I gaze around more, noticing the colorful earthenware teapots and teacups on the shelves above (in such colors as burnt orange, burnt yellow, and burnt green, a chip here and there, adding to their value); the paper, cone-shaped lights swaying in the breeze created by the fan; the local, eclectic artwork on the walls; the cute, colorful, miniature lamps on this and that table; and through the side window onto the concrete deck, where people of different aims and ethnicities drink, study, talk, and relax under patio umbrellas.

In about seven minutes total, which passes by very quickly for me (slowly, for them, I'm sure), the drinks are placed on the counter in front of me, in two cardboard containers, one stacked upon the other.

"That comes to twenty-fifty," Nathan says, after having punched a bunch of buttons on the cash register, the perspiration apparent on his brow. (I heard a customer call him by his name earlier.) "And oh yeah…the one in the bottom container with the little bubble pushed in is the one with the extra chocolate," he adds, pointing to it.

I reach in my pocket and hand him the money. "Here you go. And please keep five for yourself and Sarah."

He looks down at the money and then up at me with even bigger eyes than I had seen when I first gave him the order. "Thanks!" he says, the gratitude apparent in his voice, as he proceeds to get me my change.

"Thank you," I reply, giving them a farewell grin, "and thank Curt over at The Grill if you get a chance."

I pick up the trays carefully, and, to say the least, it's quite a feat trying to carry seven tall iced coffees by myself, even though it is a short distance back. I hold on to the trays tightly, balancing them as best I can, and walk carefully and slowly. Luckily, on the way out of the coffeehouse, someone opens the door for me. I'm not so lucky when I get to The Grill. Believe it or not, no one is walking past at the moment I arrive there (Murphy's Law and all that). So I decide the best thing to do is to gently place the trays on the sidewalk, open up the big, gray door with my right hand, hold the door open with my left foot, and then reach down and pick up the drinks, like a strange game of Twister.

Just as I'm attempting this balancing act, however,

Diana comes running toward me. "Jenna, let me help you with that," she says, and then—unable to resist singing along with Curt's choice of music for the evening—"Pleased to meet you; hope you guess my name... Woo! Woo!... Woo! Woo!" She takes the top tray and sets it down on the small bar near the wall. "Which one's mine?" she asks next, like a child eyeing her mother when she gets home from the grocery store, the bags still in her arms.

"Here you go!" I say, giggling once again, handing her the specified one, which is in the tray I'm carrying. She runs to the kitchen with it, apparently on her way to show the others her prize.

As soon as I get situated, I pass the rest of the drinks out, and I watch. Watch Marcy laugh, uninhibited, when she finishes her joke, her head falling in her hands. Watch Rolanda slip a five—without worry—into the slot machine, assuring everyone she'll win this time. Watch the calm spread over Curt's face as he raises his iced mocha to his lips. Watch as Diana bounces around the place with even more energy than before. Watch Richard stroll to the bar to join in the fun.

Watch the smiles and the bright eyes, and the nods and the glances of recognition, and the familiarity. And the "oohs" and the "aahs" that don't even need to be heard. And the way that the sharing of the rich, flavorful, smooth, cold, chocolaty coffee opens everyone up even more.

I haven't even tasted my own coffee yet, but I can't help thinking *This is so much fun!*, feeling warm, content, and happy; and realizing—once again—how far a bit of generosity flies, and the effect it can have like nothing else.

And yes!—how I relish this sweet, unorthodox, Curt-inspired night—the first of many—with delicious flavors, friends, music, laughs, and conversation.

It's a sprinkle of chocolate from heaven. ∎

THE RUSSIAN FIESTA

I *hate* carding people. I don't know why. It's like it's an invasion of their privacy or something, even though I know it's not.

I fear it's going to get me into trouble, though—and very soon. Like tonight, for example.

It's Friday, close to midnight, and there's tons of young Russians here. There were only a few at first, sitting together calmly and drinking, but now I'm almost lost in the midst of them. Did the word spread *that* quickly that I wasn't carding? Every now and then I do see one of them leave for about ten minutes, but when they return, they're never alone.

I can't take all the blame for it, though, now can I? For some reason, when the first young Russian walked in and right up to the bar and ordered a drink, Nick didn't card him, and I just stood back and watched, amazed. He is usually such a stickler about it (especially when someone looks so young), and he has scolded me several times for my failure to do it: "*Did you card them, Jenna? Well, if you didn't, you better go back and do it before I put any more drinks onto* YOUR *tray.*" Maybe it's because it was so terribly dead in here for most of dinner and he didn't want to turn any of the drinking crowd away? Wanted to liven things up a bit and salvage the night by making at least a few dollars?

I, however, don't think he ever expected *this*... And

neither did I.

I've never seen it this way.

There are beautiful young things with long, blonde hair; formfitting, brown leather jackets; tight jeans; long, fiery-red fingernails; daringly high, open-toed shoes; and sexy, mischievous smiles. There are beautiful young things of the opposite sex, too, so suave and masculine, with their looser-fitting, black leather jackets; designer jeans; slicked-back black hair; mouth-lingering cigarettes; and strong arms wrapped tightly around those beautiful girls' waists.

And there is Nick, looking irritated.

There are shouts traveling from one end of the restaurant to the other. There's Frank Sinatra bellowing from the small, hanging-on-the-wall jukebox. There are tables pushed together—and pushed apart.

And there is Nick, starting to sweat and redden.

There's money thrown about easily and heedlessly (where do they get all of it?). There's chatter and laughter abounding. There's standing around and sitting lazily. There are drink orders—Two shots of JD! A screwdriver, please! Four sea breezes and a mudslide!—rattled off without end.

And there is Nick, having a hard time keeping up, which never happens.

There's me delivering the drinks hurriedly, if I can squeeze through. There are the regulars—Gloria, Marcia, and Jayne (pronounced Jay-na)—who are Russian but are of age and are behaving (thank God!) at their favorite table near the window. There are drinks (uh-oh) knocked over and crashing to the floor.

And there is Nick, sizzling.

There's the intoxication level reaching volcanic heights. There's the smell of old beer spreading about, like in a frat house. There's a constant, action-packed, deafening din.

There are more Russians, quite a large group—oh no!—pushing in through the front door.

And there is Nick—finally—on fire.

"ALL RIGHT!!!!!!!!!!!!!!!!!!!" he erupts, practically taking off from his spot behind the bar, his face an exploded hand grenade. "Anyone who's under twenty-one has *ONE* minute to get out of here!!!!!" he yells, grabbing just-tasted drinks off of the tables and out of the hands of the youngest-looking. "But *no*," he adds, stopping abruptly, "on second thought, *EVERYONE* get out of here—and I mean *NOW!* The bar's *CLOSED!!!!!!!*" The drinks splish and splash in his hands, which are emphasizing everything he says.

Suddenly, it's disturbingly quiet, other than Frank prophesying that he did it his way. And there are no longer any words, but eyes full of question marks conversing in their place. The looks quickly answer each other, however, and in a fraction of the time it took for the fiesta to grow to full force, which hadn't been long at all, they are all out the door, followed by the enforcer Nick and his key.

I stand, dumbfounded and fatigued, in the middle of this disaster area, looking at all that I have to clean up, but that's the last worry on my mind. I have bigger problems to face.

"Jenna."

Oh, god. Here it comes.

"From now on, you *have* to card anyone who comes into this bar who looks younger than forty... Do you *HEAR* me?... And you *have* to cut people off when you think they've had too much... I *won't* have another night like this again." He says that last part looking me directly in the eye, with his head jutted forward; throws his keys onto the bar; and storms toward the kitchen and down the steps into the basement, haughtiness and distaste trailing after him.

"Okay, Nick," I reply to his back, twisting a wet rag in my hands, my words barely audible.

What else is there to say?

Well, at least I'm alone now with Frank and can clean this mess up without anyone looking over my shoulder. I mean, I'm feeling painfully embarrassed and somewhat abused, and I'm really struggling to keep the tears from breaking free. But with each task—as I methodically and earnestly empty the beer bottles and glasses and line them neatly upon the bar; pick up all of the trash from the floor; wipe off table after table; dump out the over-full ashtrays into the garbage and wipe them clean with a soapy cloth; and go over the floor again and again with the nonelectric vac—I'm starting to feel better and better. There's something quite cathartic and refreshing about all of this, these mundane tasks I do night after night. But now, for some reason, I am especially aware of them.

Soon, my feelings of doubt and uneasiness even begin to disappear, and, out of nowhere, I'm feeling rather elated.

I start to giggle. Yes. Giggle. And the more I work, and the more I think back over the night, the more I giggle…and giggle…and giggle, the held-back tears—now happy ones—rushing down my face.

You know what?

I could care less if Nick has returned yet or not. ∎

AFTER WORK

Perhaps even better than working Saturdays with Adam and Anthony is spending time with them after work, the three of us sitting beside each other at the bar, eating, talking, and drinking; discussing the events or nonevents of the day; challenging each other to a shot of Jägermeister, tequila, Sambuca, or Goldschläger (a cinnamon-tasting, pretty liquor with gold flakes floating around in it); the achiness in my feet and the diligence of the day being replaced by and rewarded with a juicy burger, glistening, thick, hot french fries, a refreshing beer, and laughter; the popular music enhancing everything.

A couple of times we hang out elsewhere after work, once at a dark, smoky billiard club in Oakland, amid pool sticks and too many pitchers of beer; another time across the street at the Manor Theatre, where Adam and I (after some serious convincing by him) go to see the crime thriller *Seven* (Anthony passes on the invitation, his eyes focused on the door; his feet moving fast under him past Adam and me at the bar, where we sit having a drink before going to the movie; his backpack slung over his shoulder; and the words "Can't stay tonight, guys. I have two papers at home waiting to be written…" following behind him. It seems that he is afraid of pausing, of stopping, afraid that if he does, he won't escape). Most of the time, however, we are perfectly content and eager to hang out at The Grill after work—for one hour, two hours, four hours, six hours!—or even, sometimes, until "last call!" can be heard traveling through the place, from the bartender, to the waiter or waitress, and finally, always, to the disappointed customers, who look up and utter, completely shocked: "It can't be *that* late already—*can* it?!"

We, too, share the customers' sentiments. Sure, we've been here all day—working—but the place brews its own kind of magic, has become—over time—a person in itself, a friend, a confidant, someone whom you just can't walk away from without a thought or a twinge…a second home—and, for some, the only place they will ever call home. There is always someone to talk to, to joke with, to flirt with, to learn from, to care for; always someone new and interesting to meet or observe; always some good story to listen to or tell, or memory to hear again; always some wonderful music—whether jazz, classic rock, rhythm and blues, eighties hits, Rolling Stones favorites, or Frank Sinatra ballads—to lose yourself in.

How I love these Saturday evenings sitting at the bar after work under the dim lights, whether with Adam and Anthony, or alone—relaxing, drinking, eating, feeling, wanting, thinking, longing, learning…and living…experiencing not yesterday, nor tomorrow, nor earlier today, nor later tonight, but the *now*, and all that it holds. ■

THE RACE

I'm in the kitchen, picking up a New York strip with a side of mashed potatoes, and there's Mary Ellen and Tommy, chomping on chicken wings taken from the large bowl sitting beside my steak.

"Hey, kiddo," Mary Ellen says. "When you're finished dropping that off, come back here and try these. They're something new we're testing—garlic-parmesan-flavored."

Tommy nods his head and licks his lips, obviously totally in favor of the new concoction. "And get the word out to the others, too, if you don't mind," he adds.

If I don't mind? Is he kidding?

I deliver the plate of food in what I think is record time, and then I go up to the bar. "Hey, Nick, guess what?"

He raises his eyebrows nonchalantly.

"Well, a little bird, there in the kitchen…that little bird told me that something good's awaiting."

Hell, that's all I need to say. He is in the middle of counting a stack of money, but he shoves it into the register, closes it, and is off.

I motion to Shane, and he understands what I mean, but he has just begun taking an order for a family of eight. Aw, the torture.

Kerry, our newest hostess, an intellectual-looking blonde who goes to the beauty school downtown, is fortunate to be let in on the secret next. She immediately stops arranging the disheveled stack of menus and redirects her attention to you know where.

As for me, I notice that a group of four was seated in my section while I was in the kitchen. Really, to be honest, I should go over there and wait on them now. But, hey, what's a few more minutes studying the menu?

So I arrive in the kitchen, and of course there the four of them are, shoulder to shoulder, huddled together in an intimate little circle around that bowl of temptation, chatting and smiling and enjoying the wings so much you'd think that's the first they've eaten in days. But, then again, it's always this way, no matter if Mare's made us a bowl of fried mushrooms, a plate of gooey, decadent, cheesy potato skins, or some hot, glistening french fries. We act as if we aren't even working, as if the customers waiting for us out front don't really exist. In fact, I bet we all completely forget about them for a few minutes. I know that I do.

"Hey, you guys," I say, nudging my way in between Nick and Kerry, feeling much more of Nick's body than I had intended, "it's my turn...okay?"

I grab two out of the four wings that are left, and Tommy grabs one, too, shooting me a feigned look of disgust.

"Fine with me," Kerry says, turning around and reaching for the spigot. "I've had quite enough." Her finely manicured nails shimmer with olive oil and specks of parmesan.

"You can't be serious...this is all that's left?... Mare?" I say.

"I'm all set, honey."

"Well, in that case..."

I greedily start enjoying the two wings I had barely retrieved for myself.

But poor Shane. He slides into the kitchen just as Nick is devouring the last one.

What a look he gives us. "You couldn't save me just one? Just one this time? Not even one?"

"Well, you know how it goes, there, buddy," Nick reminds him, body checking him rather abruptly. "You snooze, you lose."

Apparently there is nothing he can say to this, so he just starts jumping up and down. ■

A SURPRISE ENDEARMENT

I leave the bathroom, where I've just brushed out my long, wavy hair and applied a conservative spray of Baby Soft. As Bruce's "Hungry Heart" greets me, I walk up to the bar. But I hesitate. It's so crowded, regulars and coworkers laughing and having fun. Not a seat left. Except beside Nick. And he looks so different tonight, his night off, the night he goes out bowling with his league. He's wearing gray sweatshorts, a ball cap on backwards, and a tasteful red wifebeater, which reveals the expensive gold chains he always wears around his neck. There's a little bit of sweat on his temples, and his fingers are resting around one of the two awaiting shots in front of him. He picks it up and downs it, in a quite quick, skillful, and attractive fashion.

Oh, what the hell.

I walk around the bar and pull out the bar stool beside him. I rise a bit on my tiptoes and ease myself onto the stool, somehow managing to scooch my way into the tight space between Nick and the person to my left. Nick watches me, a smile on his face.

"Jenna! And how are you tonight?" he asks. "Just finished your shift, I take it?"

"Yes, Nick. Finally… And gladly. It's been crazy in here all night."

"Yeah. I can see that," he replies, looking around. "You

want a drink?"

"Oh, yes, I sure do. That's just what I need," I say.

"A bottle of I.C. Light for you tonight? Your usual?" he asks, downing his second shot and then following it up with a gulp of his Iron City.

"You know what, Nick? I've seriously been thinking about it, and I've decided that I might switch things up a bit and try a Sierra Nevada draft," I answer, nodding, my lips approaching a hint of a smile.

His eyebrows flicker upward. "Daring tonight, are we? That's the spirit!" he says, winking. "Curt…buddy…a large Sierra Nevada for the lady here… And, hey, why not?" With one large circular arm motion he collectively includes the crowd sitting at the bar, as well as the throng of people standing around it. "Everyone's next round is on me." And then to Curt: "Put it on my tab, buddy. I'll take care of it with Bobby tomorrow."

"Woo-hoo!!!" Shane yells as he raises his large Rolling Rock draft high in the air, spilling quite a lot of it, which runs down his arm. He just starts giggling.

"Thanks, Nick!" the regulars from Eat'n Park yell in unison (they seem to always be on the same wavelength, apparently the result of working through—and surviving—all of those after-bar rushes together).

"I'll have another Grand Marnier, Curt. Whenever you're ready," says Jack, for a slight moment diverting his attention from the sexy blonde sitting beside him, her legs crossed in his direction.

Laughing and talking—everyone continues doing this, even louder than before, and drink orders and fulfillments take precedence over everything else.

"Wow, Nick," I say, as I look around and touch his arm (but just for a second), "it looks like you've made everyone's day." I've seen it countless times before, but I'm still amazed at how excited everyone gets at the mention of free alcohol. "And it's really quite generous of you," I can't help adding.

"Well," he says, leaning toward me and talking very quietly. (But not that it's necessary. We could stand up and start doing jumping jacks and no one would probably notice.) "It's a special day, right? Certainly a reason to celebrate."

I look at him, my eyebrows raised.

"Yeah, Jenna. I know that you're the type to keep things to yourself, not wanting a lot of attention and all that, but," he says, pausing to drink the last of his beer, "I found out." He says this last bit even more softly.

"Found out? What…?"

Adrenalin. More than my usual overdose accosts me now.

"Nick?"

He doesn't answer me, but takes out a twenty and places it on the inside edge of the bar, and then he moves slightly backward and starts to stand up.

I slowly look up at him, not really sure what to say next. But before I have the chance to say anything, he leans in my direction, pauses, and, just as comfortably as ever, kisses me gently but firmly on the lips. He then looks me directly in the eye, whispers "Happy birthday, darling" in the most sincere, sweetest voice I think I've ever heard, and leaves.

What else is there to do?

I just sit there, feeling beautiful and special—my face flushed—just like I've been kissed for the very first time. ∎

THE CONFESSION

Sitting at the bar, an after-work I.C. Light joining me, I confide in Curt, as I've done before. I tell him how difficult it is to make it all the way through college. So much endless writing of papers and countless late nights—always feeling exhausted and stressed, worried that my dancing is suffering because of it, that maybe I'm on the wrong track. On the nights I'm not waitressing, working at my desk job in the dorms—signing residents and their guests in and answering an occasional phone call—trying to pry my eyes open as it approaches two, feeling about half crazy. Struggling over my senior thesis— almost seventy pages now—about Hawthorne's "Rappaccini's Daughter" and the way culture affected literary criticism of it, always trying to come up with ingenious conclusions. Wishing that I didn't have to take so many English courses at once—the reading and writing load is just so outrageous—and how I would love to have more time to actually enjoy them. But I am so concerned about being able to graduate on time, and I don't want to take out any more loans than I already have.

Tell him, finally, that I don't know if I can make it. That maybe I need to take some time off. That I need a serious break.

"No. No. No," he immediately responds, rapping his fist three times on the top of the bar, his eyes fixed on my eyes and nothing else. Assures me to hang in there, to see it through, that it will all be worth it. Not to even think of—much less seriously consider—taking time off just a few months before graduation, as…as…as he had done.

"That's why I'm still working here, Jenna," he says, glancing down and pouring a double shot of scotch into a thick, reflective tumbler. ∎

A FRIDAY-NIGHT SURRENDER

Here it is again, another Friday night. And as usual, I'm the late person out, which means that now that the kitchen is closed for the evening, I have to cocktail waitress until about one-thirty or two, as well as close down the waitstaff station: clean the iced tea bin and the coffee pots (by swirling a mixture of ice cubes and baking soda within them to remove the burnt remnants), soak the ketchup lids in hot water and refill the ketchup bottles, cut lemon wedges, make up place settings, restock the bins, and do anything else that is needed.

Nick is bartending, and at the bar, among a few others, sits Jack, drinking a Rolling Rock and a shot of Grand Marnier. This is usual for a Friday night as well. On his nights off, which include Friday, he often stops in for an hour or two and hangs out.

What isn't usual is that the drinking crowd is small. Believe it or not, the only customers I have now are the couple sitting in the nonsmoking section, in the booth farthest from the bar, sipping merlot; and Scott, a reserved, friendly, stocky, fluffy-haired, gray-bearded man, whom I particularly like even though I really don't know him that well, except that he enjoys chips, glasses of Tanqueray and tonic, and sitting at the small table to the left just as you enter the smoking section, from which the television is in clear view. I'm glad they're all I have left to worry about, though, because the place was packed during the dinner hours, and I am just about out of steam. Nevertheless, I know that if I keep one eye on them as I use the other to tend to my closing duties, I'll get everything finished quicker, and somehow, just somehow, the end of the night will eventually roll around, like it always does.

But wait! It *can't* be. Is Nick giving last call already—and telling me to do the same? Well, he's known to keep the bar open till the bitter end, but tonight he must have decided otherwise…and I'm certainly not going to complain. No one else will probably show up, after all, and even if they did, it would only be a few more bucks in my pocket anyway.

Armed with the prospect of finishing early, I decide to head first toward the wine-drinking couple. I quickly jog up the two steps leading into the nonsmoking section and grab my notepad out of my pocket, but when the couple notices me coming in their direction, they put up their hands and shake their heads before I get there, signaling that they are all set for the night. So I turn back around, jog back down the steps, and walk past the bar toward Scott. But when he sees me approaching, having taken his eyes off the TV for a moment, he gently drinks the last of his cocktail—the remaining ice jingling—wipes the moisture off the table, stands up, pushes in his chair, says goodbye with a shy smile, and sneaks out so quietly that I begin to wonder if he was really here at all. As for Jack, he orders another shot and beer from Nick, and lights up another cigarette.

For the next half an hour or so, the time passes by slowly (and painfully), but I keep myself busy restocking the paper products and every now and then glancing up at the couple, who are still chatting and lingering over the last few drops in their glasses. When the clock reaches almost one, however, they lazily stand up, nod to me, and leave, holding hands softly, giving me the freedom to finish up for the night.

The well-known procedure then begins: I clear their empty glasses, place them on the bar, dump out and clean any of the ashtrays I haven't gotten to, and give all of the booths and tables a final wipe with my worn-out rag. Next, I take a quick glance around to be certain I haven't missed a stray glass or beer bottle hiding in the corner of some table. When I'm sure I haven't, I head toward the back of the restaurant and walk down the failing, wooden steps into the sudden warmth of the basement, past Bobby's cluttered, heavily tacked, paper nightmare of an office (Mary Ellen gets on his case about it all the time). And finally, with a deep breath, I toss the dirty rags from the evening into one of the white cloth bins at the bottom of the stairs, and plump down onto a rolled-up carpet that is lying against the can-laden shelves. I am so relieved to have a moment to rest.

A few minutes later—or has it been longer than that?— my eyes open suddenly and involuntarily scan the room. "Man...I must've dozed off," I eventually mumble, running my hand over my face, and I slowly stand up, remembering to grab my duffel bag.

I then begin to climb back up the stairs, half believing that I have little weights hanging all over me. I make it to the top, nonetheless, and stop in the restroom, clicking the lock behind me and looking in the large mirror hanging on the wall, which is outlined in colorful, painted flowers and bright, large, bulbous dots of light. And there they are again—my unruly hair, my shiny face, and my grease-stained polo—staring back at me. "Boy do I look like a million bucks!" I grumble...but to be honest, I really don't mind. They're just evidence of how hard I worked tonight, and they're nothing that a good brush, some soap and water, and a dab or two of silky, tinted face powder can't fix.

******

IN ABOUT TEN MINUTES, not only looking refreshed but most importantly feeling it, I lazily walk to the bar. All of Nick's other customers have left, but Jack is still there, chatting with Nick as he restocks the beer cooler and takes inventory of the liquor shelves—a clipboard and schedule in one hand, a pen in the other, the sounds of "You Can't Always Get What You Want" in his ears. With an "Excuse me, Nick" I cautiously walk behind the bar and grab my basket of tips from the counter below the shelves of liquor. I then take a seat near Jack, and he gives me a friendly smile, the lines around his eyes increasing. But to be honest, I'm a bit surprised that he's still here. By this time on most Friday nights, he's usually already made it over to The Cage.

"What can I get ya?" asks Nick, the phrase streaming so naturally off his tongue. (Thanks to Bobby, we get a free drink—as long as it's not too exotic—when we finish our shift.)

"Oooohhh…how about a small Rolling Rock?" I say, nodding my head toward the tap in front of me.

"You got it."

Nick effortlessly places a small, funnel-shaped glass of Rolling Rock in front of me. There is a nice head on the liquid, but not too much. I immediately pick up the glass and feel the cold condensation on my fingers and lips as I take a sip.

"Mmmm…that's good," I softly say to myself, and then glance up, and there is Jack, giving me a friendly smile once again.

"It always tastes so good after a busy night," he says.

"You've got that right," I reply, looking down quickly, the sexy "Beast of Burden" now enveloping us.

We continue to talk, taking advantage of the time free from having any tables to worry about, when Nick interrupts us to say, as he proceeds toward the front door, that he is about ready to close up for good for the night. I swear that I've just sat down, but when I glance at my watch, it's already half an hour later, and my glass is still three-quarters full.

I take a big, hurried gulp of my beer as Jack laughs, and then both of us place our glasses on the black draining mat that lines the inside edge of the bar, push our stools in, and say a final good night to Nick as we walk past him and out the door. He stands there for a moment—with the large mound of keys hanging in the lock—propping open the big gray door with his body and taking in the night scene, like I've observed him do so many times before: the fancy, recently built two-story Barnes & Noble directly across the street; Bob, the kind, slow-speaking, mentally challenged young man strutting by and waving innocently, his hair red this week; and Silky's, the bar on the corner of Murray and Darlington, its indoor lights beckoning through its many windows. And almost instantly he looks rejuvenated, as if the Squirrel Hill spirits have given him a burst of nighttime energy.

It *does* feel wonderful to walk out into the calmly moving, thick air. It is one of those sultry summer nights that I absolutely love, the kind that always makes me feel sexy, carefree, and feminine, no matter what I'm wearing— a short, spaghetti-strapped, pink summer dress, or a pair of greasy, smoke-drenched khaki shorts and a stained white polo shirt, like I'm wearing now.

"Where's your car?" asks Jack, once we are a few steps out the door.

"Oh, it's at a meter, on the street in front of the Presbyterian church, where I usually park it," I reply, pointing in that direction.

"I'll walk you there," he says. "I'm going that way anyway."

Jack lives not too far behind the big, black, towering, stone Presbyterian church that sits on the corner of Murray and Forbes. He lives in one of those old townhouses, one among the ten or so that form the area called Forbes Terrace, which, to me, is a very ornate and pretty name. The townhouses are arranged in an oblong shape, so that, if you walk out the front door of any of them, you enter a courtyard, which is formed and surrounded by the houses. It is very private, and beautiful, especially in the summer, because it has leafy trees to shade and adorn it, but not too many, so if you want to sunbathe, you can find a perfect spot to do it. And the best part about it is that as you are walking along Forbes Avenue, you don't even know that the Terrace exists, because it is hidden so well from the street. The only indication that it's there is a fancily shaped, wooden sign that hangs on a stone wall beside stone steps that lead up to the Terrace, which reads "Forbes Terrace" in curly, elaborate lettering. But when you do walk up the steps and into the courtyard, it's as if you've entered a separate, quiet world—a land of Oz—apart from the bustle of busy Forbes Avenue.

"Oh, I'd appreciate that," I reply to his decision to walk me to my car. "My mom is always so worried about me leaving work so late at night by myself. I usually feel pretty safe, but I guess it's better to be careful."

It doesn't take long for us to arrive beside my yellow Dodge Shadow, so I begin searching for my keys. "You know, I never can find these damn—" I begin complaining, but all of a sudden, Jack interrupts me. "Hey,

I was thinking…I'm really not that tired yet. Do you maybe want to hang out for a while?" he offers.

I stop with my hand in the bottom of my purse, and look up at him questioningly. "Uh…okay. Okay, why not?" I answer, shrugging. "I do have to work tomorrow, but not till eleven, so we could hang out for an hour or so."

"Great."

I'm really not too surprised that he wants to hang out, and so late at night, because we've done that many times before, with Diana, Bianca, Vic, Curt, and, sometimes, my friend Teeli. We gather in a tight circle in his living room, dancing, sweating, and grooving to the Beatles' *Greatest Hits* or to ABBA's "Dancing Queen," each of us with a beer in our hand and a smile on our face. Then we sit on his porch in the cool, summer air, talking to the wee hours of the morning, awaiting the rising sun.

This time, though, it's different. There's no crowd to hide in. It's just the two of us.

I start to walk in the direction of the Terrace, toward the entrance on Forbes Avenue. But after a few steps, I notice that Jack isn't with me, so I pause and look back at him, my eyebrows raised. "Is everything okay?"

"I was thinking…" Jack replies, "why don't we go this way?"

"*That* way…? What do you mean?"

"C'mon, I'll show you," says Jack.

He leads me up the hill that the church sits on, on the Murray Avenue side, and then behind the church through its parking lot. It's so quiet, and vacant, that I start to feel a bit scared, really wondering whether we should be doing this. Next thing I know, we are crouching along a narrow path, surrounded on all sides and overhead by branches and leaves, and now I'm *totally* wondering what I've gotten myself into. But then, in no time at all, we end up in a small yard, right behind a tall, gray house.

"Where are we?" I ask, trying to locate myself while I stand up and brush off my clothes.

"You *really* don't know?" Jack asks, rather amazed.

"Not really—no," I reply, as I follow him from the back of the house, and around the side, until we eventually turn the corner to the front.

"Eight Forbes Terrace, madame," he says, as he moves to the side to let me pass, and bows, making a sweeping gesture with his right arm, "at your service."

"Wow!" I exclaim, my eyes opening wide and darting all around. "I had no idea *this* is where we'd end up."

"Pretty cool, isn't it?" Jack says. He steps up onto his porch and lights a cigarette, his "butler at your service" persona vanishing in an instant. "You're one of the only people who know about that secret passage, so please don't tell anyone." He exhales a long stream of smoke.

"Sure, no problem. Thanks for letting me in on it," I say, looking around and smiling, feeling privileged that he wanted to share that shortcut with me, and also wondering what other privileges are in store for me tonight.

"Come on in," he says, opening first the screen door, then unlocking the heavier door, and I can't help but notice the way he uses his lips and tongue to steady the cigarette in his mouth.

"Okay," I say, and jog up the steps and walk in after him.

"Want a beer?" he asks, throwing his keys onto his computer desk.

"Yeah, that'd be nice."

"I'll just be a minute then."

"Okay."

I slowly walk to the cushy green couch and sit down in a corner of it, take off my shoes, untuck my shirt, and curl my feet up under me. It feels cozy, and nice. As I look around, at the old grand piano in the dining room, at the stereo covered with scattered CDs, at the white, cloth curtains blowing in through the inviting window, and at the large, wooden staircase that leads upstairs, Jack's cats come to greet me, affectionately meowing and caressing me with their chins and bodies. I then remember that Jack has roommates (the cats really belong to them), but they are nowhere in sight—maybe they are out or are upstairs sleeping… It *is* almost two in the morning by now.

"Here you go," Jack says, reappearing from the kitchen, his shirt untucked as well. He twists the top off an icy Rolling Rock, hands it to me, and sits down, legs spread wide and relaxed, on the opposite side of the couch, and takes an uninhibited gulp of his beer.

"Want to listen to some music?" he asks.

"Sure…something relaxing would be great."

"Uh…let's see," he says, moving toward the stereo and kneeling in front of it, rummaging through the pile of CDs. "Well…I know. How about some Tori Amos? I love her debut solo album, *Little Earthquakes*." He holds it up for me to see. "Have you heard it?"

"No, actually, I haven't heard anything by her. I must admit that I'm usually a bit behind when it comes to those things. But I'd love to hear it."

"I'm sure you'll like it," Jack replies. He takes the CD out of its case, places it on the deck, gives the deck a soft push, advances the CD a bit, and presses play.

Chi-na…all the way to New York…I can feel the dis-tance…get-ting close…

Chi-na…decorates our table…funny how the cracks…don't…seem…to…show…

This enchanting song fills the room, and there's something about it that's so arresting, so otherworldly—so haunting, in fact—with its dissonant chords and her dissonant voice, and the message that everything in life changes and breaks too easily. Immediately, I get why Jack likes the music—such music that makes you understand the fragility of life, but, at the same time, urges you to realize how worthwhile it is to live it. That warns you not to hesitate and pass up the unexpected opportunities, however unexpected they are, that are presented to you.

"Wow, this is really beautiful," I say, enjoying my drink and taking in the music. "It really makes you think—and feel—you know?"

"Oh, I agree," Jack replies. "I listen to it all the time."

We go on, amid and within the music, to talk about many things, such as my relationship with my previous boyfriend, and its recent ending. About how controlling he turned out to be, and about how I shouldn't have gotten messed up with him in the first place.

"Believe me—if a guy showers you with expensive gifts not more than four hours after you've met him, that should be a sure sign of trouble," I say, summing up my crazy love story, as Jack nods in agreement.

Jack then begins to share information about himself, telling me about his roommates, his family, and what it was like growing up in Pittsburgh. "Yeah, I really like living in Squirrel Hill," he says. "I feel so comfortable here and know so many people as I'm walking down the street. Even though I grew up not too far from here, in Elliott, moving here was good for me and it almost felt like I was moving to another city, not just to another part of the city. Squirrel Hill has its own identity, its own special character... You know, there's all the diverse architecture and buildings and all the interesting people; the Orthodox Jews dressed in black suits and tall hats, with their extra-long beards, passing you on the street. And all of the employees from

Eat'n Park who you're bound to run into at some time or another at the video store or at The Cage. And then all of the friendly faces making eye contact with you and saying hello to you as they walk by, regardless of whether you know them or not. And, needless to say, all the smart types, the PhD students and others from Pitt and CMU—and of course the Chatham women, like you and Teeli," he teases, laughing, "hanging out at the coffee shops, completely engrossed in their laptops and books. But all in all, there's such a carefree, happy feeling about the place…and best of all, no matter what type of person you are, you fit into the mix."

"Oh—you know what? I've definitely noticed all of those things too. It's such a special, eclectic place. I'm so happy that God, or fate, or whoever or whatever's responsible, put me here," I reply.

"Well…so am I," he says, a glint in his pale-blue eyes.

For quite a while, we continue to talk ceaselessly, as I drink my beer, and Jack drinks two. But suddenly, and with no warning at all, the words finally reach their limit, and we both know there is nothing more to say.

I take a couple swallows of my beer, cross and uncross my legs, rub all the condensation off my beer, read the label on the bottle, scan the living room with my eyes, and pet Jack's cats—that is, do anything but look directly into Jack's eyes. And Jack—how is he handling it? The truth is, I have no idea. I've been too busy trying to keep myself occupied.

But then, somehow, Jack manages to get a few more words out. "You…you look…you look pretty wiped out…. Why don't you… Why don't you let me give you a massage?" (Apparently he's been using the silent time to get up his nerve to say *that*.)

My eyes shoot up, and this time I *do* look directly into

his eyes. I still don't know what to say, but, before I can say anything, he moves closer to me and places his hot, almost-steady hands on my shoulders.

"Sit down on the floor in front of me," he says, as he confidently nods his head to where he wants me to be. "That will be more comfortable for you."

"Uh…okay, okay," I mumble, hesitating, but then he guides me to the spot. And once again, I'm wondering what I'm getting myself into, but then I'm somehow sitting between his legs, my legs crossed tightly, my tense back facing him. And then he's kneading my shoulders, and I'm letting him, with no objection at all, trusting him completely, much to my surprise. But then again, I remember, that's what I had first noticed about him— wasn't it? That he was soft, and gentle, and so utterly different from the man I had been dating before.

"Ah…that feels great," I say to myself, the words coming so easy now, as my shoulders begin to round, my eyes close, and my head drops forward. All of the energy from his hands caressingly manipulating the muscles in my shoulders and neck feels like a wave of softness that is flowing all the way to my fingertips…down my legs…and into my abdomen—little earthquakes all around.

"You've got great hands…mmm…that feels really great…my muscles really need it…"

"Good. I'm glad you like it."

And as he feels how comfortable and relaxed I'm becoming, his hands become more familiar and comfortable with me. He slides them, repeatedly, from my shoulders to my hands—softly, but with just enough pressure—and then back up again. Slowly—and with a tentative aggressiveness—he leans farther forward, and farther forward, until I can see his knees, clearly, one on each side of me—until I can smell his cologne and his sweat. And his breathing—it becomes heavier and more internal—his hot breath on my neck. And his hands—they stop on top of mine, and grasp them. And his fingers—he laces them through mine—so tightly. And his palms—they lie flat, deliberate.

And all at once, I feel surrounded…protected…invited to surrender, turning my head slowly to the right, lifting my gaze over my shoulder. Meeting his eyes for an instant, and then his lips—naturally and simultaneously.

And then there's the warmth of his mouth, of his tongue—and the wetness. And the sharp, individual hairs—on top, then under—and their exhilarating newness. And the smoke…and the beer…the tenderness…the toughness.

And his sliding off the couch…and his kneeling around me…and the kissing…

And my turning completely toward him…and my sliding my arms around his neck…and the kissing…

And his arms grasping my back and guiding me—once again—to the floor…and the kissing…

And ultimately, he on top of me, and I under him…the unexplainable wanting…

And enjoying. ■

THE FLYING ICED MOCHA

"**D**amn it!" Diana explodes, a scowl appearing upon her face, a tempting iced caffè mocha resting in her hand. "I guess this will just have to wait."

I've just returned from one of my Saturday-evening jaunts to the 61C to pick up specialty coffee drinks for the employees and regulars who wanted them, compliments of Curt. It goes without saying that Diana, who is waiting tables tonight, absolutely *loves* iced mochas. Anytime I hand the cold, perspiring drink to her, she immediately gulps down the rich, smooth, fulfilling liquid, a lustiness in her eyes. Now, however, is a different story. She is in the midst of waiting on the entire nonsmoking section (eight tables in all!), which filled up in the short time I was away.

"I'll be right back," she says, and then she abruptly heads toward the kitchen.

When she returns, in what seems like two seconds' time, we get to work. I help her as much as I can by preparing salads, taking drink orders, and clearing off tables. She manages most of it by herself, though, her quick movements accentuated by her characteristic hisses, stares, and uninhibited boldness.

After about half an hour, the craziness seems to subside a bit. "Thank God," I mumble. I grab my iced mocha, which is sitting beside an unfinished *Pittsburgh Post-Gazette* crossword puzzle that Diana was apparently working on before she got so busy. Earlier, when I returned from the coffee run, I placed my drink on the small maroon counter that runs along the wall to the right as you enter the restaurant. It's opposite of the main bar and is lined with three or four stools. We store the menus and extra place settings on top of this counter, and we hang out here when business is slow, waiting for more customers to arrive. And, as I've mentioned before, it works as a kind of ancillary bar as well. Customers sometimes sit here, especially if the main bar is full.

Instead of drinking my mocha here, in plain sight of all the customers, which Nick would certainly frown upon, I carry it to the back of the restaurant, where I can be out of view. I stop in the small vestibule that leads to the kitchen. In this area is a refrigerator with a clear glass door, in which we store salad dressings, desserts, and miniature containers of butter and half-and-half. There is also a well-worn, chipping baker's table that Bobby bought for us at Staples or IKEA or someplace like that (one of those tables that you get in a box and have to put together), on which we prepare the salads and the desserts. (We initially had been using a large round tray that was situated upon one of those precarious folding tray stands: an accident waiting to happen! Put too much weight on one end and—bingo!) To the right of the baker's table are built-into-the-wall wooden shelves, on which we store napkins, straws, doilies, tiny silver teapots, boxes of place mats, and anything else made of paper that is of use in a restaurant.

I lean against the wooden shelves, glad to have a moment of privacy to enjoy my drink, which is becoming more watery by the second, when I see what appears to be another iced mocha, placed snugly in a corner of the baker's table.

That must be Diana's. Poor thing…she hasn't even had a chance to take a sip yet.

I continue to enjoy my drink, periodically glancing around the corner to the front of the restaurant to see if I am needed.

A few minutes later, Diana appears. She is sweating, part of her blue polo shirt is untucked in the front, and a bunch of grease stains are apparent. There is also a curious look in her eye. She glances at her iced mocha, at the half-gone iced mocha in my right hand, and then at me. "Okay, Jenna. I see how it is. Here I am, worn out from running around, and you're going to drink yours and then sneak a few gulps out of mine, *aren't ya?*" she says, feigning an inordinate and impressive amount of anger. "Well, we'll see about…"

She locks her jaw, tightens her hands into fists, places them in front of her, leans to the side, lifts up her right leg—as if she is a black belt (which really, in all truthfulness, wouldn't surprise me)—and shoots her foot forward…

"…THAT!!!!!"

"Diana!"

To the complete surprise of both of us—WHACK!!!—ice cubes, milk, whipped cream, chocolate, and coffee (as well as the cardboard cup that held it all) fly out of my hand and land on the floor, the shelves, the baker's table, the bathroom door, and—oh yeah—me! I stand there, quite flabbergasted, I must say.

Unexpectedly, the iced mocha took the ride of its life. But even more unexpectedly, Rambo Woman of Terror immediately and magically turns into a wide-eyed little girl right in front of me, shrinking into herself and asking for my forgiveness, holding her untouched mocha toward me, begging me to accept it as a peace offering. "Dear *god,*

Jenna… I'm so, so sorry!"

Just then, Curt appears, on his way to the kitchen. He stops abruptly, seeing me clad in mocha, the sweet liquid dripping from my hair and running down my face. "What in the hell happened here?!… And why are you all *wet?*" he asks, thoroughly amused. I relay the story to him, and from that moment on, I know that Diana will never hear the end of it. ■

TIME TO QUIT

We can hardly believe what we've just heard, but then Nick says it again to assure us. "Yes, I've decided to quit drinking."

Nobody moves. Apparently we aren't convinced.

What? He means no more effortlessly downing beer after beer, in what seems like two swallows each, when all of his customers have left and he is doing the closing duties? No more sitting at the bar with Jack and savoring a few snifters of thick, orange-flavored Grand Marnier? No more tying one on with Anthony at The Decade? And no more lounging at home watching the Steelers with his Iron City comrades sitting comfortably by his side?

Really?

"To lose weight," he says, when asked why.

That's a good answer, I guess—he has put on a few pounds—but I don't think it's the truth. I mean, if I remember correctly, didn't he disappear a couple of months ago and nobody would really say where he had gone, just that he wasn't feeling like himself and needed to take some time off? Doesn't it seem to be more of an issue of control, of feeling that the alcohol is starting to be in charge after so many years, and he not wanting it to be? Not wanting it to ruin his work, himself, or, most importantly, his family?

Will he be able to do it?

Well, I certainly hope so. Being out of control definitely has its time and its place, but not if you're not in control of it. ■

THE ERUPTION

I've just arrived to hostess, dressed in a pair of black slacks and a short-sleeve, V-neck, hot pink top. I'm sitting at the ancillary bar, waiting for the dinner crowd to appear. Curt's behind the bar, and Richard, dishwasher-turned-cook—a humorous, nice-looking, twenty-something, laid-back guy with lots of hair (complete with a mustache, a bit of a beard, and unencumbered dark brown, wavy locks)—is sitting at the end of the bar closest to the front of the restaurant, hanging out, smoking, and drinking a cup of coffee before his shift begins. He is smiling as well (a very nice smile, I've always thought), talking to Curt. Nothing is out of the ordinary tonight—it's just a usual, relaxed, early Saturday evening.

First on my list of things to do is to look over the "Specials" sheet. It's important to familiarize myself with it in case any of the customers have a question. *Bratwurst, sauerkraut, and biscuits, $8.95*, I read, trying to imprint it in my mind. *Linguini with mussels and spicy marinara sauce, $10.95*, my eyes take in next, and even though I ate before I got here, my mouth is watering. *Chicken Marsala with mush—* I begin to utter softly, but I'm unexpectedly interrupted by an unbelievable sight coming to me out of the corner of my eye.

But *c'mon*, it can't be, I think. I must be seeing things. Why on earth would Curt reach out from behind the bar and push Richard in the chest, even if it was just a light push? And why would Richard still be smiling, still be talking to Curt? I can't hear a word they're saying, but all I can figure is that they must just be joking around, although I've never seen Curt lay his hand on anyone.

I stare at them for a little while, but then I resume studying the "Specials" sheet, realizing that the dinner crowd will soon be walking in. Okay, where was I?... Oh yeah—*Chicken Marsala with mushrooms and a side of creamy mashed potatoes, $9.95.* And a *New York Strip with onion rings and freshly steamed brocco*—

But unfortunately, this is all the further I get.

I look up, and Curt is heavily and intently walking out from behind the bar—his steps quite audible—and his tanned face and long legs are covered with splotches of red. And I can't take my eyes off him as he continues around the perimeter of the bar toward Richard, abruptly and feverishly pushing in any jutting stools along the way, as they rebound against the bar and then back. Richard is staring at Curt, still smiling, although I can't tell for sure whether it's a genuine smile or one of those ironic, at-the-end-of-your-rope smiles I've seen before.

In not more than a few seconds, Curt arrives where Richard is sitting, and he grabs him by the arm and jerks him off the stool—just like that. "You feel like fucking around, Richard? *Do you*, Richard?" he says, his eyes bulging, the sweat streaming down his face, the fury-ridden "You Oughta Know" fortifying him. He then starts pulling Richard and then pushing him—turning him into a rag doll—his fingers gripping Richard's shirt, the front of Richard's shirt nothing but a wrinkled, jumbled mess. And it's so pathetically easy for Curt to do, because Richard can't be more than five-seven. At best.

Richard smiles all the way through this landslide of

events—and I don't know if I'm more shocked by this phenomenon or by Curt's actions—but then finally, and suddenly, as if a match is struck inside his head, Richard understands that Curt isn't joking. It's no wonder he's not fighting back, though—the awe-stricken, damaged look on his face explains it all.

Curt continues this back-and-forth game for quite some time, and the entire bar is eerily motionless, amazed, silent. But Curt certainly isn't. While he does what he wants with Richard, words continually erupt from his mouth—essentially a stream of consciousness in anger mode. "Okay Richard is this what you want Richard I've had enough of it Richard don't mess with me anymore Richard," he begins. "You've fucking taunted me for the last time Richard it isn't going to happen again Richard get out of here Richard and don't come back Richard," and so on and so on, until he has completely driven Richard out the front door and onto the sidewalk, throwing him around the entire way. Mary Ellen then hurriedly appears from the kitchen, a distraught, questioning look on her face, her hands entwined in her apron. All heads turn and stare at her as she raises her eyebrows and hands in utter confusion.

But then the heads, including mine, abruptly return to their starting point as Curt powerfully pulls open the front door. It swings open—as far as it can—hits the wall with a loud "Crack!" and then rebounds back. Curt reappears, taking huge, giant-reminiscent strides, and stares straight ahead, making it back to his usual position behind the bar in no time at all. I try to avert my eyes from him the best I can, but it's no use. His body's being supported by the counter behind the bar, his full weight against it. But as for his drooping head, it's on its own. And Richard. Poor, poor Richard. He's pacing back and forth in front of the window—his hands in his hair—obviously shattered and frazzled by what has happened and wondering what he should do next.

It doesn't take him long. He walks calmly through the front door and stops just a few feet from it. As he looks directly at Mary Ellen and crosses one hand over the other, palms down, and then uncrosses them, he informs her of his decision.

"I quit," he mouths, and he turns and walks back out the door.

Curt doesn't even look up. ∎

A NEW LIFE

"**I**'m going to beauty school."

Cathy, who is filling in for her husband tonight, announces this as she stands behind the bar and busily washes a few small draft glasses in a sink of sudsy, steaming water.

"Beauty school?" asks Billy, a kind, cute, curly-haired carpenter with an always-innocent air who comes in for a large Bud draft almost every night.

"Yes, beauty school," Cathy repeats, "starting next week." She places the glasses on a dish mat to dry and wipes her red hands on a white, just-laundered cloth.

"Oh, how exciting," I say, a bit woozy from my half-full glass of merlot.

Harold, sitting comfortably in his paint-covered jumpsuit and nursing his large Rolling Rock draft, looks at her curiously. "Is this a new idea, Cathy, or something you've been throwing around in that head of yours for a while now?"

"Oh, god, Harold," Cathy says, reaching for the bottle of Jack Daniel's, "it's been more than a while now, that's for sure." She pours a few-seconds-worth of the liquor with one hand while she presses the Coke button on the fountain gun with the other. Both liquids meet in a rocks glass full of ice. She applies a lime to the glass's rim and places the drink in front of Bianca, dressed in blue jeans, a tight, sleeveless white top, her long hair, and a hint of lip gloss.

"Yeah, Cath," Bianca says, removing the stirrer from her drink and taking much more than a sip, "I can remember you talking about doing this years ago, back when we first met... So I guess you decided it's about time?"

"Yeah, actually, it *is* about time," she answers, putting her hands on her hips. "Now that the boys are a bit older, I think it's about the perfect time." She cocks her head to the side. "But not that it's going to be easy, I know."

Billy tips his empty glass in her direction.

"Another one?" she asks. She picks up his glass, places it under the tap at an angle, and pulls the handle toward her. "Yeah, I mean, thank God Nick agreed to sacrifice a bit and help me...otherwise...otherwise...there'd be no way I could do it." She releases the handle back into its original position, puts a fresh bar napkin down, and then places the tall, golden draft on top of it.

"Thanks, honey," Billy says. He takes a couple of bucks out of his pocket and pushes them toward her.

"No way you could do what, Cath?" Walter, who has just walked in, asks. As he sits down, he takes his comb out of his back pocket and quickly runs it through his hair.

"No way that I could go to beauty school, Walter," says Cathy, who is now busy pouring a large Rolling Rock draft.

"Ah, your dream...beauty school. Finally getting the chance, are you?" he says, massaging his beard with his hand.

"That I am, Walter, thanks to—as I was saying when you walked in—Nick." She delivers the draft to Walter and then proceeds to prepare its never-ending companion, a CC on the rocks. "Yeah...he's really surprised me. I mean, really, he's agreed to get up early in the morning, after not getting home until around three, and watch the kids while I'm at class. He's agreed to make his own meals. And—I mean it's just wonderful—he's even offered to work a few extra shifts to cover the tuition." She places the CC on the rocks in front of Walter with a smile. Then, abruptly, she turns around.

I could be wrong, but I think I saw her gratitude in the corner of her eye. ∎

TWO FAILURES UNKNOWN

"You know, Jenna, I think that we should try and show Nina that we appreciate her…that is, a little more than we're doing now… You know—make her feel that we realize how much she helps us out each night."

I am sitting in the back booth counting the tips that I made during the course of the evening when Bianca comes up to me and says this, a tray tucked under her arm. I stop midway through my tallying, dollar bills in my hands, and look up at her, wide-eyed.

"Oh…okay…really?" I reply, almost without thinking. "Well, no, of course… Sure. Sure… That sounds good. I think that you're right."

"Okay, good," she says, immediately walking away. But I pause for a moment, a bit confused. Nonetheless, I quickly decide that I'll make it a point to thank Nina for her help even more than I'm doing now, and then I turn my attention back to my basket.

******

BEFORE I KNOW IT, it's Friday night once more and I'm sitting at the bar, again counting the tips in my basket (enjoying the melody and lyrics of Alanis's "You Learn"), and again being visited by Bianca and her out-of-the-blue comments. "Jenna," she says, as she situates herself on the stool beside me, not completely sitting on it, but only halfway. She says my name in an almost motherly tone, as if I'm her child and she's cautiously approaching me to talk about the wet sheets she found, once again, on my bed in the morning.

"Yeah, Bianca… What's up?" I put down my money and turn toward her.

"Well," she begins, looking me directly in the eye. "Do you…do you remember what we talked about last week…about Nina?"

I'm amazed she's bringing this up again, but I answer, "Well yeah, of course…of course I do."

Seriously, though—how often does she need to be thanked?

"Well, to tell you the truth, I really thought that after I talked to you…that you'd…"

That I'd *what?* For the life of me, I can't figure out what in the world she's talking about, and I just sit for a moment—motionless, perplexed—waiting for her to say something more, my mind in jumbles. I mean, don't I already realize that because Nina seats customers, clears my tables, and helps me take drink orders, deliver food, and get change, my hectic Thursday and Friday evenings are so much more manageable? And don't I already sincerely thank her throughout the evening as much as I can, and especially before she leaves for the night?

"*Jenna*," she finally says, and the motherly tone has left. "Why don't you just go and talk to Nina about this yourself. She's in the back booth, waiting for you."

******

I APPROACH HER, and she's sitting there, hands crossed tightly, dark eyes angry. I've never seen her look at me like this before. Other people, maybe—but not me.

"Nina?" I say, sitting down cautiously, my throat beginning to constrict. "What's going on? Is…is there something wrong?"

She just stares at me for a moment, but then she replies. "Yeah, Jenna. There's something *very* wrong." And from the way she says it, it's apparent that there has been something wrong for quite a while now.

"Oh, okay… Well…tell me what it is then."

"Oh, I will. Don't you worry. I've had just about enough of it now… Six months of it is enough."

"Six months…what?…six months of *what?*"

At this, her eyes grow big, her mouth opens, and she utters a disgusted "Uh! You have *got* to be kidding!"

"Kidding about *what?*" I reply, really starting to feel rather sick to my stomach.

"You mean…you really can't be that…you mean you *really* don't realize that you've been stiffing me for the past six months?"

"*Stiffing* you…what, what do you mean?"

"Oh, c'mon, Jenna. Here I've been racing around for you, *every week*, and you've been making seventy to one hundred bucks a night, and you can't even give me a five-dollar tip for it? I mean, what have you been thinking?"

"Nina... I… I…"

"And I'll tell you what else, Jenna. It really makes me *so* crazy that you insist on consistently standing *ten* feet from the table when you're taking an order… Other people do need to get by you—you know! You're not the only person who works here!"

And with this last statement, she lets out an enormous, exasperated sigh. As for me, I think I might throw up—or pick up something and throw *it*.

"Nina," I begin, desperately wanting to explain myself. But just then, Bianca shows up, and my feelings of angry horror instantly turn into defensive, belligerent ones.

"You know, Nina, if you've had such an issue with me this entire time, you should've just come out and said it to my face, like you're doing now, rather than getting Bianca to do it for you. And *Bianca*," I continue, flashing my eyes at her, "if you were going to do it, you should've told me exactly what you meant from the beginning, rather than beating around the bush. *Besides*," and I consciously try to calm myself down and lower my voice, "do you guys *truly* believe that I was doing those things on *purpose*? Do you— *really*?"

And they just look back and forth at one another, waiting for the other to answer.

******

AROUND MIDNIGHT, I stop at Jack's, my heart and ego completely shattered. My mind is full of what took place earlier, and I don't think I'll ever quite forget about it. I walk in, and Jack takes his attention away from his computer and looks at me, instantly recognizing that something has happened. The volume is low, but I hear "Little Earthquakes" emanating from the stereo.

"Honey…what's, what's wrong? You look so totally worn out." He gets up from his seat, walks over to me, takes my hand, and leads me to the couch.

I sit there for a minute or so, sinking into the cushions, staring down at my lap, until he lifts my chin gently with his hand and waits for me to say something.

"Jack," I begin, looking for someone or something to blame, "why didn't you tell me… Why…why…why didn't someone tell me?"

"Tell you what, Jenna…tell you what?"

"That we were supposed to tip the hosts and hostesses! Here it's been now, all this time…and I haven't tipped her once!… Oh god, I feel *terrible* about it…just terrible… Why couldn't someone have told me?"

"Well…" And he starts to squirm around a bit, obviously already completely aware of the situation, which makes me feel even worse. "Well, we…we just all thought that it's something you decided…something that you decided not to do… After all, really, when it comes down to it, it is your prerogative, you know."

"Well, yeah—of course it is…I guess. But so is tipping the bartenders who work with you, something which I *always* do, because I was told from the beginning that it was the proper and expected thing to do. If only I were… I just never thought that we were expected to tip the hosts and hostesses, especially since I was never expected to do that any place else I've ever waitressed, and since they currently make more than three times an hour what we make. Don't they?… Plus, now that I think about it, the few times that I've hostessed, I really don't recall ever being given a tip… I just… I mean it just…it just never occurred to me…and now…now…now I feel like such a damn fool."

He waits a moment, but then he takes my head in his hands and kisses me lightly. "You…a fool?" he says. "C'mon, get serious. I know that we've been dating only a little while now, but if there's one thing I'm certain of, that's one thing you're not. Misunderstood—certainly—but not a fool."

"Well," I say, smiling at him weakly, feeling a bit better, "I'll just be sure to make up for it from now on. Yes, when I work with her, I'll give her double of what's expected… And as for her claim of my standing too far from the tables and being in her way all the time, well—oh, so did I forget to mention that?—well, I really can't believe I do that. I mean, I am a dancer after all, and wouldn't I be aware of something like that? But oh well, it's entirely possible, and

I'll definitely try to avoid doing it… And then…maybe—just maybe—" I say, shaking my head, wringing my hands, "this whole embarrassing, horrifying mess will blow over."

"Oh—it will—don't you worry," Jack replies, chuckling wryly, his gaze turned inward. "Take it from me. They always, always do." ■

FORGIVENESS

I can't quite believe it, but Richard's back—after a three weeks' absence—not only hanging out, but cooking again as well.

I don't know if I could've done it myself.

I mean, did Mary Ellen and Bobby talk to him? Coax him into it? Offer him more money?

"Hey, Richard!" I say, walking into the kitchen to pick up a vegetable plate (thick slices of carrot, celery, and green pepper, and chunks of tomato). I grab the plastic container of ranch from the fridge and give it a downward shake, and as the creamy dressing flows through the long, thin neck into the small porcelain dish situated amid the vegetables, I tell him I'm so happy that he's back.

"Well…me too," he agrees, smiling. "To tell you the truth, though, I didn't think I'd be able to, you know…didn't think I could deal with it…but then something happened that completely changed my mind."

"Oh yeah?" I ask, setting down the dressing container—and staring at him in spite of myself. "What…what…what was that?"

He walks over to the charcoal grill, flips a hamburger sizzling on it, tops it with a couple pieces of cheddar, and then turns around and looks at me.

"Curt…" he begins, "well…well…he apologized."

And I can't argue with that. ■

WALTER

In many respects, Walter is The Grill's Norm. Like the well-known character, he stops in for a drink just about as often and is known by just as many people. And even though he isn't nearly as "healthy" as Norm was, the evidence of his daily consumption is there (sorry, Walter). But instead of hearing "Walter!" in unison as "Norm!" was heard time and again on *Cheers*, when Walter walks through the door you hear "Hi Walter What's up Walter Good evening Walter Hey Walter"—greetings from about eight to twelve people, from this corner and that, one after another, often overlapping each other—as Walter's nods and accepting eyes recognize the words falling through the air.

His ritual after being greeted by practically everyone in the place is to remove his long wool black coat and either hang it on the shiny gold coat rack or put it on the back of a bar stool, remove his black beret and place it on the bar, and take his white handkerchief out of his pant pocket, adroitly remove his glasses, and quickly but gently massage his lenses with that handkerchief, holding it between his thumb and index finger, removing the spots that have formed during the day or the moisture that has been put there by the rain. When it's nice outside, he simply has a light jacket to take care of, or nothing at all. But no matter what time of year it is, whether he is dressed in a conservative black suit and tie or a pair of faded blue jeans, a white pinstriped button-up cotton shirt, and old tennis shoes, he never forgets to quickly take a black comb from his pocket and, with a swift motion, smooth the top layer of his hair back, away from his forehead, covering the bald spot that is beginning to appear, as his eyes once again greet everyone and take in the mood of the setting in an instant.

"A shot and a beer, please." That's all Walter has to say as he pulls out a bar stool and sits down upon it. Whoever is behind the bar knows exactly what to give him: a CC on the rocks and an Iron City. Sometimes he stays for one round of drinks, sometimes many, depending on the day of the week and the time of day. During the week he usually stops in between four and six, to take advantage of happy hour, coming from work or having just returned from the airport and a business trip. Walter is a lawyer (a very good one, as far as I can tell) and fairly well-known in Squirrel Hill. Recently he was named "Squirrel Hill Citizen of the Year," an honor he is very proud of. So our Walter is very different from Norm when it comes to the career world. He is definitely not a slacker, as *Cheers'* Norm was portrayed to be. But, like Norm, he is a constant friendly face sitting at the bar, and he enjoys the refreshment and taste of a good beer—there's no doubt about that. I don't know if Walter is aware of this, but each and every time he takes a tasty swig of his beer or a generous sip of CC, he swishes the liquid around in his mouth, quickly swallows, and then satisfyingly smacks his tongue and the roof of his mouth together several times in succession, finishing the enjoyable, routine procedure by quickly licking his top lip and the mustache that protects it. His right hand then finds a familiar spot on top of his blond-gray beard and scratches for an instant, and then returns to resting on top of the bar. A flash of contentment appears in his kind eyes.

Walter especially enjoys hanging out at The Grill on Friday nights, particularly ever since his favorite Friday-night hangout, The Decade, closed. The Decade was an intimate rock and roll club on Atwood Street in Oakland, near The University of Pittsburgh. Rock stars such as Bruce Springsteen, U2, and the Iron City Houserockers performed there. The walls were covered with sheet music and rock paraphernalia, including an autographed photo of Jon Bon Jovi. A small, silver metal bucket that hung above the heads of the bartenders accepted tip after tip. Quickly, pointy corners of green could be seen reaching out of the bucket. And everyone in the place knew when a tip was being pushed into it. "Drop the tip, ring the cowbell" was the bartenders' ritual. It was a sad day when The Decade's doors closed, and it seems as if customers who were regulars there now come to The Grill for comfort. There is no ringing of a cowbell here, but there are plenty of smiles and good laughter and the playing of soulful blues and jazz on the music system, especially when Curt is behind the bar.

Walter also appears here on Saturday afternoons, around two or three, and stays for a couple of hours, visiting Adam, Anthony, and me, always curious to see what interesting movie Adam has decided upon by surfing through the channels of that old, dusty TV that sits high atop the beer cooler. "Well, you have your choice of a Western, an Elvis flick, or *Talk Soup*. What d'ya think?" Adam asks me, Saturday after Saturday, when we are both finished with our opening duties, waiting for the lunch crowd to arrive. Of course, the movie choices vary each week, but it is surprising what an eclectic mix we have to choose from.

Anthony also appears from the kitchen to say hello to Walter when he has a moment and there aren't too many customers in the place, dressed in his white T-shirt; white, full-bodied, stained apron; gray sweatpants; and ominous, black, metal-toed shoes ("For safety, in case I drop anything heavy on my feet," he explained to me once, "like a gigantic pot full of soup or a sharp knife"). On many occasions he asks Walter for advice and info about landlord and tenant rights and responsibilities because, unfortunately, he is often having problems with his landlord. Walter is always very helpful. It is obvious that he gets enormous pleasure from elaborating on any subject that comes up in conversation that he is knowledgeable about, which, in fact, is just about anything you can think of. No kidding. Whenever someone has a question, you will hear—it never fails—"Ask Walter." I often think that it must be so cool to be equated with an encyclopedia. Not only is Walter The Grill's Norm, but he is also The Grill's Webster.

However, Walter is often rewarded for his knowledge and advice. After the lunch crowd disappears, Anth brings out a medium-sized Styrofoam container filled with the homemade soup of the day, sometimes chicken noodle, with large, tender pieces of chicken breast; cream of mushroom, flavored with a touch of Burgundy (Mary Ellen's specialty); or beef barley, rich and hearty. He hands the soup to Walter—"Want some soup, Walter?"—and Walter always graciously accepts.

Usually Walter comes to the bar alone on Saturday afternoons, but every once in a while during the summer he walks in, followed by his tall, skinny, somewhat-shy fourteen-year-old daughter, Kristen, who is decked out in rollerblades, shorts, a glittery tank top, and windblown golden-blonde hair. "We're here for some quality father and daughter time," Walter says with a smile, as he gestures to the two-seater closest to the front window.

They sit and relax for a couple of hours, casually chatting and gazing out of the window, Walter relishing his usual round of drinks, and Kristen enjoying a pretty, pink Shirley Temple with lots of cherries (in a highball glass with a straw), and either crispy chicken fingers with both honey mustard and barbecue dipping sauce, or tender, cheesy, gooey potato skins with refreshing sour cream. It is such a happy and comforting sight to witness and be a part of (I wait on them often): a father and daughter feeling comfortable enough to spend some time alone together and learn more about each other; a father feeling secure enough to drink in front of his daughter and to share with her his favorite place to hang out; a daughter not embarrassed about being seen with her father. What particularly impacts me is the mixture of the innocence (the pink of the Shirley Temple) and the maturity (father and daughter enjoying a drink together in a grown-up place). *After all*, I think, as I watch the two of them together, *that's what life should be all about. You should grow and learn, improving yourself, yet never lose touch with the innocence and idealism within you that makes life so special and inspires you to reach and grow in the first place.*

Frequently, Walter's stay is cut short on Saturday afternoons because he has "an appointment with the kitchen," as he puts it. Either it is his turn to make dinner for his family, or he is going to help prepare a fancy meal for a dinner party that he and his wife, Katy, are hosting later that evening. Elaborate dishes such as duck à l'orange and coq au vin come to life in Walter's kitchen. I've never visited Walter's home, but he's told me that he owns one of those very large, old, full-of-character Squirrel Hill houses that have multiple floors. He once said that he can be on the fourth floor working in his library and feel as if he is the only one home, even though his son and daughter are watching TV on the second floor and his wife is in the bedroom reading. The house's expansiveness, which allows for privacy and calm when he needs them, is one of the aspects that Walter particularly loves about the house and about living there.

I sometimes imagine what Walter's dinner parties are like. In my mind, doctors, lawyers, and psychiatrists comfortably sit at the rectangular, glossy, cherry table, which is adorned in the center with a crystal vase full of bright gold, red, and purple flowers. The red of the flowers matches the women's red lips, and the gold matches some of the men's shiny ties, which hang loosely around their necks. The guests, as well as the china, glasses, and silverware, are elegant and refined, but not pompous or overbearing. There is a happiness and brightness in the room, enhanced by the light from the simple chandelier, which reflects off the silverware and puts a glow on each person's face. Statements and questions such as "Mmm…this is really delicious," "How's business, Walter?" "The flowers are so beautiful," and "Has your son decided upon a college yet?" intermingle and flow, as course after course are presented and then enjoyed.

After dinner, the friends sit on the soft, white couches, surrounded by rows and rows of literature arranged on wooden bookshelves that line the walls. They drink Burgundy, cognac, and Baileys Irish Cream—and, of course, a CC on the rocks is present. The lounging and chatting lasts until ten or ten-thirty; then, just as smoothly and easily as the evening has progressed, the guests give their thanks, say their goodbyes, and leave the warm, enticing household. Walter and his wife smile at one another and exchange a soft, sweet kiss, acknowledging that the evening has been a success.

Whether Walter's dinner parties are like this at all, I really don't know—I've never conveyed these particular musings to him. But I often think that I picture his dinner parties to be this way because my reflections are an embodiment of what Walter is—elegant and refined, intelligent and sophisticated, yet laid-back and friendly: the best of both worlds. He doesn't limit himself to certain types of people or places but feels free to associate with both the professional sphere and the service sphere, with his lawyer colleagues and with young waitresses like me who are working to put themselves through school and are aspiring to unconventional paths in life.

In fact, Walter always gives me a boost and is encouraging to me, because he seems to be genuinely interested in my life and the goals I am pursuing. It's amazing how much someone can give to you—confidence, worth, inspiration—simply by taking an interest in you and your interests. I especially need a motivational boost now, because a little more than two months ago I began my adventure (or should I say, *crucible*) at Point Park College, on my way to attaining a dance degree. The dance classes are difficult and extremely demanding, the students I am taking classes with are so talented and much better trained than I am (as I expected), and I am tired (to put it mildly), dancing anywhere from three to five hours per day, then waitressing two to three nights per week on top of that. It's been very socially challenging for me as well. I'm a few years older than most of the dance students there (I already have one BA, having received an English degree from Chatham College not too long ago), and I really don't fit into any particular "group." The freshmen all stick together, and the upperclassmen have already made their set of friends. Some of the dancers, particularly the better, highly trained ones, can be deliberately unkind as well. Plus, unlike when I was attending Chatham, I now live off-campus, so I haven't had the opportunity to get to know anyone outside of class time (although I guess I could probably make more of an effort). I am particularly shy and introverted, too (it's getting to be more of a problem as time goes on), which obviously doesn't help. And to make it even worse, the dance department recently took an informal survey of its students, with categories ranging from "the funniest dancer" to "the shyest dancer." Well, I was one of the people listed under "the shyest dancer" category. Luckily, I don't think I won.

Given the difficulty I'm having (to be completely honest, I've had quite a few crying bouts in my apartment before heading out to the bus stop in the morning!), Walter has truly been a comfort. "Are you physically and mentally dealing with all of the classes okay?" "What classes are you taking this semester?" and "Are you going to be in any shows soon?" are all questions he asks me. It certainly helps to have someone to talk to about my life at Point Park, because I don't feel that I know anyone well enough at the college yet to discuss things with. The best thing he's said to me, however, is what he told me just last week. "You look and seem a lot more energetic and healthy now," he began. "The first month or so, you really looked like you were dragging, but you seem to be handling the rigorous schedule much, much better now. Good for you, Jenna. Good for you." I appreciate those sentiments the most, because he's affirmed my own feelings that I am improving, am facing the challenge I've set up for myself, and will eventually be able to achieve what I so yearn to achieve.

So thanks, Walter. You've done so much for me, simply by being yourself: concerned and curious, genuine and friendly.

I won't forget it. ■

NO TIME TO WASTE

At approximately 4:05 I jump off the 61B at the corner of Forbes and Wightman and rush to my building and up the stairs to my second-floor apartment. Once inside, I peel off my tights and my stretchy dance top. There's no time for a shower, so I wash my face, fix my hair a little (it's already pulled back), and apply some deodorant. What's the use of a shower, though, really? I'll be saturated with grease and smoke by the end of the night anyway. It's just a shame that I don't have time to eat anything substantial. A raspberry breakfast bar will have to do for now. So I inhale it without a thought and then grab the ironing board, realizing full well that I should've ironed my clothes the night before. For some reason, I can never get myself to do it.

As I press my clothes, the odor of cigarettes and french fries hits me in the face. Oh well. Apparently I need to do laundry more often, or get more work clothes. The pressing done, I turn off the iron and unplug it, pull on my toasty khaki pants, and put on my light blue Oxford shirt, buttoning it up quickly and tucking it in. Then I start taking down the ironing board, then immediately decide that I'll do it later. I grab a pair of white socks out of the top drawer of my dresser, plop down on my bed (the box spring sinking, once again, beneath the frame—I've had this bed since I was a kid), and put them on. Damn it all to hell!

This pair has holes in the toes too. Nonetheless, my ugly, black, super-arch-support-laden shoes find their way on my feet, which take me into the bathroom for a swish of mouthwash and a dab or two of ruby lipstick. Then I'm out the door, my purse and bag (today containing *The Vagabond*, by Colette) thrown over my shoulder.

I walk into The Grill at 4:27, three minutes to spare. ∎

HUNGRY

The overwhelming smell of fries, burgers, pasta, wings, steak, and ribs taunts me, and my stomach growls—earnestly—hoping tonight will be like some other nights, when Tommy or Mary Ellen pushes a dish toward me, saying, "You want this Reuben? The customer decided he didn't want it after I had already started making it" or "I misread the slip and put the wrong kind of sauce on this pasta. You want to take care of it for me?" In these situations, I am always so grateful. I stand at the baker's table, just outside of the kitchen, trying to be as much out of everyone's way as I can, feeling some energy come back to me as I devour the hot, juicy food. Otherwise, after having danced all day without the time to eat before arriving at work, I'm forced to run around on an almost empty stomach until the dinner hours are over and it's time for my break, carrying plate upon plate of delicious, steaming food on a tray in front of me, which is the perfect spot for inhaling all of the tempting aromas.

Mistakes? Well, thank God for them, that's all I can say. ■

KEN

On my short walk home after work—especially if he hasn't been in for a Heineken—I almost always stop to see him. Sometimes I'll pick up a package of gummy worms or sour fish, but that's always secondary.

He works at the Gulf Station, which inhabits one of the corners shared by Murray and Forbes, and which is three doors down from The Grill. When I arrive there, he's usually standing in front of the main window, in his blue uniform, either in the luxurious summer breeze or the biting, noncaring chill (depending on the time of the year), calmly watching the people and the cars go by.

Most of the time he quickly spots me as I pass the bagel shop and then walk toward the pumps and the front door of the station. Other times, he doesn't, so I'm free to study his interesting, exotic, middle-aged looks, with his slim build; prominent nose; black hair and mustache; dark, tanned skin (year-round); and American Indian subtleties.

And then I get to hear him talk. It's deep but not too deep, relaxed but not too relaxed, Southern-mixed-in-with-Pittsburgh accented—that voice of his. I've never heard anything close to it before, but what I think I like most about it is the longing and yearning that's in it, and not just in the words themselves, but in the sound and tone of them. Plus, I love what we talk about, one of my favorite things.

"Ahhhhh, Jenna…the breeeeeze is just wonderful tonight…isn't it? Makes me just *cra-zy* for the coast…"

"I know what you mean, Ken," I reply, following his example and looking out toward the busy street, but seeing only sunshine, waves, shimmering sand, and sailboats, as I'm sure he is.

Yes, when we learn that we share this intoxicating love of the ocean—and everything associated with it—we can't help but discuss our obsession each time we see each other, sharing bits and pieces of our adventures, until the stories, one day, are completely told. I tell him about my many trips to Rehoboth Beach in Delaware with my mom and our friends—one night describing the exhilaration of diving into the waves, another night describing the beautiful boutiques that sell precious earrings, soaps, and candles, and another night describing the way we sit at the Rusty Rudder eating hard-shelled crabs by the open window that lines the ocean and allows a view of the setting sun—as he nods and shakes his head, it all just sounds so wonderful. He then returns the favor and tells me about his many trips to Stone Harbor. When he has the chance he goes there with a few of his friends. They enjoy lazy days under the sun, long drives along the coast, and evening campfires on the sand. He usually goes in late September or early October, "the absolute best time to go, when the beaches are empty, there's peace and quiet, and you have time to think—when that glorious mixture of cleansing air and beaming sunshine rejuvenates you more than anything else." And I stand there smiling, feeling that environment surrounding me, forgetting that my nose is turning red and my fingers are aching. "Ahhhhh, there's nothing like that coast, Jenna," he says again and again, and I know exactly what he means.

On a rare occasion, I won't stop to see him, especially if I'm exhausted or I don't notice him standing outside the station or inside waiting on a customer. But in these instances he always seems to see me. As I walk by the pumps, a familiar, clear, thick voice suddenly escapes out of one of them, saying: "Oh there she is, that Jenna, that pretty one—that ocean-lover—just watch her walk by." The first time this happens, I look up, startled, my heart racing, and I am rather confused and scared. But after the first time, and after I figure out what's going on—and by whom—I quite like it.

Some nights, when it's really slow at the station, he'll even start to walk home with me, but he never ventures too far. "Yep, this is it," he says, not quite touching the tips of his black shoes on the line that separates the station's lot and the sidewalk. "This is all the farther I'm allowed to go. One step past this, and my job's history." He says this in a joking manner, but I can't help but feel that he is actually very serious, that if he allowed himself to invade that boundary, he'd never go back. And it's then that I completely understand why he loves the ocean so much—the infinite, ever-moving, boundary-less ocean.

"Sweet dreams…" he calls to me, as he watches me depart. And I'm positive this won't be a problem, because he's already given me so many. ∎

A BIT OF ADVICE

"**D**on't feel so bad about it," Nina says, looking me directly in the eye. "It was just a kiss. I mean, I've cheated on every boyfriend I've ever had..."

"You *have?* Really?" I respond, quite shocked by her admission.

"Oh yeah. So don't you worry," she says, taking her lip gloss out of her purse and applying it nonchalantly, as we sit facing each other on the rolled-up carpets in the hot basement. "You'll get over it." ∎

THE THREE OF US AND PRIMANTI

"Ready, Jenna?" Mike asks.

It's now approaching two o'clock in the morning. I worked the late shift, but for the past hour I've been talking with Beth and her boyfriend, Mike, a sweet, kind, gentle, intelligent, attractive, and extremely funny guy who likes to tell innocent jokes. They often come to The Grill together around eleven o'clock or midnight on Friday nights and hang out and drink a few beers until closing, and they always offer to give me a ride home.

"You bet, Mike. Just let me grab my things."

I go downstairs into the basement and gather my purse and my duffel bag and, in no time at all, reappear upstairs.

"All set, Mike."

So we are happily on our way. Nick locks the door behind us—"Good night, guys"—and we walk to Mike's old, grayish-blue Cadillac, parked tonight in Mellon Bank's lot, which is across the street and about half a block to our right (it's okay to park there while the bank is closed). Other times, Mike parks directly across the street at a meter in front of Barnes & Noble, or at a meter in front of the Gulf Station.

Once we're all safely in the car, we head toward the light at the intersection of Murray and Forbes. It never fails—it always turns red just as we get there. The streets are practically deserted by this time of night, but Mike is always patient. He waits for the light to turn green, saying that you never know where a cop could be hiding out.

When it's safe to proceed, Mike makes a left onto Forbes Avenue, and in a matter of seconds, Beth and I will be home (Beth now lives in the first-floor apartment below mine, in our three-floor walk-up). Even though the "trip" is so short, I thoroughly enjoy the stillness, rolling down the window in the back seat to allow the cool, refreshing, almost startling air to flow over me, getting rid of some of the smoke that has penetrated my clothes, hair, and lungs.

Mike pulls up to the curb in front of our building, but before we get out of the car, he asks us the usual question: "So, you two, what flavor of Primanti will it be tonight?"

Beth and I look at each other eagerly.

"I'll have a corned beef," Beth says, giving Mike a kiss on the cheek.

"And I think I'll have a pastrami tonight," I say, unlocking my door.

"Okay, you got it; a corned beef and a pastrami coming right up… Why don't you two go in and relax and I'll go pick them up and be right back."

"Okay, honey," Beth says.

"Thanks, Mike," I add.

We get out of the car, close the car doors behind us, and head up the concrete steps. Once inside Beth's apartment, which sits just to the right of the entranceway, we go into her kitchen and bring out whatever we need for our gathering, setting everything up on the small coffee table in the living room.

Primanti Brothers—especially on the weekends after the bars let out, when people of all ages are in the mood for some satisfying and hardy sustenance to soak up all of the beer, shots, and mixed drinks they've sustained themselves with for most of the night—is the place to go. There's corned beef, pastrami, roast beef, kolbassi, knockwurst, turkey, grilled chicken breast, fish, and egg and cheese—your choice—piled high on rye bread, with coleslaw, hot sauce, and thick, juicy french fries on top. Yes, french fries. They are the unique ingredient that has made the sandwiches so famous. There's a Primanti Brothers in the Strip District (the original location), but Mike always goes to the one in Oakland, a straight shot down Forbes Avenue.

Beth and I chat for a while, and in about half an hour, Mike is back, the warm, abundant sandwiches with him.

I can't wait.

******

"YUMMY!" I say without fail as I take a bite, having already quickly grabbed my sandwich out of the paper bag and unwrapped it from the wax paper in which it was held. There's almost always a pint glass full of Pepsi sitting on the coffee table in front of me (unless I'm in the mood for a beer), among an issue of *Cosmopolitan*, two Budweisers (one each for Beth and Mike), three stoneware plates of varying bright colors, and a jar of Tabasco sauce, which Mike swears is the perfect addition to the delicious sandwiches, and which I have to undoubtedly agree with. Beth sits on the couch with me, to my left, and Mike pulls up a chair across from us.

"Yeah, they certainly hit the spot, don't they?" Mike says, and then he likewise takes a big, juicy bite.

These after-hours socials with the two of them mean so much to me, the three of us sitting in our intimate circle in Beth's open but cozy apartment with the colorful painting by Monet above her fireplace; enjoying the thick, flavorful sandwiches; chatting and laughing as Beth's black, petite, friendly cat, Stormy, joins in our conversations by looking at us curiously, meowing at us happily, and affectionately rubbing up against our legs. I feel especially at ease with the two of them, comfortable enough to untuck my shirt, take off my shoes, and curl my feet up under me as we talk. Beth tells me about her job at Carnegie Mellon and how well she is doing, having recently been promoted to a management role. She even has her own office now with her very own name displayed on the door in fancy letters, and she is traveling occasionally to Toronto to speak at seminars and to lead computer training courses. There is even the possibility that she may be offered a permanent position in Toronto in the near future, after she completes her master's degree. Both she and Mike are so excited about it because they think that Toronto is such an amazing city.

We also talk a lot about The Grill. It is during these conversations that I find out about the histories and secrets of many of its employees and regulars, such as who used to date whom, when and why they broke up, what the true reason is for a person acting a particular way, and on and on. I even discover what Beth's true feelings about having worked at The Grill are. "Boy, Jenna," she casually says during one of our late-night feasts, as she sits down beside me, having just returned from the kitchen with two more Buds for herself and Mike, "I just bet you can't wait to get your dance degree so you can get out of that place."

I put down my sandwich and look at her, not exactly sure how to respond.

"Well," she says, recognizing my surprise, "I just know that I was so happy to quit working there myself."

"Really?" I say, thinking. "I mean, I realize that working there was very tiring and quite a juggling act for you, but you really didn't like it?"

"Oh…well of course I did sometimes, but most of the time I just got so tired of people asking for this and that and telling me what to do, especially the rude customers. And then there was trying to deal with Nick and his arrogance, and then the sleazy guys who would come in at night and gawk at me and say sexist things." (Mike can't seem to avoid raising his eyebrows when she says this…) "I mean, I really liked most of the people who worked there, but I just didn't want to be in that environment anymore."

I don't say anything for a few seconds. "Wow, Beth, I…I can completely understand your frustration with Nick and how utterly rude he can be sometimes…and some of the customers, too…but I really haven't run into any guys who harass me or give me any major problems, except every now and then, of course," I reply.

"Well, you know what? I did notice that things were starting to get much better right before I quit, compared to when I started working there, and things seem to be really good now. Bobby, he has…yeah, he has really cleaned up the place and enhanced the menu, which has brought in a lot of respectable customers and turned away some of the *utter* creeps who used to go in there." She shakes her head, obviously still disturbed at the thought of them. "Actually, it's much more of a 'restaurant with a bar' now rather than just a bar, like it was before, so…I suppose working there now wouldn't be so bad. But I was just so eager to get on with my career. Yeah, I think that my desire to move on was probably the main reason I was dissatisfied working there… I have to say, though, I like the place much better now that I can go in as a customer, have a few drinks, and hang out for a while without the pressure of making sure that no one's glass is empty," Beth says, picking up her beer and taking a drink, pausing for a moment. "But, Jenna, really? You… You particularly enjoy working there?"

"Oh yeah, Beth, I really do," I say, wiping my mouth with my napkin. "I mean, I get tired of it some days, especially when someone is unexpectedly nasty or I go to clean off a table and a tip is nowhere in sight—not hidden under the sugar container, or misplaced under the place mat, or accidentally on the floor or under the table, *nowhere*—but, to tell you the truth, I'm quite taken with the place. I really get a sense of satisfaction at the end of the night when everyone has left and all of the tables are cleared and wiped off, and I'm sitting at the bar having a drink while either Curt or Nick is behind the bar finishing up, and the music on the radio is playing. I think about the many different people I served, joked with, observed, and talked to during the night, and I feel like I really got a taste of life. And then to count the pile of tips that were waiting for me all night long in my basket, and to put the money in my purse and take it home with me, feeling more secure because of it than I had felt before I got there…it's such a good feeling. And, most of all, on the nights when I'm the early-person-out, to come home to my nice, steamy apartment, especially when it's freezing outside, and wind down with *David Letterman*—there's no beating that," I say, leaning back against the couch, folding my hands in my lap, feeling absolutely content, having really been talking to myself rather than to Beth and Mike. Eventually, however, I do realize where I am, and how long I've been going on (very unusual for me), and the sense of calm I feel is immediately overshadowed by a tinge of self-consciousness. I glance from Beth to Mike, and then back. But, really, I can tell there is nothing to worry about. They sit there smiling, looking at me thoughtfully. ■

SEEK AND FIND

It's 3:45 (and extremely sunny outside—the glare is amazing!), and I've just finished my last dance class of the day at Point Park College and am on my way to the bus stop on the corner of Forbes and Wood, right in front of the Boyer Candy store. I almost walk right by him in my haste (I have to be at work in less than an hour), but I catch him out of the corner of my eye.

"Tommy!!! What are you doing down here?" I ask, surprised, stopping abruptly. (I usually run into him only in Squirrel Hill.)

"Oh…I was just looking for *you*," he replies, squinting mischievously. "I've come to tell you a joke." ■

THE MEETING

Three boxes of powdered and glazed donuts sit open on the bar. A pot of just-brewed coffee permeates the air. Nick, dressed in a blue fleece and a white ball cap and smelling good, sits facing us, his hands crossed.

"Well, guys," he begins, "thank you for coming in." He moves around on his stool a bit. "I realize it's Sunday morning and everything, but I thought it'd be best to meet before we open later this afternoon… You know, to discuss some issues that have gotten quite out of hand."

I glance at Jack, who is rubbing his bloodshot eyes. He shoots me back a questioning look. Shane, however, can't quite seem to quit staring at the cream-filled donuts in front of him, and Bianca is gripping an empty coffee cup. The smoke in our faces comes from Diana's third cigarette since she got here. As for Nina, she is busy removing her sparkly black scarf, with the help of Adam's big hands. And Anth—where is he?—he hasn't shown up.

"You see," Nick says, removing his cap, "to get right to it, and to not waste your time this morning, I know that Bobby and I have always been pretty lenient about you guys drinking a Pepsi or a glass of juice or whatever you want while you work—and as many as you want, too…"

We all nod. The constant supply of caffeine and sugar definitely keeps us going.

"But, the truth is, guys, we need to be professional about it… Over the past couple of months, we've become way, way too casual. You know, what I'm trying to say is, this is a respected establishment and we need to think a little more about our actions and how those actions affect customers' perceptions of this establishment."

Just then, Anthony walks—stumbles—in. "Sorry, Nick," he says, as he climbs onto a stool, using Bianca's shoulder for support. We all look at him, trying not to laugh, except for Shane, whose hand is inching, sort of like a caterpillar, toward you know where.

"As I was saying," Nick continues, at the same time giving Anthony a look conveying that he could care less about his lateness (they've had some palpable male bond ever since they got crazy drunk together that one night quite a while ago at The Decade), "there will be no more sitting your beverage of choice on the secondary bar while you work—in plain sight of *everybody*—and especially no more taking a swig, or a sip, or a gulp, or a—you choose what to call it—out here on the floor. From now on, that will be reserved for the kitchen area only. Nobody needs to see it… And I mean it, guys, for the kitchen area only. Got it?" He pauses for a moment, then places his cap snugly back on his head. "And, of course," he adds, again lifting his cap up for just a second and placing it back on his head again, "it goes without saying that Curt and I will do the same."

"Sounds fair," Shane says, shrugging his shoulders, as his hand makes a dive into the closest box of donuts.

"But there's one more thing," Nick says, with a glare in Shane's direction. Shane retrieves his hand suddenly. He glances around, caught unawares, apparently at a loss of what to do with his empty, powder-covered fingers.

"This eating-and-snacking-in-the-kitchen habit while

you're on the clock—you know, the mess-ups, the extras, the taste tests, the 'he changed his order,' the 'she doesn't want it,' the whatever—it's stopping today."

Quite flabbergasted, we all drill him with our eyes. Even Shane looks shocked. He inadvertently sticks his fingers in his mouth.

"Well, guys, c'mon," Nick says, sensing our absolute reluctance to the idea. "I mean, I'm not going to pretend. You guys know as well as anyone how much I like to eat, and I, too, thoroughly enjoy taking a bite out of a tasty New York strip that was cooked a little too much, or trying a new version of wings that Mare has concocted—especially those jalapeño-lime ones she made that—"

"Yeah, they were *damn* good," Shane interrupts, emphasizing his expletive with a smack of his fist on the bar, an action quite out of his character.

"*But*," Nick continues, trying his best to ignore this last interjection, although his utterly wrinkled forehead betrays him, "you *do* all have to admit that it takes your mind off of serving our customers, and it's really not all that sanitary…and besides, the biggest problem is that it stops the flow and causes too much traffic in the kitchen, and even sometimes not enough coverage out here on the floor. We just can't have that. So, as I said, it stops today… Period."

"Okay, Nick," Anthony says in his slumped-over position, his voice but a whisper. We all collectively shoot him a "What in the hell are you agreeing to?" look.

"Well," he says, his eyes barely open, "I work in the kitchen, you know. It does get freakin' crowded in there sometimes. A little more breathing room would be nice." Apparently, he has used all his energy to defend himself. Exhausted, he lays his head on the bar.

"Well, after five years of doing that," Bianca says,

running her finger around the rim of her still-empty mug, into which she is blankly gazing, "it'll certainly be a hard habit to break."

"I agree, Bea," Jack says, shaking his head, his long hair moving freely.

Me, I don't know what to say, so I just sit there wondering how I'm going to survive not eating anything until I have time to take a break, or—when it's extremely busy—until after my shift is over, especially after having danced all day.

"Well, if that's the new rule, that's the new rule," Adam contends, at the same time wrapping his arm around Nina's waist.

"Yeah…I guess… I mean…what can you do?" Nina adds, unconsciously playing with her large, silver hoop earring.

"Well, then," Nick replies, getting ready to stand up, "good… And don't forget, it's in effect—immediately… And, guys, there's one last thing…"

We all look at each other, wondering what horror will befall us next.

"Oh, good *god*, Nick." Shane stands up abruptly, throwing his hands in the air. "I mean, really, how long are you going to make me suffer? Can't I just take a bite already?"

Nick stands up too and laughs. "Go for it," he says. "And enjoy it while you can."

Shane seizes a donut and devours it greedily. ■

SYNCHRONICITY

On a similar lazy afternoon many, many months later, I hear them talking about it again. (About Craig's former career as a professional bowler, that is.) But it's no surprise. It's just like them, these two—trying again to convince me. I can't help but notice, however—this time—a heavy dose of excitement infusing their conversation. And why not? According to my friends here, a couple of Hollywood producers called Craig last week and made him an offer he can't refuse. They are in the midst of preparing for the shooting of an upcoming movie called *Kingpin,* which—what do you know?—is going to be about a professional bowler. They want Craig—*our* Craig—*our* Globy—to come out to Hollywood for about three months to work with the star of the movie, to train him and teach him the ropes of bowling.

Just guess, though, who he is going to get to work with. (Do they really think I'll fall for this?) Woody Harrelson, who, as we all know, played the painfully naive but lovable bartender on the TV series *Cheers.*

I start laughing. "C'mon, guys, really? Couldn't you have picked some other star for your story? I mean, the coincidence is too much. It's rather pathetic, actually," I say, teasing them.

Craig and Curt look at each other. "Pathetic, huh?" Craig says. "Well, see if you think this is pathetic." He grabs an envelope out of his back pocket and pushes it toward me.

"What's this?" I ask, picking it up. I notice that it's addressed to Craig, and—of course—the return address is from Hollywood. It looks utterly professional, too.

Wow, they're really working hard on this one. They've resorted to using props.

"Go ahead, dear," Curt says, grinning. "Open it."

"Oh yeah? I have your permission, do I?"

"You do, sweetie… You do."

I proceed to peel off the piece of tape that is holding the back flap closed, and I take out the thick document, which is made up of many pages. I just can't wait to see what they've concocted. Off-color jokes? Pages ripped from a coloring book? Comical pictures of Craig and Curt at the neighborhood bowling alley, doing all kinds of fancy under-the-leg and behind-the-back feats with the bowling ball?

But it's not what I thought it would be. I look through the pages quickly, and I just don't know what to say.

"This, this…" I begin. "This is a real contract, isn't it? I mean, at least it looks like one."

They nod in unison, not saying a word, looking directly at me.

So I stare at them for a few more seconds, still not quite sure if they are telling me the truth. But then all of a sudden I see the confirmation in Craig's eyes.

"Well, well, well…that's just…AMAZING!" I say, unable to hold in my excitement. I start jumping up and down, and we all just start laughing.

And wouldn't you know it? Their happiness—and mine—is contagious.

For the next couple of months, Craig and his new, thrilling opportunity are the talk of The Grill. Everyone thinks it's wonderful that Craig is getting to go to Hollywood to work with someone famous, but it's even more fabulous because this unusual and fun form of employment has been offered to him at such a perfect time. The Decade closed about a month ago, and he's been anxiously wondering what to do next with his life, when out of nowhere this adventure has fallen into his lap. "It must be another one of those mysterious workings from above," I mutter to myself, having witnessed (and experienced) too many other situations such as this one to think otherwise. What's more, he suffered a tragic event a couple of years ago when his wife passed away from cancer, and he's been raising his five-year-old daughter alone. An exciting excursion into the world of cameras and lights is probably just what he needs.

And they weren't jagging me. How about that? Perhaps anything is really possible. ■

AN UNEXPECTED OUTCOME

She is dunking a tea bag up and down in the hot water of her mug when I walk up behind her and the fresh scent hits me. This is quite unusual for her, who always sips a Pepsi while she's hostessing. Plus, I'm surprised that she's brought her tea out to the front, especially since Nick is working tonight.

"Hey, Nina," I say, as I casually return the menus to the corner of the ancillary bar. "I don't remember ever seeing you drink peppermint tea before. Do you have a cold or something?"

There is a pause, but in words rehearsed and said many times before they get to me, she answers. "No, Jenna, I don't have a cold........................I'm pregnant."

******

I'M LEANING AGAINST the ancillary bar, beside Bianca, waiting for some customers to appear, when what does appear is a sight of shocking white. No, it's not a snowball, thrown from the kitchen (this did happen once), or a figment of my imagination; it's Adam appearing from the kitchen—dark-haired, brown-eyed Adam—his hair a definite, defiant platinum.

******

SITTING ON NICK AND Cathy's porch, amid blooming flowers and flickering candles and friends, I watch Nina, belly apparent, surrounded by gifts, center of attention. She looks happy, confident, and okay with her situation, and I can't help but admire her for assuming the responsibility and accepting it so well.

******

I'M STANDING AT THE ancillary bar, again beside Bianca, but this time we're in our street clothes. Adam's hair, however, is still in white. The next minute, I overhear Bianca whisper something to Adam, something very curious and intriguing. And Adam nods, seemingly a bit scared.

"Hmmm, hmmm," Bianca begins, clearing her throat. "Could I have everyone's attention, please?"

It takes a few minutes, but eventually the noise dies down, and everyone looks at her expectantly.

"Well," she says, as she lays her hand on Adam's shoulder, "I have some news to announce for our good friend Adam here."

She pauses and looks at him for a moment, but then she says it.

"At exactly this time next week, Adam will no longer be a single man."

******

I SWEAR THAT IT WASN'T very long ago that I saw them together, at the bottom of the steps leading up to Forbes Terrace, as I was on my way to Jack's after work. They were standing there, looking at each other, talking, surrounding his bike. They flinched a bit when I turned the corner, and looked at me sheepishly. Undoubtedly they had just experienced something wonderful together (Nina lives in Forbes Terrace in the townhouse beside Jack's), and didn't want anyone intruding on them as they were saying their goodbyes for the night. So I just glanced sideways, said a quick hello, and passed through the intimacy-thick air and left them alone.

And then, about a week after that, I actually went out with them, to an interesting dive called Luna, which is located in Bloomfield, a cityish, downtrodden area just outside the Pitt campus. I don't remember too much about the club, except that it was extremely crowded and that we had a good time grooving uninhibitedly to disco music as we drank freely. But what I do remember clearly is the way she gently and affectionately put her head on his shoulder after we got into the Pitt shuttle bus much later that night, and the way he gently and affectionately wrapped his arm around her. I got off on one stop, but she didn't get off with me. Apparently, she had decided otherwise.

And for good reason, I suspect. As we worked together one Saturday afternoon, he had told me that the first moment she had walked into The Grill for an interview—with her short, dark, feathered, stylish hair; large, gold-hooped earrings; and curvy, busty body in the latest fashions—he had wanted her. And, from behind the bar, as he watched her talking and interviewing with Bobby, he had wanted her even more. And that he had realized, in those moments, that if he had ever imagined the perfect woman for him...she was it.

So, to tell you the truth, I just don't understand it one bit. Don't understand how it is that this weekend—I still can't believe it—he will marry the pretty, blonde, artsy Colorado girl, the one he grew up with, in a simple, private ceremony.

Don't understand how the flirty, fiery brunette will have

her baby—a healthy, beautiful boy—with the father, whom she doesn't want to marry, by her side.

Really, it's crazy the way things work out sometimes, but I'm sure that someone must know what made them break apart—so suddenly, and so permanently, and so absent of the lingering, the wavering, the backtracking— before her passionate, daring weekend with her new love interest, and before his reunion with his childhood sweetheart. But even though their lives are going to be so separate now, from what I witnessed when they were together all those months, I know that their connection will always be there, somewhere deep within each of them.

To separate and move on with such quickness, such decision, such intent…it couldn't be otherwise. ∎

CRAIG BROCKLE

It's late and I'm behind the bar drawing a Sierra Nevada Pale Ale from the tap when Craig walks in, looking cute as always in jeans, a white button-up shirt, and cowboy boots. I glance at him and smile.

"Hi there, Jenna," he says, rather softly. "What? Are you bartending tonight?"

"Oh no, not me!" I say, laughing. (I can draw draft beers and make a few mixed drinks—probably more than the average person—but to bartend alone for an entire evening? I wouldn't feel comfortable doing that.) "Actually, Nick is in the basement getting another keg of Budweiser," I explain. "We ran out of it a little while ago, so I'm just trying to hold down the fort until he gets back, which shouldn't be hard, since things are extremely quiet right now," I say as I place the Sierra Nevada on the bar in front of Chuck, one of our late-night regulars, a blond, full-bodied guy who often comes in after his shift is over at the Barnes & Noble bookstore directly across the street, where he is a manager. He wears his name tag on his shirt with much pride, never seeming to remember to take it off.

Craig stands in the entranceway for a moment, then he heads toward the last bar stool to his left, quite far away from where Chuck is sitting. This really surprises me, because Chuck is the only person sitting at the bar, and Craig is usually quite sociable. Plus, I'm almost positive that the two of them have met before. Craig does acknowledge Chuck with a friendly hello, however.

"So, Craig," I say, placing a little square napkin in front of him. "Will it be your usual tonight?"

"You got it," he replies.

I turn my back to him, walk a few steps, open the door to the cooler—which sits to the right of the shelves of liquor and the cash register—bend down, and grab a Red Stripe from the bottom compartment. I then stand up, close the door, grab the bottle-cap opener and pop off the cap, take a small beer glass from the shelf under the cash register, turn around, walk a few more steps, and place both the glass and the beer on the bar in front of Craig. As I do so, he says thanks but glances away rather suddenly. I get the funny feeling that he was intently watching me the entire time.

"Sure, no problem," I reply, watching him pour the pretty-colored liquid out of the short, fatly round, dark brown bottle with the teeny opening at the top and the flourish of orangish-red on the side.

Just then, Nick appears from the back, heavily striding toward the bar, carrying a large silver keg against his stomach, his face beet red. I move out of his way.

"Craig!" he says, in his macho, exuberant tone, as he bends over and places the keg behind the bar, a deep sigh escaping. "What's going on, buddy?"

"Not too much, Nick. Just thought I'd stop in for a drink on my way home from work," he replies.

They continue to chat, and—amid Mick advising that "we all need someone we can lean on"—I busy myself greeting four customers who have just walked through the door. They ask to sit in the front of the restaurant, near the windows, so I lead them in that direction, which is not too far from where Craig is sitting. As we walk by him, I notice that he quickly glances at them, an uncomfortable look on his face.

What's bothering Craig tonight? I try to concentrate on taking the customers' drink orders, but I wonder if I should approach Craig and ask him if something is wrong.

After I take the orders, I walk around to the other side of the bar, across from where Craig is sitting, and I call out the drinks to Nick. I stand there leaning against the bar, waiting for Nick to make the drinks, occasionally looking at Craig. Strangely, he is looking down, playing with the ends of his bar napkin.

Well, I'm definitely going to ask him if everything's okay. I decide that I'll say something to him after I get the table in the front all taken care of.

In a matter of minutes I put the drinks on a small round tray and deliver them to the table. After I ask the customers if I can get them anything else, and they shake their heads no, not really even looking at me because they are already completely consumed with trying their drinks, puffing away, and chatting, I put the tray down by my side and am about to turn around and walk in Craig's direction when…

"Jenna—uh—when you have a minute, could I talk to you?"

I turn in the direction of the voice, and there is Craig, looking over his shoulder at me. I pause for a few seconds, taken a bit off guard, but then I reply, "Well, sure…I have a minute now."

As I walk the few short steps to where he is sitting, he reaches his right hand into the right back pocket of his jeans and quickly takes something out. He then, just as quickly, places his hand safely in his lap.

"What's up?" I ask, as I slither onto the bar stool beside him, trying to act as natural as possible.

"Well, I—" he starts, glancing around, as if to be certain

that no one is watching him. (Nick is now busy examining the liquor shelves, taking stock of what liquor he needs to order.) Craig then hunches over a bit and turns toward me slightly, so I turn toward him in response. Cautiously, he raises his hand from his lap, eventually revealing what he has been keeping hidden. He places his secret on the bar but makes sure to keep it within the space he has created between the two of us.

Extremely curious by this point, I look down slowly, and on the bar are two skinny, rectangular, yellow tickets, with the words "Illusions Dance Company" printed on them in black, bold text. Pleasantly surprised, I look Craig in the eye, but he doesn't say anything, apparently feeling more comfortable to let the tickets do the talking for him. So I say something instead.

"Craig—two tickets to the Illusions concert. That's so cool... Come to think of it, I'm pretty sure I read a short review about the concert a few weeks back, but I really don't know that much about the company, except that they are from Canada, I think, and they're an all-male company, if I remember correctly...but you must be really interested in them if you got tickets for the show..."

"Well, actually," he begins, clearing his throat, "*In Pittsburgh* gives out free tickets to its employees every once in a while—one of the nice perks about working there—and it was my turn. So I thought it would be fun to check it out, to do something different for a change...and, well, to tell you the truth, you immediately popped into my mind. I know that the company may be a little too modern and avant-garde for you, according to what we've discussed before about what kind of dance styles you like, but the more I thought about it, the more I realized that you were the only person I knew who would truly appreciate going to a show like that, so...so...what do you think? Do you think that maybe you would you like to go?"

His eyebrows rise in expectation.

"Oh yeah, of course—I'd love to go! Going to the theater is one of my favorite things," I immediately reply.

"Yeah?" he says, apparently shocked by my quick answer.

"Yeah," I answer.

"Well, that's great…just great," he says, nodding and smiling. He picks up his beer, himself once again.

******

I AM ALMOST READY, applying another coat of my favorite long-lasting soft-plum lipstick, which I always wear (it makes my eyes look even bluer than they already are), when my cranky buzzer buzzes. I quickly put the cap on my lipstick, throw it in my purse, grab my white, pearl-buttoned sweater and keys off my bed, and take a final look in my bathroom mirror. Looking good! I run my fingers through my silky curls, the result of my trusty hot curlers.

I open my apartment door, hastily walk out, and then close the door and lock it. Next, I rush down the crooked, winding stairs to the first floor, pull open the blue, solid front door, and then push open the screen door. There stands Craig, looking very polished in a trendy black suit, white shirt, black tie, black sunglasses, and black, leather ankle boots. "Wow!" I can't help saying. "You look great!" He walks toward me and steps just inside.

"So do you," he replies, taking off his sunglasses and furtively taking me in, glancing first at my face, then at the rest of me, his eyes traveling all the way down to my feet, and then all the way back up again. "That's really a great color on you."

I'm wearing a lime green outfit that my mom bought for me, which consists of a rather tight, ribbed, short-sleeved top with a short turtleneck, and a pair of those flowy harem-like pants with a tie around the waist that are so comfortable but make you feel so elegant at the same time. And on my feet are a pair of light brown, blocky-heeled, open-toed sandals that lace from just above my toes and all the way up to my ankles so that most of each foot can be seen peeking out through the laces. I absolutely love these sandals. They look stylish and dressy (and more important, make me feel that way, no matter what I wear them with), and the best part is that I bought them at the Payless shoe store located in my hometown, and they were only five dollars, part of a "Two Pairs for $10" sale. I've already worn these sandals for a few summers, not wanting to give them up. I know that it will be painful for me to commit them to the garbage.

"Thanks, Craig," I say. "My mom got this outfit for me."

Suddenly, the door to my left opens, and Beth walks out. She stops—abruptly—looks at me, and then at Craig. "Jenna— Craig— You two look really nice… What… What's going on?" She looks confused.

"Craig and I are on our way to a dance concert at the Benedum Center," I begin.

"Yeah, I got a few complimentary tickets from work, so we thought we'd check it out," Craig adds.

"Oh! Well," she says, giving us a nice smile, "that sounds like a lot of fun. I'm sure that you two will really enjoy it."

"Oh yeah, I'm really looking forward to it," I reply. "And what are you up to tonight, Beth? It looks like you're on your way out too."

"Yeah, I am, actually. I'm on my way to CMU to take a swim. I've been working so much lately, plus trying to keep up with school, I really haven't been exercising like I should," she explains, locking her door.

I want to ask her more—it has been a while since we've chatted, and she's such an interesting person—but I notice Craig glance at his watch.

"It's getting kind of late, right?" I ask him.

"Yes, yes it is. And sorry—I don't mean to be in a rush, but we actually should really get going," he says.

"You got it," I reply.

The three of us walk out the door, down the front steps, and onto the sidewalk, where we stop for a moment.

"It was really nice to see you again, Beth," Craig says, shaking her hand. "I haven't seen too much of you at the bar lately, although I have run into Mike a couple of times… You should try to stop in a little more."

"Oh, I will, once my schedule eases up a bit," Beth answers, sighing, as she glances up the street. "Oh! There's the bus." She begins to walk quickly toward the bus stop at the intersection of Forbes and Whiteman. "I can see it rounding the corner. I gotta go!"

"All right, Beth, take it easy," Craig says.

"I will. And you two have fun… See you later, Jenna!" she softly yells.

"Bye, Beth!" I softly yell back.

She breaks into a slow run, her very long, wavy brown hair reluctantly following her.

As I watch her, and as Craig opens the passenger door of his black Volvo for me and then shuts it after I am seated comfortably in the silky, form-fitting, cushy leather seat, I can't help but think what a good girl she is.

******

THE VOLVO STOPS ABRUPTLY, at a light that has just turned red.

I lurch forward.

"Dammit! Sorry about that, Jenna! Damn!... I thought I could make it through the light, but then I suddenly changed my mind… Are you okay?"

"Oh! Yeah, sure. Sure…sure, I'm okay. No problem, Craig. No problem at all," I say, glancing at him, noticing that he is blushing, and feeling like I've been awoken from a dream. "That kind of stuff happens to me too when I drive," I offer, trying to make him feel better.

I look out the window, and we are already in downtown Pittsburgh, on Grant Street, about five miles from my neighborhood. We've been chatting casually since we left my apartment, but he's been much quieter than I expected, and so have I. To be honest, I can sense that he is nervous, and I've been feeling rather nervous myself, which has surprised me. I've always felt so comfortable talking with him at the bar, but the instant he got into his car beside me and put his key into the ignition, I suddenly saw him in a different light, and a forceful wave of attraction overtook me.

Curiously, though—the unexpected can sometimes turn out to be good—the abrupt stop at the traffic light seems to have somehow helped ease the intense atmosphere in the car, because, as we round a corner, Craig points to a unique stone building across the street and comments on it just as naturally as ever. "That's a beautiful building, isn't it? It would be even more beautiful if someone would take the time to clean it up a little… I just don't think that the architecture in this city is appreciated enough," he says, a very sincere look on his face.

"That *is* really a beautiful building, Craig," I reply, looking intently at it, never having noticed it before since it is located a few blocks away from Point Park College, where I am pursuing my dance degree, and I've never made it down this way.

We keep going at a slow pace, stopping every now and then because of the traffic, when we eventually pass by a building that, this time, catches my eye first. "Oh, dear god, Craig," I say, my head almost completely out the window, "is that the *Cricket* that Nick and Curt and some of the guys at The Grill are always talking about?"

Craig slows down a little, looks past me, and out my window. Once his eyes set on the building, he looks away and says, "No, that's not the infamous place, but a place just like it. The Cricket is in Oakland." He almost sounds irritated.

"Oh, I'm sorry," I reply, feeling like maybe I shouldn't have brought it up. "Apparently you're not a fan of the place like the rest of them are."

"Well, you know, it's just that I can't understand why they feel the need to go there. I mean, I can *understand* it. Naked women are beautiful, of course, and to be honest, I enjoy looking at them too" (he glances at me, immediately recognizing that maybe he's said too much), "but to go and drink and stare at them all night long, to belittle them like that… I know that they just do it as a form of fun, and the women are essentially allowing themselves to be belittled by having that job in the first place, but I just don't think it's right, and I have no interest in doing that kind of stuff."

Wow! Given the subject matter, I feel a twinge of embarrassment, but I'm completely impressed with his frankness, and I know, from conversations that I've had with him before, that he isn't saying all of that stuff just for my benefit. I can tell that he means everything he's saying, and I appreciate being with someone who isn't afraid to be himself with me. I know now that the evening is going to turn out to be even better than I had expected.

When we get to the theater, we find our seats and talk until the show starts. He tells me all about a book he's reading on Nikola Tesla. He is obviously completely fascinated by the engineer and inventor and all he created. We also talk about his design and advertising job at *In Pittsburgh*, the Burgh's weekly news and entertainment newspaper, which I always enjoy reading, and about the spacious warehouse he rents and lives in on the North Side. Jane Smiley and her Pulitzer Prize–winning novel, *A Thousand Acres*, are also a topic of conversation. He completely loved the book and promises to bring his dog-eared paperback copy into The Grill for me to read. As I begin to tell him that I would really appreciate that, the lights dim and the curtain rises.

The dance concert is definitely unique, different from anything I've seen before, and I've seen quite a few dance companies perform, including the Dance Alloy, the Paul T. Jones and Arnie Zane Dance Company, and Slippery Rock University's dance company. To begin with, the show is only forty-five minutes long, with no pauses or intermissions like most shows have. And for this entire time, a group of fifteen dancers (all male), dressed in yellow overcoats, stand shoulder to shoulder in an unbreaking line, walking in unmistakable unison on one platform and then the next, as the platforms rise and fall and move in various diagonals of varying heights and slopes. What is most unusual is that during the entire show the dancers' faces are as expressionless as stone, and they keep their arms stiffly to their sides.

Craig was right when he had predicted that the style of dancing wouldn't be my favorite. I love it when the choreography allows for the arms and faces of the dancers to change freely and frequently according to the music and what is being felt within. But I am nonetheless fascinated by the exactness with which the men move and stay together, forming one unit. Not one step is out of place or is executed at the wrong moment. It is a display of the utmost discipline.

"Impressive," Craig says. The dancers have just finished taking their final bow. "That was certainly something."

"You've got that right," I say as I stand up and start to put on my sweater. Craig gently assists me. "I can't even imagine how many hours of rehearsal it took to reach that level of precision. It's quite remarkable if you really think about it."

"It is," he says, smiling, "and I knew you'd appreciate it."

It takes a while, but we eventually make it out of the theater and head toward the parking garage. "So," Craig says, as he places his hand on the small of my back, "we could always stop in at The Grill for a drink if you'd like before dinner…but I…"

"Yeah, Craig," I say, not needing for him to explain any further, "I don't think it's the best idea either." We both know that Jack might be there. True, Jack and I broke up a while ago, but Jack still doesn't seem to be okay with it. Plus, Craig and Jack are pretty good friends, and there is really no point in causing problems between friends if it can be avoided.

"Let's go somewhere else then," he says.

"Sounds great."

We get in the car and head to one of Craig's most favorite places to eat: Kaya. It is a Caribbean restaurant that opened a few months ago on Smallman Street in the Strip District. The Strip District is a one-half square-mile area near downtown Pittsburgh, between the Allegheny River and the Hill District. It is the city's market district, selling— among many other delicious items—fresh fish, meats, fruits, olives, cheeses, breads, and coffee. Smallman Street is one of the Strip's most unique streets. It is lined with warehouses on one side, and dance clubs, restaurants, and bars—many of which used to also be warehouses—on the other. In the evenings, lit by a few streetlights and a few red neon signs, it has a dark, alluring, and mysterious feel.

"Ever been here?" Craig asks as we unexpectedly find a parking spot almost directly in front of the restaurant.

"No, but I'm surely looking forward to it," I reply.

"You're gonna love it."

We sit at a small square table not too far from the fancy, people-lined bar with the colorful tile backsplash and the colorful bottles of varying vibrant shades. The lights are low and soulful, and Spanish guitar music is softly playing. I order a margarita on the rocks with salt, and he has his usual. Our appetizer of choice is grilled alligator—"You just *have* to try it," Craig tells me. I'm a little skeptical, but I decide to be daring, which pays off. The alligator is absolutely delicious: tender, juicy, dripping, marinated pieces served on a couple of long, pointy skewers.

For our main course, we share the special of the evening: soft-shelled crabs, asparagus, and brown rice. As we eat, gently taking small pieces from the large plate between us, we comfortably chat and laugh, talking about The Grill, talking about our mutual acquaintances, talking about our expectations for love and work, pausing every now and then to comment on how perfectly the food has been prepared.

Later, after our dinner plates are cleared and the waiter slides that delicate little knife-like tool across the table to remove the stray crumbs, Craig leans back in his chair and smiles. "Delicious, right?" he says.

"Yes, delicious," I agree, gently wiping my top lip with my napkin. "I'll definitely be coming back here again, you can be sure of that."

"And how about some dessert?" he asks, moving

toward the table and resting his forearms and weight upon it, a look of satisfaction in his eyes, which are looking directly into mine.

"Of course," I say, looking directly back. "It's a must—always."

We enjoy two steamy, frothy cappuccinos in feel-good-to-the-touch mugs, and a picture-perfect crème brûlée. I do the honors of cracking the crispy, caramel-colored covering, exposing the creamy, delicate perfection within.

More than an hour later, the check arrives. I hesitate for a moment, but then I reach under my seat for my purse and start to open it.

"Jenna," Craig says, gently putting up his hand, his wrist still resting on the table. He takes his wallet from his back pocket, opens it, and slides out a credit card. Instead of looking at the check before placing the credit card on top of it, he looks at me and says, "It's my pleasure."

******

AROUND ONE, we pull along the curb in front of my apartment. Craig turns off the car. We sit there for a minute.

"Well," he says, glancing over at me.

"Well," I say, glancing back.

"Well, Jenna, I must say, I had a really great time."

"I did too, Craig. I did too…"

I involuntarily look down at my hands. And then: "Do…do…"

Craig involuntarily coughs.

"Do you maybe want to come in for a little while?"

Did I just say that?

He doesn't say anything, but a few more involuntary coughs escape, and eventually he shakes his head no. "Jenna…I…I…that sounds great, but it's late, and I really

270

need to get up early in the morning to finish some work for the paper."

"Okay, Craig, no problem," I say, feeling this strange sensation of relief and rejection.

He does walk me to my door, though, and as he says goodbye, he gently but firmly shakes my hand. So I enter my apartment building, but instead of heading for the stairs, I stand in the small vestibule for a moment, peeking out of the skinny, vertical window that lies just to the left of the front door. Then, with a warmth and an excitement in my heart that have been put there by a night full of both elegance and realness, I watch him walk down the steps, get into his car, and drive away. ∎

USHER OF LOVE

One night after a Pirates game at vibrant Three Rivers Stadium, he walks through the door in a new ball cap and a shiny, bright-yellow jacket that reaches down to his knees, with large, enticing pockets. He smiles at me, reaches into his right-hand pocket, and takes out an extremely dense, inviting roll of bills. He then holds the money up in front of my face and fans through it with his thumb, like it's a deck of cards. I see ones, fives, tens, and even a few twenties flashing before my eyes.

"Look at the night *I* had!" he utters proudly, his tanned skin glowing.

******

ANIL, my CMU Ballroom Dance Club partner, receives free tickets to a Pirates game. I tell Tommy that I'm going to be at the game and will look for him.

"*Look* for me?" he asks, surprised. "Come to my section and, if I'm able to, I'll fix you two right up."

Boy, he isn't kidding. When he spots me quite a few rows above him, as I'm looking around, a bit bewildered, he quickly heads my way, up the wide, concrete steps. I hand him our tickets (which are for about three levels higher, as far as I can tell). But he glances at them, squeezes my hand discreetly, and whispers in my ear, "You two just wait here for a second, but keep your eyes on me." So we do. And he walks down the steps as if he owns the entire stadium, including the people in it, and he surveys his section—with such an air of professionalism, and seriousness, that I begin to wonder if it is really him, if a Tommy look-alike hasn't taken his place. But soon, the familiar, happy smile is there again, as he turns around and signals to us with his eyes, his hand placed firmly on the back of one of the seats he has chosen, just a few rows from the field—and directly behind home plate.

"*Thanks*, Tommy!" I say, intensely but softly, once we reach him, and as he passes the ticket stubs into my hand. "This is so great!"

"You're welcome, sweetheart," he replies. "I hope you two really enjoy the game."

With seats like these, how could we not? Just to be able to see the players' expressions so clearly, to feel the speed and the accuracy with which the ball is thrown and hit, to witness the way the athletes move so freely in their bodies—it doesn't matter who wins.

******

AS PART OF A LATIN festival, and as members of Pittsburgh's Latin American Cultural Union, my friend Mariano and I have been invited to perform a short salsa routine. But it isn't going to be just any salsa routine performed just anywhere. We are going to dance between innings at a Pirates game, on top of one of the dugouts!

"Guess what, Tommy?" I ask him one day as he's leaning against the bar, sipping a Pepsi.

"What's that, honey?" he responds, giving me his complete attention.

So I tell him all about the upcoming event, my hands flying everywhere, and he says that he's scheduled to work that night and will keep an eye out for me, giving me a general idea of what section he'll most likely be in.

"And I'm so glad I'm finally getting the chance to see you perform," he adds, winking and kissing me affectionately on the cheek.

******

FOR THE NEXT FEW WEEKS, Mariano and I practice hard, dancing the routine countless times in his living room, mercilessly wearing down the carpet. And then after each rehearsal, over beer and hot wings, we imagine how exciting it will all be, discuss just what we will wear, and feel so fortunate to have such a unique opportunity.

Therefore, when the big day arrives—a sunny, warm, beautiful day—we are ready, Mariano dressed in slim, black slacks; a black, collared, silk shirt; and black Cuban shoes; and me in a short, colorful, flowery dress with a flared skirt, a black cotton sash tied in a knot around my waist, and black character shoes, the choreography fresh and imprinted on our minds.

Waiting behind the scenes, going over the steps again and again (just to be sure!), it seems to take forever, but eventually the third out—of the bottom of the fourth inning, to be exact—is called, and we jog down the steps toward the field and wait for our cue. "Please welcome Pittsburgh's one-and-only Latin American Cultural Union giving us some salsa!!!" the announcer booms over the loudspeakers. With our adrenaline and excitement in full force, we run onto the home dugout through a small gate in the iron fence that separates the first row of seats from the field, as Marlon and Nancy (two more members of our group) do the same on the opposite side of the stadium. The music starts, with its varying rhythms and syncopation, and our feet begin to move. Unfortunately, we don't have much room (the edge is *right* there!), but somehow we don't have to try even a little bit to remember the choreography—it just appears on our bodies. And really, it's no wonder I like to dance so much: Performing in front of all these people and being in the midst of all the bursting energy that ball games are so good for—I don't think I could feel much better.

After the performance, however, Mariano and I are walking around the inner perimeter of the stadium, past all the food and souvenir stands—trying to calm down and catch our breath a bit, excitedly talking about what we just experienced—when I notice Tommy to my right, standing at the top of one of the sloping entrances to the stadium, looking around expectantly. "Tommy!" I yell. Almost as if on cue, his face lights up and he opens his arms wide.

Without a moment's thought, I run toward him and fall into his hug—his warm, welcoming, and soft hug. "It's so good to see you—did you see us dance?" I ask.

"I sure did… That was *wonderful*! You were even up on the big screen for a few seconds! And what an amazing dancer you are!"

"Oh, I'm so glad you didn't miss it, Tommy!" I reply.

"Miss it? Now why would I ever do *that*…" he says, smiling and giving me another big hug.

Tommy has proved me wrong. ∎

CAUGHT

Here we are in the kitchen, Mary Ellen and I, both of us enjoying "Build Me Up Buttercup," which is being piped through her little radio and the oldies station she's so committed to. She's singing freely and twirling her apron strings, and I'm grooving to the music, totally engrossed in the song, my hips doing things they most probably shouldn't be doing at my place of work.

Nick. (Oh god.) What? Here he is with us, suddenly, like what seems out of nowhere. And not only does he see my hips of abandon, but here I am—oh, the horror—a couple of juicy, thick french fries hanging halfway out of my mouth.

Nick stops abruptly, and I stop swaying, trying to inconspicuously chew and swallow the rest of the fries, as if it's really possible for me to do that. I can feel the hot grease all over my lips.

"You—of all people—*you* know better than that," he begins, a look of disgust…and disappointment…on his face. "You were already told not to do it."

So here I stand, once again—speechless, my heart pounding—feeling like I used to feel when my first-grade teacher, Sister Eileen, scolded me for not knowing an answer to an obvious question during her rapid round of questioning she executed every day before lunch.

I guess I let him down. ∎

THE NEXT LEVEL

She's been a waitress here at The Grill for almost five years now, and I've worked with her for the past two. Tomorrow, however, she says goodbye to this station and enters the big leagues—as a bartender. And it's about time. At least I know she thinks so. She certainly has all the skill, knowledge, and personality necessary for it, and the fact that she's a woman isn't going to be held against her any longer. Now that Adam is marrying Tanya and leaving for Colorado, she's finally being given her long-overdue chance.

I know she'll be a wonderful bartender. How could she not? I mean, if she bartends like she waitresses, she'll be going home with overflowing pockets each and every night.

I can just see it. There'll be the *Monday Night Football* games, and she'll be standing behind the packed bar, cheering, rooting, clapping, laughing, and yahooing for the Steelers as if she were one of the guys, her eyes bright and active, fitting in perfectly. There'll be the calmer Wednesday nights, with only two or three people at the bar, and she'll be chatting and commiserating with a lost soul. There'll be the chaotic Friday and Saturday nights when there's no time to talk to anyone, but she'll be adept at making drinks quickly and correctly and will always stay in control.

And then there'll be the pride—that pride of hers—oozing out even more than it already does.

In her defense, being a bartender is, I have to say—in practical and monetary terms at least—quite a step up from being a waitress. First of all, she won't have to run around like she's on speed anymore—well, not as high a dose. Secondly, she will certainly be paid much more an hour, probably more than twice as much as we waitresses and waiters get paid, and will often make as much serving a person a few drinks as she used to make waiting on a table of four. Plus, most of the regulars who sit around the bar know her well and like her, so that obviously won't hurt. And neither will her looks.

On top of all that, she'll possess the increased authority that comes with the job. In fact, she'll be in charge of telling the "early person out" when he or she can leave—depending on how busy we are—something that she used to be told to do. She'll have the power to give the "almighty last call." And she'll be the person who does the credit card report, who takes stock of the liquor, who closes the place. That's right—the one who turns out the lights.

So watch out, everyone. Here comes Bianca…Bianca times two.

Are you ready? ◼

MY SECRET TREASURE

"It happened, didn't it?" he says very quietly, but directly, standing close—almost touching me—as I stuff the "Specials" sheets into the menus.

I turn my eyes away, and continue with my task, not saying anything for quite a while. "How…how did you know?" I eventually ask, very perplexed, my voice—and my hands—shaking.

"I just knew. I could just tell."

He is, to be honest, the first—and the only—person who knows. The only person who knows that it finally happened, and that it happened with my ballroom dance partner. (It was just a matter of time, after all.) Not even Teeli knows, in fact, because I'm scared to tell her. And I don't know why. Maybe it's because I've always felt, and probably unfairly, that she too has been holding me up to the moral standard I've set for myself—one that she wouldn't even imagine setting for herself—and I'm afraid of letting that image down.

And then forget about my parents. Not that I couldn't tell them *anything* if I really needed to. But what in the world would they think of me?

But Tommy—he's figured it out even before I've had the chance to tell him (you do have to be careful what you say around here, and when you say it). And he's been so supportive and comforting about the whole thing, not laying a judgmental eye or word on me for a second.

How lucky am I, then, to have him, to have someone else in the world I can unapologetically share my secret with, to have a person I can tell all the good and none of the bad? And so what if this person is a mischievous, older man I've met through work? Come to think of it, that's probably the main reason I'm not freaked out that he knows. Because, when it comes down to it, he has no connection to my family or to any of my really close friends. Sure, he knows most of my coworkers, some of them very well, but that's okay, because he's like a cherished, private journal that holds my sacred news. In essence, he's even better than a journal, because the information he possesses can't be searched for in my drawer and stolen by any other person, can't be mistakenly left available on my writing table in a moment of heedlessness. The only way that my secret will be revealed is if he voluntarily reveals it, and I know, in my heart, that he won't. ■

THE LATE-NIGHT ENCOUNTER

My boyfriend and I walk in late to Samantha and Mark's New Year's Eve party (Samantha and Mark are good friends of my coworker Bianca; they hang out at The Grill often). We spent most of the evening salsa-ing and merengue-ing at Cozumel's, a restaurant cum nightclub on Walnut Street in Shadyside. Guaracha was playing, one of Pittsburgh's best Latin bands.

Samantha, Mark, Bianca, and Jack (who shoots us quite a look), as well as a few other guests whom I don't know, are sitting around a card table in the back of the apartment, laughing, drinking, and playing board games. Diana, however—she's standing in the front of the apartment by the Christmas tree, gazing at the lights, an almost-full beer in her hand.

Samantha, an interesting young woman with short, straight, black hair, who is totally into tarot card reading, rushes over to greet us. (She often sits in one of The Grill's booths in the nonsmoking section, doing a reading for a daring soul, her colorful and detailed cards spread out on— and completely covering—the table in front of her.) "Hey, you two! Thanks for coming. Could I start you off with something to drink? We've got just about anything you could want."

"That'd be great," Anil says to Samantha. Then he looks

at me. "What would you like, Jenna?"

"An I.C. Light would be fine," I reply.

"Okay, but I'm not exactly sure what I want yet, though," he says. "Could I take a look at what you've got, Samantha?"

"Sure, no problem. Come on into the kitchen with me. It's all in there."

"Okay," Anil responds. "Are you coming along, Jenna?"

"Actually…would you mind getting my drink for me? I think I'm gonna chat with Diana for a few minutes," I softly say, motioning in her direction.

"Yeah, that would probably be a good idea," Anil whispers, glancing at Diana, whose back is toward us.

"Hey, Diana, how's it going?" I say, walking over to her.

"Oh, Jenna!…" she says, rather startled, looking over her shoulder. "What, me? Oh, I'm okay… Yeah, I'm okay." She turns to me and weakly smiles. Her eyes look on fire, though, and she seems totally different.

"Is everything all right? Why are you standing over here all by yourself?"

She looks at me for a few seconds, then down at the floor, then back at me again, then away. "Oh, well, I…I…uh…I have a lot on my mind…"

Apparently. "Oh, okay," I answer, trying not to be too intrusive, but then Diana doesn't seem to know what to say, so I offer, "Do you maybe want to talk about it?"

"No, no…no…I don't think so…" she says, looking at her feet. But then she quickly looks up, her eyes still glowing. "Well, actually, you know what? I can trust you, right?… And besides, what does it *really* matter? It will be general news at The Grill in no time," she says, raising her eyebrows.

I couldn't agree with her more, thinking to myself how

incredibly fast any type of news (especially juicy news) travels through that little place.

She must sense my agreement, because, suddenly, as if she were a bull just let out of the pen, she throws off whatever is restraining her and tells me all about the wonderful, crazy, impulsive, totally fabulous night she had with—

"CRAIG??? Craig BROCKLE???!!!" I interrupt her, trying to keep my voice low, although there is no disguising its intensity.

"Jenna!!! No, no, no… Not *that* Craig—the *other* Craig," she says, her lips pursed, her eyes widening, and a sharp nod of her head trying to enlighten me of the name without her having to actually say it.

"The *other* Craig?"

I pause for a second, thinking. But then it comes to me. "What?… You don't mean Craig…" (take a breath) "*NEWBERT?*" (take a breath) "*Do you?*" (take a breath) "*GLOBY???????!!!!!!!!!!!!!*" I burst out, amazed. (In case you're wondering, "Globy" is the nickname that Craig's best buddies have given him because of the size of his head… You know—you get it, don't you? Large, like a globe…. But—then again—maybe it's simply because he used to always have a bowling ball in his hand. In all honesty, I really don't know.)

"Shh… Shhhhhh… Not so loud—*please*, Jenna," Diana says, quickly glancing around to see if anyone has noticed. But everyone seems pretty engrossed in a game of building blocks, watching Bianca try to remove one of the center blocks without causing the entire tower to collapse. And Anil is at the food table, happily filling his plate with cheese, crackers, and olives.

"Sorry, sorry… I just…"

"Oh, I *know*, Jenna. He is just…beautiful. And the

whole experience was just…beautiful," she says, shaking her head, "and so unexpected."

Two weeks prior, she and Craig and some others had been hanging out at Curt's apartment on Northumberland Street one night after she and Curt had gotten off of work (which would have been around two o'clock in the morning). They were all enjoying themselves—drinking, smoking, laughing, and listening to music—the usual spontaneous, after-work party scene. By four or five in the morning, though, most of the partyers had gone home, and Curt had given up and finally gone to bed, having to be back at The Grill by eleven. Diana and Craig were still hanging out, however, lounging on Curt's black leather couch, turned toward each other, talking, enjoying the calming music, getting to know a little more, and a little more, and a little more about each other. And, as so often happens when youth, loneliness, alcohol, music, fatigue, and the mystery of that in-between time, between dusk and dawn, collide—a volatile mix, for sure—one inadvertent, soft brush of the arm leads to another brush…maybe not so inadvertent…and all sense of rationality is tucked away under the covers, under as many layers as you can put it, and desire wins.

"Unexpected?" I say. "Well, yeah, those kinds of situations always are that way…so unexpected…totally unexpected… But what…what do you think will happen from here? Are you guys gonna start going out?" I ask, dying to know.

"Oh, Jenna, I would *love* to. But…you know…he says he needs some time to think about it and doesn't want to rush into anything—as if we haven't *already* rushed into something. You know how all of that goes, though. And, really, what can I do? I'll just have to wait and see what happens," she says, her voice saturated with hope. ■

A BETTER QUESTION

Now, when I run into Tommy on the street—in what I believe is an unorthodox, serendipitous loop of fate, it just happens so often—instead of asking me, "How's that boyfriend of yours?" like he used to do, he always gets that sly look on his face, moves back a few steps, lowers his chin, and says under his breath, "How's your sex life? You're being careful, aren't you?" Of course, he can never let go of his joking nature completely. In addition to this bit of concern and advice, he never forgets to add, in the most humorous and flattering tones available, "That boyfriend of yours is so…*damn*…*lucky*. If I were in his shoes, I'd…and I'd…and I'd…"

Well, I'm sure you can fill in the rest. ∎

JONATHAN

His black hair is so greasy. Greasy and stringy. So much so, that as he sits contentedly at the bar for two hours and sips from his pint glass full of ice, Pepsi, and a straw—as he does almost every day—it practically clings to his fingers when he brushes it to the side, out of his eyes.

He's really not unattractive, however. About five-six, not dangerously overweight but a bit chubby and out of shape, he dresses decent enough and wears serious, smart glasses. And although he's quite reserved, eccentric, and unusual, I've never seen him be mean to anyone, and never can imagine him being so.

Plus, today he has a thick, cream-colored hardcover along with him, keeping company with his Pepsi…

I'm so glad for this. For the past week, he's been his other self—glassy-eyed, hollow, vacant. Leaving almost as soon as he sits down. The Pepsi and the surrounding people failing to help. The familiar words—*he must not be taking his medicine again*—coming from Nick, as he sadly watches him disappear out the door.

But today there's the book.

"Hey, Jonathan!" I say, as I rinse a rag out in the sink behind the bar. "How's it going today?"

He looks up abruptly. He has been staring down at the top of the bar, as he's prone to do.

"Oh, Jenna…I'm good… Yeah, I'm good… How are you?"

"Can't complain, Jon," I reply, walking around the bar and sitting halfway on the stool beside him. "You know, the usual workday."

It's amazing how much better his eyes look today—like there's actually someone inside.

"What's that you're reading, Jon?" I ask as I point to the book. I'm really very curious.

Slowly, he picks up the book and turns the spine toward me.

"*The World According to Garp*," I read. "By John Irving… Oh, how cool, Jon… What do you think of it?"

"It is *really* great, Jenna," he replies, his eyes becoming even more alive as he flips through the pages. "Yeah, some of the stuff in it is really pretty crazy…just crazy—but you just have to guess where I got this."

"Oh, I don't know, Jon," I reply, thinking. "How about at Barnes & Noble across the street?"

He shakes his head mischievously.

I try again. "Okay, then. The Squirrel Hill Bookstore on Forbes."

"No!" he says, unable to wait any longer. "The Squirrel Hill Library!… And for only *fifty cents*! Can you *believe* that?"

"Wow, Jonathan. That's awesome!" I say, thoroughly impressed, realizing how much a good hardcover costs these days.

"Yeah, they have a few shelves in the entranceway set up with used books on sale, and every now and then, if I look hard enough, I come across a great find, like this one," he says, holding up the book once again.

"Oh *yeah*, Jon, now that you mention it, I have browsed those shelves before, but the only things I ever found of use were a few computer and math books, which I used to prepare for exams that I could take to test out of the requirement to take the actual courses at Point Park. You know, so that I wouldn't have to spend the extra money on the courses. But anyway, I'll really have to go back and check it out again… Maybe I could find some good literature there, too… But you know, Jon, I've actually been meaning to read the *Garp* book. I saw the movie with Robin Williams a few years back, and it seemed so interesting. Besides, I usually always enjoy the book much better anyway."

"Oh, me too…me too," he comments, nodding his head. "Well, you know, as soon as I'm finished—I'm about three-quarters of the way through now—you're welcome to borrow it. And then…" (almost all of the life has returned to his eyes now) "…we can talk about it!"

******

FROM THE FIRST SENTENCE, I'm enraptured by the book—and its author. The sexuality. The humor. The reality. The exaggeration. The crudeness. The unfathomable imagination.

I take it with me on my trip to Boston when my boyfriend, Anil, moves there. While he's enduring his first week at work, I spend the afternoons reading in the beautiful, sunny Public Garden—surrounded by weeping willows, unending flowers, swan boats floating on the lake, painters and their canvases, and dreamy cherub fountains—or on the hot, front steps of the old, stately brownstone on Marlborough Street, where we are staying for two weeks. Reading about Garp's first trip to Vienna—his detailed descriptions of the stately buildings, mansions, culture, and museums—I feel that I am in a Vienna of my own.

Back at The Grill, in quite another Vienna, I laugh and

laugh and Jon chuckles and chuckles as we go back and forth, and back and forth, discussing and relating scene after scene to each other: "Could you believe that incident with the pigeons?" "Have you ever heard a prostitute described like *that* before?" "How about all of that couple swapping…and Garp and Helen seem surprisingly so okay with it?"

There is just so much crazy stuff in the book to talk about, and Jon and I are having plenty of crazy fun doing just that.

******

I'M DROPPING A TIP into my basket behind the bar and I hear "Guess what, Jenna?" excitedly coming toward me.

I turn around, and there sits Jonathan, his usually passive hands laced tightly behind—could it be?—a thin, tall glass of cranberry juice.

"What's that, Jon?" I reply, looking at him expectantly.

"Well…" And he pauses, as if he won't be able to go on if he doesn't. "Earlier today…yes, earlier today…I went for an interview at the high school nearby. You know, the one on Friendship Avenue."

I nod quickly.

"Well, they're looking for people to teach chess to the students there during club time."

"Wow, Jon, *chess*? I didn't know that you played chess." I am so surprised, but, on second thought, not really. "A friend of mine tried teaching that to me once and I found it extremely confusing and difficult."

"Oh sure, it is at first. But I've been playing chess my whole life. It does take time, you know, but once you get it…"

"Yeah, I can see that. But chess—it just seems so complex, like you have to have a pretty mathematical mind to really excel at it. There just seems to be so much…so much…strategy involved in it," I try to explain.

"Well, you're right about that. But, you know…" (and the words seem to come to him so easily now) "…give it time and practice, and lots of patience, and you learn to think ahead, to try to predict what is coming next, or what difficult position your opponent is going to put you in."

"Okay…"

"Yeah, some games, you fail, of course, and you are stuck, with no way to get out, and you feel defeated for a while, not wanting to play again, not wanting to touch the pieces or the board *ever* again… But the next game comes along, the next challenge, and something inside you, some overwhelming urge tells you to try again, and there you are, feeling better and more confident, like you could actually win…and you play, and think, and calm yourself, and work not only from your own energy but likewise from the energy of the person sitting across from you… And sure, the fear of losing is there all of the time, never quite leaves you, in fact, just cannot be completely washed away no matter how many times you try, but every once in a while, in some fortunate moment, before you know it, you're free from it, completely in control…and it's 'Checkmate!' and you've overcome the challenge."

✳✳✳✳✳✳

"IS EVERYTHING OKAY, Jon?" I ask, standing beside him.

It is a few days after the interview, and Nick has just placed a fizzing glass of Pepsi in front of Jon, having sweetly said as he did so, "There you go, partner."

"Thanks, Nick," Jon replies. His voice doesn't sound quite as happy as it did the other day, his back is a bit rounded, and his hair is all over the place.

"Jon," I repeat, softly. "Are you okay?"

He looks at me, saying nothing for a while, but then—

"I didn't get the job, Jenna," he says finally, shaking his head slowly. "No—they gave the main position to someone else."

"Oh, Jon," I reply, pulling out a stool and sitting beside him. "I'm so sorry…but at least you gave it a shot, you know. It's better than not having tried."

"Oh, I know, Jenna. I know."

Surprisingly, he is handling it much better than I expected.

"Besides, it's not all bad news. The woman I talked to this morning said that I could come in every once in a while and help out as an assistant if I wanted…which, after I thought about it, sounded like a pretty good thing to do… So, yeah, I decided that I'll probably do that. You know, meet some new people and be back in an academic environment again… It'll be fun."

He pulls the piece of paper off the tip of his straw and then takes a much-needed sip.

"Ah, Jon, now *that's* the spirit," I reply, touching him on the shoulder, so thoroughly proud of him—and so thoroughly inspired. ∎

SAME NAME, BUT DIFFERENT

I don't mean to, but I overhear her say it. "Yeah, Walter—Craig and I moved in together just about a week ago." I walk away quickly, not wanting to eavesdrop (plus, I have a just-made martini with a twist to deliver), but I, in all honesty, am shocked! "They moved *in* together?" I mutter to myself. "How did that happen…? Boy! I must *really* be out of the loop!" I add, inadvertently passing right by my customer.

But after fighting with myself and thinking about it for what must be at least two hours, I decide that the most up-front (and foolproof) thing to do is to walk right up to Diana and ask her about it directly.

"Hey, Diana, how's it going?" I begin. She is reaching into the refrigerator to take out an already-prepared salad.

"Not too bad, Jenna… How's everything with you? I haven't talked to you much lately. You've been really busy with school and all of your dancing, I guess?" she asks, glancing at me for a moment.

"Oh yeah, you bet. It's always a challenge trying to keep up with everything," I reply.

"I know exactly what you mean. I just *finally* finished moving all of my stuff into Craig's place—what a damn lot of work that was…" she says as she bends over the baker's table and pours some pepper-parmesan dressing into a little plastic container.

"Yeah, well…that's what I heard you telling…well I heard you telling that to Walter earlier this evening," I say, sheepishness spreading all over me.

She turns around quickly, looking straight at me, the shallow glass bowl of salad waiting patiently in her hand. "*What!* You mean you didn't know? I didn't mention it to you? I—"

I can't help but notice that through the radio in the kitchen, Alanis Morissette is just at that moment asking, *And isn't it ironic... Don't you think?*

"Well…no, Diana…no….but that's okay, you know. I just—I just thought that—I got the impression that Globy didn't want to get seriously involved with anyone right now…did he?"

"Globy!" she exclaims, laughing, almost dropping the salad. "No, no, no…no, Jenna. Not Craig Newbert—not Globy. I moved in with Craig. You know. With *Craig*. With Craig Brockle." She looks at me expectantly.

"Craig Brockle?" I reply, completely bewildered and not knowing what else to say, but seriously feeling like a lethal case of déjà vu has thumped me hard on the head.

"Oh, god, Jenna," Diana says, lightly punching my shoulder. "Don't worry; you don't need to say anything. Besides, I've already been teased to death about it—'What? It didn't work out with one Craig so you thought you'd sample another?'… 'What? We just bet you're playing the both of them, aren't you, you little salacious devil…' But why should I worry about what other people think?" she asks, almost seeming to direct the question to herself rather than to me. "But, in any case—you know how Craig usually comes in after midnight on Friday or Saturday nights to drink a Red Stripe or two?" she continues.

I nod.

"Well, we just started talking, and then talked some

more, then went out a couple of times, and really hit it off. We both knew that it was really quick, but we decided to give it a try and move in together, and then—oh freakin' shit! I better get this salad out before someone starts cursing me!" she says, grabbing a tray, suddenly realizing where she is. "Anyway, Jenna, he's so gentle, intelligent, and nice, what other choice did I have?" she adds, shrugging. She then quickly takes off, once again being swallowed by the commotion just beyond.

I stand on the spot for a moment, trying to take in everything she's told me, and I think about Craig Brockle—my mind suddenly being flooded with details of that night that he took me to the dance concert and to dinner—and I start comparing him to Craig Newbert. Although he looks much different from the other Craig— much, much shorter, a lot stockier, and a bit heavier—he's definitely attractive. And whereas Diana's first Craig (as I've mentioned before) has a mysterious, daring, intriguing masculinity about him, which makes you (or, *me*, to be candid) quite hesitant to sit beside him and start chatting (I don't remember ever having a really deep conversation with him), Diana's current Craig gives off a disarming, natural openness that assures you he'll be easier to find out about. He's quite shy at first—there's no mistaking that— but all you have to do is ask him about himself and he'll open up to you, and he likewise makes you feel comfortable enough to do the same. And the more you talk to him, and the more you see what he's all about, the more utterly attractive he becomes.

I don't blame her. ■

DIFFICULT TRANSITIONS

Tommy's here today—finally—but something's definitely wrong. I mean, why isn't he next to me, telling me a joke and giving me a squeeze? Well, this time, I'll just have to be the one who hurries over to him.

I sure have missed him. Strangely, for the past few months, he's stopped coming to The Grill as often as usual, and I can't remember the last time I ran into him on the street. I've really been wondering what's happened.

"Tommy? Hi… Where have you been?" I ask. I hope I don't sound too demanding. But he starts talking to me just as if we saw each other yesterday.

"Remember when I told you that my wife and I were thinking about moving from our home in Squirrel Hill to another house out in the country?"

"Yes, I do," I reply.

"Well, for the past two months we've been in the process of signing over the papers and moving all of our things. It's been really busy…" he says, his voice trailing off.

"A new home…wow! That must be nice… But you…you seem kind of sad. Is everything okay?"

"Well, no…not really. But yeah…oh I don't know. I guess I'm just having a really hard time with the change. I miss Squirrel Hill so much and miss being able to walk right out the door whenever I want and come over here to visit and go to Giant Eagle and all the other places I've been used to for so long. And it takes *forever* for me to get to Squirrel Hill now. I have to take two buses… Plus, it's so *damn quiet* out there. It's so damn dead…. But, oh well—what can I do now? More than twenty years in that beautiful, old house—and then we just get up and leave it. But what can I do now? I would've never moved in the first place if it had been up to me," he says, looking down and shaking his head.

"Oh, Tommy. I'm *really* sorry…so, so sorry. It'll probably just take some time to get used to it. Hang in there," I reply, putting my hand on his shoulder.

"I'll try. I'll really try," he says, as his eyes once again meet the floor.

I feel so bad for him—it's obvious that he's aching. My heart hurts for him, and I'm now being hit with that sick, regretful, nostalgic feeling that I see on his face and hear in his voice. How I wish I could do something, because I can understand, at least a little, how he is feeling. I'm also one of those people who gets so attached to particular places, and to all of the individuals and familiarities associated with the places: the coffee shop on the corner, the bank with the welcoming teller, the tree-lined street with the unusually structured houses, the music you can hear in the air as you walk home from work. There are those who don't—and I've met them. They can move from one location to another, leaving everything behind without a thought, so completely enamored with the excitement of something new.

"Well," he begins, without warning, a few minutes later, "it's about time for me to get going." And now, I am even more disturbed, because he hasn't told a single joke, hasn't cracked a single smile, hasn't flirted with me even a little bit. So I helplessly watch him pass through the front door and then wait for him to walk by the front window—which takes him so long to do. But then it takes me just as long to walk up to the bar and sit heavily onto a stool, and eventually look up at Curt. At least it's an extremely slow afternoon and no one else is around.

"He's pretty down today, isn't he?" Curt says, cocking his head to one side and propping his right foot upon the box of empty beer bottles sitting under the sink.

"Boy—you said it," I reply, wringing my hands. "I've *never* seen him like that before."

"Oh—I have," Curt replies, almost before he knows what he is saying. But then he adds, "And much worse than that."

"You're kidding."

Curt is silent for a moment as he looks at me searchingly, but then he says, "You're not one to gossip. Right?…Well, let me fill you in on a few things."

Curt confides in me that Tommy has suffered much in his life. He's been dealing with alcoholism for a very long time (although he seems to be winning the battle now), and his son…his only son…died from cancer—leukemia—a few years ago. As he tells me all this, I suddenly remember a little episode that probably would've never again passed into my consciousness otherwise. It's the time that I asked Tommy if I could get him an afternoon cocktail to cool him off, and he replied, the displeasure apparent in his voice, "I don't *touch* the stuff." Yes, after I seriously begin to think about it, I realize that the only thing I've ever seen him drink, other than a glass of water, is a glass of Pepsi, filled with lots of ice. "Give me a little bit of that, would ya, Curt?" he'll ask as he leans on the bar and points toward the tap gun, a look of expectancy in his brown, Italian eyes.

"But don't worry, Jenna… He'll be all right," Curt assures me. "You just watch. He'll be walking through that door in no time at all, armed with a new joke. Trust me. I know." ■

THE PHOTO SHOOT(S)

"I'd really love to get into a dance company. That's been a dream of mine since I can remember," I tell Walter. "Or even better than that—to dance on Broadway."

It's a Saturday afternoon, nearing the end of my shift, and like so many other Saturday afternoons before, Walter and I are casually talking about my dance classes at Point Park College, when I expect to graduate, and what I plan to do in the future.

"Wow—that sounds great, but it also sounds like a lot of hard work. Do you think that you're going to try to find something around here first?" Walter asks.

"I'll try, but there really aren't that many dance companies in Pittsburgh, especially jazz dance companies. There's the Dance Alloy, which is a modern dance company, and they only have around four or five dancers, so it would be really competitive to get a spot…and then there's the Pittsburgh Ballet… But, you know, I've actually been thinking about moving to Boston. My boyfriend moved there a few months ago to start a new job, and he really likes it there so far. And from what I saw of it in April when he and I went to a ballroom dance competition at MIT, I think I'd like it too. Of course, there aren't that many jazz companies there, either—if any—but dance in general has more of a presence there than here, so I could

298

probably train more there and see what happens. To tell you the truth, I don't think I'm ready to move to New York City yet, so Boston would be a good 'in-between' city, sort of a step up from a small city like Pittsburgh, and it would prepare me for a big city like New York. Plus, there are tons of publishing companies in Boston, so I could get a job at one of them to support myself and my dancing."

"Well," Walter says, nodding his head and scratching his beard, "it sounds like you have a plan."

"Yeah, I've been thinking about it for a while. But, you know, come to think of it, I really need to get some headshots taken soon so that I can take them with me when I go to auditions. They're so expensive, though," I say, shaking my head.

"That's what I've heard..." Walter replies, as his eyes turn inward and his right hand rests on his chin, lightly massaging his beard once again.

"Yeah, I really wish I could get some decent pictures taken, but for a decent price as well," I say. "However, that's not so easy to come by these days."

"Hmm, you're certainly right about that. But...but you know what?... I was thinking... Maybe I could help you out a bit. It just so happens that I have a camera and tripod at home and some black and white film, and...why don't I take some headshots of you? My camera is a bit old—but it's a quality camera—and I've been known to take a good picture in my time. Photography has been a hobby of mine for quite a while now, in fact... So," he asks, his face lighting up even more, "what do you think?"

I consider it for a quick moment, quite pleased by my fortune.

"Well, that sounds great, Walter!" I reply. "It would help me out so much!"

"Okay. Well then, it's settled then. Let's just figure out a time to do this. But, you know what? Maybe we should wait a few days until your face decides to cooperate," Walter advises.

Remmy is sitting nearby, waiting for new customers, and she can't help but overhear this comment. "Walter!!!" she bursts out, as her eyes get bigger and her mouth opens wide. "You shouldn't say that to someone!"

I don't know what to say, but blush in response, as usual.

"Okay, okay, but it's true. The fewer blemishes on the face, the better the picture… I was just being honest," he admits, shrugging his shoulders.

In the past, I would've been extremely hurt by such a comment, but considering my experiences so far at Point Park, where most of the dance professors are critical all the time, and brutally honest—"You look very boring," my theater dance professor told me not too long ago as I did some grand battements to the side—I take Walter's comment in stride. Anyway, I know that Walter isn't trying to be cruel but simply wants the photos to look their best.

******

WE DECIDE TO DO the "photo shoot" one Saturday afternoon that I have off, around four o'clock. We pick this time because it is usually a slower time of the day: The main dinner crowd doesn't start arriving until around five or five thirty. Obviously, we don't want to disturb anyone's drink or meal; plus, we want to avoid as much embarrassment and staring as possible—at least I know I do.

"Hi, Walter," I say as he walks in, a large black leather bag slung over his right shoulder, carrying all of his camera equipment. I arrived a few minutes ago and have been chatting with a few people at the bar. Honestly, I feel a bit out of place. I'm used to being dressed in a white or blue button-up, collared shirt; khaki shorts or slacks; and ugly, comfortable, black "old lady" shoes (as my brothers like to call them, teasing me), with my hair pulled back, away from my face. Now I'm dressed in a stretchy, tight, U-neck, short-sleeve, light pink top, and my hair is down and curled. I'm also wearing bright-pink lipstick and my dangling, maroon, East Indian–style earrings that my mom bought for me. I feel as if my current persona doesn't fit the persona I'm used to exhibiting in this place.

"You look nice," Walter says.

"Thank you. And thank you so much for coming," I reply.

"My pleasure," he says, looking me directly in the eye. "So, you want to get started?"

As Walter unpacks his bag, sets up the tripod, and adjusts this and that knob on his black, old-fashioned camera, I choose a spot that I think will be ideal for taking the photos, if there is such a place in a restaurant. Luckily, Bobby has taken the large picture of the whirling nightclub scene (in which a Black jazz musician—playing an oversized trumpet and surrounded by circles and circles of dancers, instruments, and other jazz musicians—is the focal point) off the wall in order to clean it. This has left the cream-colored wall in the front part of the restaurant free for the taking. So, without a moment's hesitation, I push to the side the two small tables and four chairs that line the wall, and set up a bar stool in their place. I take a last look at my hair and makeup in the small mirror that is conveniently located on the inside flap of my blue leather purse that I love, which I bought over a year ago at Hit or Miss around the corner on Forbes Avenue. *Your hair looks really beautiful today,* I think to myself, *and luckily your face isn't very broken out... Walter should be pleased.* Satisfied with how

I look, I happily jump up onto the stool, fold my hands in my lap, and sit up straight against the wall.

"Okay, Walter, I think I'm ready," I say, grinning.

"All right. Just one more adjustment and we should be all set to go."

Walter turns a dial slightly, looks through the camera, and moves it a bit forward.

"Okay. I think we're ready now…. Smile!"

I smile, Walter clicks, and…

I'm being very patient, waiting for something to happen, but there wasn't a flash, and the camera isn't advancing.

"Uh-oh," Walter says.

This doesn't sound good.

"Something doesn't seem right," he then adds, his head completely hidden behind the camera. "Well, I, uh… Well, let's try it one more time," Walter suggests, adjusting a few more knobs.

"Okay. Sounds good to me," I reply, and I get ready with another big smile.

Click!

No flash. No nothing. Once again.

"Oh gee. Something is definitely wrong," I hear, followed by a heavy, confused sigh. And then, after a long pause, "You know what, Jenna? I'm really, really sorry. But I just don't think this is going to happen today… I mean, gee whiz. The camera was working fine the last time I used it." He continues to examine the camera, his forehead a wrinkled mess. "I'll have to take it to the shop and see what's wrong with it."

"Okay, Walter. Okay. That's no problem. Thanks for trying anyway. I really appreciate it," I say.

"You bet. I'm just so sorry to bring you in here on your day off, and then the camera doesn't work. I mean, I should have tested it out. It's been a while since I've used it," Walter explains. "How about we try this again in a few weeks, once I figure out what's wrong with it?"

"Sure. Of course. Thanks for going to all of the trouble anyway. Let me know what you find out, Walter."

I jump down from the stool, disappointed—but the logical side of me realizes that these kinds of things are bound to happen sometimes.

Nonetheless, this minor event reminds me, for the umpteenth time, that this dance dream of mine isn't going to be easy.

******

FORTUNATELY, after a lot of speculation on Walter's part, which finally results in a trip to the camera doctor, it turns out that all the camera really needs is a good cleaning. "Apparently, it works just like anything else. If it hasn't been used in a while, doesn't get its exercise, and isn't taken care of, it weakens and won't function," Walter explains to me a week later. "It should be ready to be picked up on Friday. I'm going to be busy this coming Saturday, but why don't we try to take the pictures again the Saturday after that?"

"Okay. I'm pretty sure I'll be free then. Want to try four again?" I ask.

"Yeah. That sounds good to me."

The second time around we set up in the nonsmoking section, against the back wall, because there are customers sitting in the front of the restaurant. This wall is vacant too, for the same reason that the wall near the window was vacant a few weeks before. The gargantuan painting that is usually on this wall is of a majestic, powerful, genie-like woman, enrobed in a swirling, silver cape with many folds, and a silver cloth surrounding the top of her head. There are also swirls of glittering color—blue, hot pink, and silver—encompassing her. It seems like she is floating, maybe in the heavens, in control of the atmosphere and everything near her, and has magic powers. What I like best about her is that she has a calm, all-knowing look upon her face, and a hint of seduction in her eyes. I often wonder who this woman is supposed to be and what the painting signifies. I think that many of The Grill's customers wonder the same thing, because I notice them staring at the painting a lot, and I even hear a few of them discussing it every now and then, speculating about what kind of wishes she could grant them. *In any case, I hope that she uses some of her magic and helps us to take some nice pictures today,* I mumble to myself as I position the bar stool against "her" wall. I make sure my stretchy top is smooth and tucked into my slacks properly, and I climb onto the bar stool and start to get situated.

"Okay, okay, okay," Walter says, adjusting the camera. "Let's give it a shot and see if it works this time."

Click! Click! Click!

All of a sudden, Walter takes three pictures in succession.

"Walter! Oops! I really wasn't ready, Walter," I say, a worried look upon my face, I'm sure. "I don't think they're going to turn out very well."

"Of course they will," he says. "In fact, sometimes the best pictures are the spontaneous, natural ones—the ones you aren't prepared for."

I have to agree with Walter on that one. However, I have a problem that Walter isn't aware of. I'm rather photogenic (or so I've been told), but if I'm caught too off guard (or even when I'm not), my eyes rebel against me and close as soon as the flash goes off. I don't know how many pictures I have of myself in which my eyes are shut, or halfway shut, or partially shut, or one eye is open and the other is shut, or one eye is open and the other is halfway shut, or I look like a complete moron, or I look like I'm three sheets to the wind, or I look like I just got off a terrible roller coaster ride—and on and on and on and on, there are just too many variations to mention. It just seems to happen over and over again: I'm always eager to get a picture taken of myself, because I love to keep scrapbooks and photo albums and chronicle my life, the places I've been, and what I've experienced, but when the flash goes off and my eyes shut, that familiar regretful, sick feeling ensues. "Well, at least the other people in the picture probably look awake and happy," I habitually comfort myself. When I actually have both eyes open in a picture, and they look natural, not two times bigger than they actually are—because this is the other problem: I try so hard to keep them open that sometimes I turn out looking like a lizard or a frightened gorilla—I am truly thrilled.

"Walter, to be honest, I think that it would be better for me if you gave me a little advance notice," I comment.

"Oh, okay, Jenna," Walter replies, his eyes popping from behind the camera for just a moment. "Okay, sure. We'll give that a try too." So he follows my suggestion. He directs me at various times to sit up straight; to turn my head slightly to the right, or to the left; to look up to the right at a forty-five-degree angle, "for an artsy effect"; and to look directly at the camera.

He even brings Tommy and Bobby onto the scene—tall, Black Tommy, and White, not-so-tall Bobby (they make quite a nice picture themselves)—as they are walking out of the kitchen together, on their way to dinner. "Would you two like to help?... Great... Bobby, stand to Jenna's left and tilt the light that's hanging over the back booth toward her face. Tommy, do the same thing on her right. This will give us a more dramatic lighting effect."

"Wow! I not only own The Grill on Murray Avenue, but The Studio on Murray Avenue as well!" Bobby jokes.

"That's right! If we're going to do this, we might as well do it right," Walter responds, laughing, and he continues directing and clicking.

This major event in the life of The Grill lasts about twenty minutes to half an hour, at the most, and then Walter, Bobby, Tommy, and I return to behaving normally, and people eventually quit gawking at us, to my utter delight.

******

IN ABOUT TWO WEEKS' time, Walter brings the proofs into the bar for me to review. To put it bluntly, I can't stop giggling. In half the pictures my eyes are shut or partially shut (big surprise!!!), and in a few my bra strap is showing ("I should have noticed that," Walter comments. "Like I said, it's been a while…"). In one, I swear I look like I'm constipated, and in a few others, I undoubtedly think I'm Audrey Hepburn (although I have to admit I really like those ones). In another—how should I describe it? Well, actually, I think Walter describes it best: "In this photo, you can be perceived as being either stoned or very, very sexy."

Despite the fact that a lot of the pictures are very comical (*hilarious,* even), there are a few that look quite nice, and Walter is very proud of their clarity and sharpness. And, as he puts it, "You only need one good one."

Walter gives me some time to take the pictures home to decide which one I like the best. I'm torn between two of them. In the one, my head and my focus are directed at a forty-five-degree angle to the right, and my neck, my shoulders, and the top part of my torso are included in the picture (not including my chest). The other picture is very similar, except my face is turned only slightly to the right, therefore showing more of my face and a more direct view of it.

After changing my mind countless times (indecision is a big part of my life, I confess), I eventually decide on the first picture, mainly because I like the expression in my eyes, which is a combination of contentment, wonder, naturalness, and eagerness (a dreamer, for sure). In the other picture, I have a very expectant, almost starstruck expression, which I think would possibly give some casting directors a feeling of doubt or uncertainty on some unconscious level when they looked at it. In both pictures, my blemishes are apparent (unfortunately, my face wasn't nearly as clear as on the day we first tried to take the photos). There's a rather large one in the area between my lower lip and chin, another under my left eye, and still another on the bridge of my nose between my eyes—not in the center, thank goodness, but on the side closest to my left eye. If I'd had the photos professionally done, I assume that the developer could blot out the blemishes. But I'm not going to worry too much about them, at least for now. They've been a regular part of my life since I can remember, and probably will be for many years to come (adult acne, and all that stuff), so I'm just going to allow myself to think that they add some character, and let it go at that.

Having made my decision, I show Walter which photo I prefer as he jingles the ice in his almost-gone CC.

"Good choice!" he says. "I would've chosen that one too... So, just give me a few days and I'll get some larger ones made for you. Okay?"

"Yes, of course. But do you want me to give you some money for them now?" I ask, as he places the chosen proof snugly within his black bag.

"Oh, don't worry about it now, Jenna. We'll take care of that another time, after the copies have actually been made," he replies, smiling kindly, as always.

******

A COUPLE OF WEEKS later, Walter hands the sturdy white envelope of newly processed photos to me, ten black-and-white eight by tens, which are protected between two thick sheets of cardboard. I unwind the tan twine that secures the envelope and take out one of the glossy pictures. "Wow! This looks great, Walter! It really makes me excited to start auditioning… Thank you *so, so much*."

"You're certainly welcome, Jenna. And really, it was no problem. It was actually a really fun experience," Walter says, taking a big gulp of his Iron City.

When I finish looking at the photos, I ask Walter again how much I owe him for the reprints, the roll of film he used, his time, and, most importantly, his efforts and kindness, and again he delays, telling me that he'll let me know later, after he calculates the total cost.

Well, wouldn't you know it? Another two weeks pass right by, and he still makes no mention of the money. "So, how much do I owe you there, Walter?" I ask yet again, one quiet Saturday afternoon, as I casually lift up his glass and place a fresh bar napkin under it. But before I can finish doing so, he places his hand on top of mine, rubs it fatherly, and says that he's thought about it, and that I don't owe him anything—that it's his gift to me and my dancing.

I expected as much, having known Walter long enough to realize what he is made of.

The same substance as that genie on the wall. ∎

308

CONSEQUENCES

She races from table to table, absorbing herself in her job, looking you in the eye only when she has to. But she's so utterly patient as she's filling her drink orders, actually showing mercy on the bar gun, and I haven't heard her swear in almost two weeks. Plus, she's been eating lots of salads and fish, and she now drinks herbal tea, sipping it calmly. And what did I see her reading the other day? It was *The Lives of the Saints*—the unabridged version…

"What's going on, Diana?" I finally ask her, seriously not able to stand it anymore, "Sunny Came Home" emboldening me.

"He said it wasn't working out for him, that he rushed into it too quickly," she tells me, softly shrugging her shoulders, her mouth turned downward. ∎

NECESSITIES

Ever since my conversation with Curt, I've been puzzled about something. About how, given what his life has dealt him, Tommy is so happy and carefree.

Don't get me wrong, though. I do know that he's sometimes in a sad, even despairing, mood—such as when he was adjusting to moving out of Squirrel Hill—but over the three years that I've gotten to know him, the majority of the time he acts as if nothing tragic has ever touched him or jaded him, that his only mission is to enjoy himself, others, and the life he's been given. And even if he is down and out one day, the next day he is himself more than ever.

I mean—if Curt hadn't told me—would I ever have known about the searing pain that Tommy has experienced, especially through the cruel loss of his son? Where is that all-consuming bitterness, that overwhelming anger, that lingering sadness, that give-it-away despair that clings to some people and rules them forever? Most of the time I just don't see it. How has he conquered it so well, not let all of it take him over? Would I be the same if it had happened to me?

But then, earlier tonight (why didn't I realize it before?), he came up to me, like he's done countless times in the past, his eyes, actions, and words sparkling and on fire— so natural, so easy, so himself. And then it struck me.

It's the joke-telling and the flirting and the laughter. *That's* what it is! The laughter and the flirting and the joke-telling. Not used as a cover-up, or a device, or a roundabout way to forget and drive out what has happened, but is constant, never-failing, in him from the beginning, on which he depends, and which depends on him. As much an integral part of him as…as…my relentless drive to dance! Pieces of us that we couldn't deny no matter who or what tried to convince us otherwise. Friends that, when some difficulty or tragedy befalls us, we turn to naturally and immediately, because they're what makes us *us*, the essential parts of our beings that we rely on to save us and pull us through, because although they are comforting and familiar, they are, even more, invigorating and life-renewing, crucial and undeniable. They are the gifts that we've been given to go to when nothing else, or no one else, seems able to make life right again. Or to go to even when everything *is* perfect and our choices are innumerable, because—when it comes down to it—these particular gifts are not our choices, and never really have been. Sure, we can try to push them away, give them up, act like they don't matter anymore, that they're just not worth the effort, that there are more important things on which to focus, that there's no place for them in the here and now; but if we start to head in that direction— we find out—it's never for very long.

So I finally understand it. Understand what draws Tommy and me to each other above all else. Understand what makes me trust him so much. Understand—and it's just so clear now—that his laughter and his never-ending efforts to put a smile on my face make me feel so carefree, so alive, so valuable, so myself, without worries or regrets or fear of the present or the future, giving me an abundance of self-worth, contentment, challenge, and abandon always—just like my beloved dancing does…and just like it always has.

******

I SENSED IT FROM the first day I met him—that dose of recognition that shot through me out of nowhere—but now I know without a doubt that whenever I must leave The Grill, and Pittsburgh, to pursue my dancing goals, to fulfill that necessity, Tommy will be one of the people I miss the most. But what I know even more than that, and most of all, is that he'll never betray his passion to laugh and to make others laugh, no matter what else comes his way, wonderful or terrible—a comedian for all time. Yes, when I return to Pittsburgh to visit, which I'd never be able not to do, I'm positive I'll round the corner one cool, dreamy afternoon (my dance bag in hand), and there my Tommy will magically appear, rushing toward me, flirting and laughing. ■

THE SEQUEL

In her hand is a green Barnes & Noble bag, and on her face is the hint of a smile.

"Hey, Jenna, what's up?" she says, approaching me as soon as she walks through the door.

I'm sitting at the ancillary bar, in the middle of assembling place settings, taking—with my right hand—a paisley place mat from the cardboard box in which it is held, putting it on the counter in front of me, and then placing—with my left hand—a napkin on top of it, sometimes on the right, sometimes on the left, so that the stack doesn't become too uneven. I've been doing this for at least fifteen minutes now, so there is a towering stack in front of me. I actually feel rather dizzy from glancing to the right, then down, then left, then down, over and over again. So I look up whenever I hear my name being called, happy for the distraction.

"Hey, Diana," I say tiredly, glancing at her. "What's up?" But I don't stop what I'm doing. My hands are so used to this place mat–building routine, that they just keep going and going and going (muscle memory and all that).

"Well…" she says, as she proceeds to open up the bag and then reaches inside. "Look at what *I* just got across the street."

"Oh, okay," I say, with a little more energy than before. I turn toward her slightly. "So, what is it?"

She pauses, looking at me furtively, her hand just beginning to show out of the top of the bag. "It is…" she begins, and then looks directly at me.

"Yeah?" I say back to her, rather curious, waiting for her to divulge.

"It is…" she says again, still looking directly at me.

My god, this one—is she ever mischievous.

"Yeah?" I repeat, very intrigued at this point, my hands slowing down considerably.

But would you believe it? She continues to stare at me, completely composed.

"*Diana*," I say, in what I consider to be quite a stern manner (well, at least for me).

Apparently she doesn't agree. She just starts laughing under her breath, utterly amused and downright defiant.

There's pity hidden in her somewhere, however, because she eventually lets me in on it.

"It is…" she says, "…you're finally ready now?… Well, I think so… It is…the…*Tropic of Capricorn*!" She quickly pulls out the book as she makes this announcement, and then puts it on display, the fancy letters and colorful design right in front of me.

I immediately snatch the book from her, examining its front cover and then the synopsis on the back, completely abandoning my mundane place mats—finally. "This one sounds even more ribald, sensuous, and vulgar than the first!"

"I know!" Diana says, laughing and rubbing her hands together. "I just couldn't wait to get it—you want to borrow it when I'm finished?"

The Henry effect is in the works once again, and my Diana is finally back. ∎

A LONGING, UNNAMED

It's almost midnight, and the guttural guitar sounds of Jimi Hendrix fill the room. The lights are dimmed, enhancing the mood. Curt leans against the liquor counter behind the bar, his left foot propped upon a box of empty beer bottles, his left arm resting on his knee, holding a lit cigarette in his right hand—his characteristic pose—the smoke seductively rising in front of his face, a cup of coffee on the bar in a white stone mug, also steaming. His look is attractive, thoughtful, and mysterious, with his deep black hair, dark eyes, and black moustache—his gaze totally lost in the melancholy music.

This is my most favorite time of all.

I don't have to talk to him one bit. Through the music—the painful, bluesy, touch-you-to-your-core music, the music that talks to him like nothing, or no one, else— I can feel what he is feeling. Through the drawn-out, deliberate drags on his cigarette, alternating with mouthfuls of strong, untouched coffee, which reflect the sounds and changes in the music, I can sense his rhythm, and my own. So I walk slowly and lazily from table to table, clearing and cleaning each one in turn, slowed down in thought and in action. And there is the bittersweet longing in the strings, which vibrates within me as the longings I too hold securely within me—the longings to dance, to succeed, and to find love. What I'm not quite sure of, though—although

I keep searching—is what Curt is specifically longing for. Is it a different life? A lost love? A more fulfilling job? The parents he never really knew? Whatever it is, we spend many a soulful evening together—with his music, coffee, and cigarettes—trying to find it.

I just hope that one day he does. ■

THE GOODBYE NOTE

Soon.

Soon, it will be here. A week more, and I will no longer be able to call myself an employee of The Grill, no longer be able to proudly tell others, "You know the bar-and-grill with the great food on Murray Avenue? Well, that's where I work." It's really so difficult to believe, and so sad and painful, too, but in my heart I know it's time—time to move on and see what else is waiting for me…

In an instant I look around at everything: at the glistening taps, at the colorful pictures on the walls, at Nick busily and expertly making drinks and change, at Bianca drinking and laughing as she sits at the bar with her hair free and flowing, looking beautiful. At my sweet, sweet friend Mariano, sitting at the middle table in the nonsmoking section—softly asleep—his head leaning sideways against the wall, his face on fire from the two Beck's Darks he drank with dinner, his hands comfortably resting on top of his devoured *Economist*. At Bobby, my wonderful boss, who's eating dinner in the back booth with Tommy B., baby-skinned and ornery. At the three characters who come in every Thursday evening to eat after playing competitive-but-friendly racquetball together at the Jewish Community Center around the corner, neatly dressed in buttoned-up shirts and pressed slacks, always ordering the same thing: a chicken sandwich (lettuce, tomato, and raw onion) with french fries for the short, thin, dark-haired man with glasses; a plain chicken sandwich with potato salad for the tall, thin, satirical, graying fellow with glasses; and a Cajun chicken salad for the stocky, easygoing, friendly faced, fully gray-haired gentleman, also with glasses. At the eccentric, not-sure-how-to-take-them guys who come in together late on Friday nights, the one: dark-haired, tall, skinny, dressed in red flannel and suspenders, missing a few teeth—and the other: short and big-bellied, with his buttoned-up shirt stretched and not quite fitting (a wrinkled undershirt peeking through), his round-framed glasses covering most of his round face, and his almost-no-longer-there gray hair sticking up in different directions; both of them incessantly gawking around but somehow still intently listening to each other, as they share two pitchers of Bud and talk a mile a minute about politics, sports, or whatever—"Can you believe what that President Clinton's gotten himself into? Well, you can just bet that..."—their opinions buzzing around like an overcrowded beehive. At Jack and Adam, working together on Sunday nights amid episodes of *The X-Files* and its distinctive theme song; Jack tossing an empty pitcher high in the air from the front of the restaurant to Adam behind the bar, and then Adam catching it and performing a few more tricks with it before he refills it, as if he and Jack are characters in the movie *Cocktail*. At Jack once again—spontaneously grabbing me one evening in the nonsmoking section to slow dance with him to Annie Lennox's *Why* when the dinner rush is over. At Mo, an overweight, deaf, simple, mentally challenged but-always-happy Black fellow, who sits at the bar with his headphones on, ordering nothing, but singing loudly, moving his head side to side as Stevie Wonder does, and grooving to the music as if he can actually hear it, always making Nick laugh in spite of himself. At Rachel, one of those prima donnas who really isn't one—her hair platinum and bobbed and smoothed perfectly—sitting sideways with her legs crossed, a fancy cigarette in her nonchalant, raised hand, talking so seriously. At Steve, a cocky lawyer with glasses and curly, rather long black hair, who never comes in to eat but can always be seen on Sunday afternoons at the bar with a beer in front of him, telling jokes that he thinks are hilarious but that, inevitably, no one else does. And finally, at Jonathan, my unusual friend Jonathan, whom I have to thank for introducing me to my delicious love affair with John Irving, and—most importantly—for not giving up no matter how tough things are.

And so there is Jonathan, so there he is—amid the yearning of "Wish You Were Here"—and he's motioning me to him—shyly—offering me something.

My hand takes it.

It's a small, folded piece of cream-colored, thick stationery, held together with a small piece of tape, with my name written on it.

My eyes look down at it, and then back up at him.

"Just a little good wish and farewell before you leave— that's all," he answers quickly.

So, slowly, my fingers undo the tape and unfold the note, and lightly run along the fancy, sharp, in-and-out pointy triangles that are its border, and then over the black fancy letters, in the lower-right-hand corner, that spell out Jon's entire name. My mind registers the fact that, before this moment, it didn't know what his last name was. Somehow, over all these years, it didn't seem to matter.

But now, what *does* matter is what's written inside, in a clear, pretty, intriguing hand:

16 January 1998

Dear Jenna,

It is with sincerest wishes that I wish you good luck in your new job that awaits you in Boston. May you ever stride in your pursuit of happiness and fortune. I'm sure that you will succeed in all that you do in your life's journey. A new chapter in your career is ahead of you, so look toward it with a clear mind and a good heart. My only regret is that I didn't get to know you better.

Affectionately yours,
Jon

My eyes look up at Jon slowly, but nothing will come out of my mouth. The note is so well written, so inspiring, and so encouraging, and expresses so much confidence in my abilities, that my heart is amazed by it.

A few days ago, even though my mind didn't really care, my heart realized that there was no farewell party, no farewell dinner, no card with everyone's signature and goodbye message, no nothing planned for it. But now, my heart doesn't need any of that anymore. Now it has this note—this sincere, kind, deeply felt, wonderful wish for its new life…and all from Jonathan.

It is more than enough. ■

JOHANNA MCKENZIE is a writer, a dancer, and an editor, and the author of the blog *Personal Yummy: Pursuits and Delights That Bring Me Joy*. She lives in New York City.

personalyummy.com

9 798988 285700